The Wrong End
of the Rainbow

The Wrong End of the Rainbow

Finding Love During Lockdown

SANDRA SALTER

Published by Team Siandra Publishing

A CIP catalogue record for this book is available from the British Library.

ISBN: 978-1-3999-9583-2

Cover design by Joe Finbow

Prepared and printed by:

York Publishing Services Ltd
64 Hallfield Road
Layerthorpe
York YO31 7ZQ

Tel: 01904 431213

Website: www.yps-publishing.co.uk

To my mum, Joy,
for always believing I could do this.

NOTES FROM A PANDEMIC

It is funny what you take for granted. Going to the shops, finding what you want on the shelves, being able to pick up everyday products, like toilet rolls and paracetamol, without a problem.

Both were always plentiful before, but in March 2020 that all changed. The shelves were bare, as supermarket after supermarket was stripped of not only these, but almost all their products.

Britain was at war. Not a war like the First or Second World Wars, but a war against a new enemy – a virus. With daily news coverage and facing the fact that this scary new virus was heading their way, people started to panic-buy. Even though the government insisted there was enough food for everyone, lockdown was coming, and everyone wanted to be ready.

We would eventually all have to learn to 'live' with the virus, but in those early days of 2020, it was all very new, scary even, as our lives changed in a very dramatic way. We now know that there are certain things we shouldn't take for granted. Hugs, shaking hands, being able to invite as many people as we wanted to a wedding, being able to sit on a bus without a mask, to name just a few of the things which were suddenly prohibited.

It was December 2019 when the World Health Organization first became aware of a cluster of cases of a pneumonia-like disease of unknown cause, originating in China. It was first reported as a novel virus – SARS-CoV-2 coronavirus, for the scientifically minded – but by the time it had reached pandemic proportion it had become known as Covid-19 and, eventually, just plain Covid.

All around the world 1st January 2020 would have been like any other New Year's Day. The clock would have struck midnight, and we would all have been singing Auld Lang Syne, popping open bottles of champagne and welcoming in the New Year, whilst promising ourselves that this year we would stick to our New Year's resolutions. This year we would not fail.

But most would be destined to fail, especially if those resolutions involved anything to do with leaving the house.

Chapter One

From as far back as I can remember, my New Year's resolution had always been the same. I resolved to get married. In fact, even before I hit my teens, I felt that I really needed to get married. When I turned 18, and every year after that, on 31st December, when the clock struck midnight, I would swear that this would be the year.

My wedding plans started to seriously take shape when I was 12. By then I had designed the dress I was going to wear, I knew the month I was going to get married in and I had planned every fine detail of my wedding day. The only thing that ever changed was the groom. When I was seven, I was going to marry the Prince in Disney's Cinderella. He was only a cartoon character, but he was gorgeous. I used to say he looked 'kind and handsome'. Then as I got older, while the wedding details remained the same, the victim changed. One year it was John Travolta, another year Pierce Brosnan. Then there was Ronan Keating, Hugh Grant and Ben Affleck. And so, the list of mostly dark-haired pin-ups and prospective husbands went on.

Of course, not everything in life is guaranteed. Life is not guaranteed. I now have people in my life who mean more to me than Pierce or Ben ever could. Recently, I almost lost everything and that has taught me an important lesson. Things are not always what they seem.

My name is Sally, and I am the eldest daughter of my beautiful mum, Grace, and my adored dad, George. I grew up in the seaside resort of Hove in East Sussex. Not much happens in Hove but it has some lovely, pebbled beaches and many well-maintained parks. For people who need more than that, then Brighton is right next door. Brighton has always been far livelier, with the Pier and lots of things to do on the promenade. I have lived in Hove most of my life. Not much happening suits me well. All I need is a small beach or park to take myself off to so I can people watch and daydream.

My dad passed away when I was seven. He apparently died from a massive heart attack, but all I understood at the time was that one day he was alive, and the next day he wasn't. I don't remember the ups and downs of my dad's character, but I do vividly remember what he looked like. He was handsome and stood out in a crowd. He was a foreman on a building site, big, strong, and tanned, partly because he was outside all the time and partly because his father and grandparents were Spanish. To me, nobody was as good looking as my dad. He had brown eyes, long eyelashes and shoulder length black hair. He called me 'Princess'. He was my hero, and he spoilt me rotten.

I think that might have been why I decided quite early on that my perfect husband would have to be someone who looked just like my dad, and who would look after me, spoil me rotten and treat me like a princess. As you have possibly figured out by now, I have an active imagination. And in my world, the idea of being treated like a princess meant that I would want for nothing and never have to lift a finger in my life. Presumably, the only way this would happen would be if I met an actual prince. Surely only a prince would be able to treat his bride like a princess? And, in my mind, there was no doubt I was a princess.

Going through life believing I was a princess involved a lot of work for my Mum. When I was young, I insisted on wearing tiaras which, of course, only look their best on long, flowing hair. I wouldn't let Mum cut my hair at all. It's only recently that my hair has become short. Until then it has always been black, shiny, and long enough to sit on. With some good looks I had inherited from my dad and my luxurious locks, my appearance got a lot of attention. I was told I was a 'stunning' child, and I guess I grew into a stunning teenager and a stunning young adult as well. I didn't try very hard. I was just lucky.

A young Sally would always have a special dressing-up wardrobe full of beautifully coloured long dresses. When I was very young these were easy enough to come by, but as I got older Mum often had to resort to buying me second-hand bridesmaid's dresses. I would dress myself up in a long dress, put a tiara on my beautiful long hair and then just stare at myself in the wardrobe mirror. Princess Sally. Waiting for her prince.

Young Sally also had a bookshelf full of Disney-style princess books and I would insist Mum read these to me repeatedly. Just as we would watch and rewatch videos of Snow White, Cinderella, Beauty and the Beast, etc. Any film that had a theme of a prince and a princess, any film where they all lived happily ever after.

A slightly older Sally would read love stories and watch her favourite – somewhat more mature – films repeatedly: Sleepless in Seattle, Notting Hill, Jerry Maguire, Ghost, Romeo + Juliet. I was beginning to appreciate that a man didn't really have to have dark hair to be handsome and got the serious hots for Leonardo DiCaprio. I adored Titanic. Leonardo played Jack and Kate Winslet played Rose. I was so jealous of Rose. Even though I realised she was a fictional character, I vowed to steal him from her – one day Leonardo would be mine. In my imagination it was never Rose and Jack. It was Sally and Jack. Deal with it, Rose.

Unfortunately, my fantasising was not without its problems, it used to get me into trouble at school. Daydreaming my teachers used to call it. "Sally is a day dreamer… Sally is easily distracted… Sally would be top of her class if she spent as much time staring at the blackboard as she does staring into space." And my favourite, "Sally is always away with the fairies."

I often got detention, but it didn't bother me. It just gave me a chance to make up more stories. I didn't see anything wrong with having an active imagination and I used it to make people laugh, which I enjoyed doing. If you exaggerated in the right place, you could make a dull as dishwater real-life event into something exciting and hilarious. I enjoyed the happiness my flights of fancy brought to others.

But it wasn't just a problem at school. Mum and I have always been close, but we would argue about my active imagination and particularly my need to exaggerate a story to make people laugh. "Lies Sally, blatant lies," she would scold me. Mum has always hated lies.

NOTES FROM A PANDEMIC

In the pandemic there have been far too many blatant lies and, yes, these were lies – not exaggerations. And they were not done to make people laugh. Just nasty, unsettling, downright unnecessary lies.

We had the Dominic Cummings scandal, which saw the chief adviser of the prime minister deciding to travel from London to County Durham for childcare, when everyone else had been told to stay at home, and then lying about it.

We had the Matt Hancock saga. As Health Secretary, Mr Hancock often made moving speeches about the work of the National Health Service. He was the one who told us clearly to, "Stay at home, protect the NHS, save lives." He also advertised the 'hand, face and space' routine we all had to adopt – wash your hands, wear a mask and make sure you stay two metres apart from other people.

But apparently, he wasn't paying attention to his own words, as he was caught snogging his aide from a distance that was definitely not two metres. Again, his initial reaction was to lie.

Then it was discovered that whilst we were told we could only have up to six people at a time inside a house, the very people in Downing Street who gave these instructions were having regular knees-ups. During this time Prince Philip died and poor Queen Elizabeth, his wife of over 70 years, was photographed sitting alone at his funeral. Nobody was allowed to sit with her, as those were the rules. It was heartbreaking to see, but as she sat obediently in solitude, the government itself was abusing the situation. Followed up by, you guessed it, lies.

Chapter Two

All these lies would have grated on my mother's nerves and many other people's nervous systems as well. Nobody likes unnecessary lies.

It wasn't only certain members of government that lied during the pandemic. Much closer to home others were also lying, including my sister Belinda. I think Mum is now beginning to appreciate the difference between an innocently exaggerated story and the blatant web of deceit Belinda was spinning.

Belinda's lies almost broke Mum at the time, but now we are learning to live with the outcome of the untruths Belinda told and, like the rest of the world, moving on. Leaving the memories of past hurts behind us.

Belinda and I are actually half-sisters, with a ten-year gap between us. My Mum met Phil one year after my dad died when her friends took her to salsa dancing lessons to cheer her up. Although she had a job in the local post office, after work she never went out. She had been moping around for a year, going nowhere and just doting on me, making sure I was OK. Her friends said she needed a life outside of the house.

Phil was American and had come over as a part of a team from New York to set up a company in the UK. Phil looked nothing like my dad. He was bald for a start, and short, and he wore glasses, but he seemed to make Mum happy. She laughed a lot when he was around.

Going from a family of two to a family of four happened quite quickly as Belinda was born the same year Mum and Phil got married. It didn't cause me any inconvenience at the time and my friends were jealous I had a little sister, so it felt good.

As stepdads went, I felt Phil was OK. He put food on the table, treated us all well and made it known from the day Belinda was born that he considered me to be as much his daughter as she was. He genuinely tried to treat us the same, but she was undoubtedly his princess. And that was OK because I had enjoyed my turn of being my dad's princess – it seemed fair.

My friends would often say, "She is so cute... isn't she a doll... it must be lovely having a little sister". But I can honestly say that I never felt any of those things. I had a little sister, the end. But she got me noticed so it wasn't all bad.

However, by the time Belinda turned six and I was 16, I could already see that being spoilt wasn't a good thing for her and she was actually turning into a monster who was on a path to who knows where, but wherever it was, it wasn't likely to be pretty. She acted like an entitled brat and had tantrums whenever she didn't get her own way. She liked nothing more than coming into my bedroom and scribbling on my posters. She used to kick off if I didn't let her hang out with my friends. I loved her, of course I did, and I did my fair share of looking after her. I just didn't feel particularly enamoured by her.

Belinda and I were not alike in looks or any other way. I had long dark hair and she hated her hair to get long. From a very young age she would ask Mum to cut it regularly. She liked it to be bobbed and it suited her like that. Her hair was strawberry blonde and often looked gold in the sunshine.

As a teenager Belinda designed her own bedroom in jarring reds. She had a double bed with a black silk duvet, and her walls were covered with records. She liked to listen to and play music. She also liked to make things. She was very good with her hands and could make wonderful clothes out of scraps of material, old curtains and other odds and ends. Unlike me, she was very talented in making things and she seemed to enjoy it.

As she entered her teenage years, the thing Belinda enjoyed most of all was to fight with Mum and Phil. She rowed with them about everything, and I could tell they both found it exhausting. She didn't want to go to school, and when they thought she had finally conceded and gone, they would get a phone call from the school asking where she was. At the age of 13 she spent more time on the beach busking than she did at school. She smoked and although she wasn't allowed to do so in the house, when she went into the garden to light up, she would blow the smoke into the house through the back door, just because she could.

When I was 24 and Belinda was 14, the family travelled to New York to visit Phil's mum, who had been unwell. Surprisingly, Mum and Belinda loved the place. And even more surprisingly, it was decided that the family would sell up and go live there. The theory was that as Belinda didn't really have many friends in England, she could make new friends there. She would be happier there in a new place and with a new start. It would be an opportunity for her to settle down and start focusing on her studies.

I hated the place. It was far too big, too busy, and too unfriendly. I had no intention of moving. Fortunately, just like Paddington Bear, I had an Aunt Lucy, who stepped in and saved me.

Aunt Lucy was the elder of my dad's two sisters, with Aunt Charlotte being the younger.

Aunt Lucy and I had always been close and when Dad died, she stepped in and helped Mum to look after me. It was Aunt Lucy who picked me up from school if Mum had to work late and when Mum started going to salsa lessons it was Aunt Lucy who suggested we redecorate the spare room so I could have sleepovers.

We decorated her spare room together in pinks and lilac. The two chests of drawers were literally covered in dolls and the wardrobe was full of dressing-up clothes. The final touch was a big sign on the door saying, 'Sally's Room. Do not enter', which one of Aunt Lucy's church friends had carved for me.

My most precious doll stayed at Aunt Lucy's house. She was my special Barbie bride doll, who I loved. I would always wash my hands before playing with her, to make sure that her wedding dress stayed beautiful and white. As I got older, I got rid of most of my dolls but kept her. I didn't play with her anymore, but she remained my pride and joy.

When Belinda was old enough to notice and be jealous, Aunt Lucy changed the sign on the door from 'Sally's Room' to 'Girls' Room'. She persuaded me to give Belinda one of the chests of drawers to keep her special bits in – mainly colouring books and felt-tipped pens.

One day Belinda used one of those felt-tipped pens to colour my Barbie bride doll's dress bright red. I was mortified. I screamed, I cried, and I tried so hard to scrub the colour off, but to no avail. My precious Barbie bride was ruined.

Mum told Belinda off, but Phil made excuses, as he always did. She was only a child and didn't understand what sentiment was. She wouldn't have understood how important it was to me and, anyway, I shouldn't even have had dolls at my age, I was a teenager now. I knew that Belinda understood perfectly well. She had a certain way of looking at me when I was upset, especially when she was somehow the cause – a look of smug satisfaction.

Aunt Lucy eventually brought me a new bride doll for my 18th birthday, which I somehow managed to love even more. This one wasn't going on display though. This one was locked away.

Aunt Lucy didn't mock me for cherishing that doll at my age, or for constantly chatting away about brides. In fact, she loved me talking about my wedding day. We were very alike; she was an old romantic with a vivid imagination just like mine, and we often made-up stories to entertain each other.

So, when Mum, Phil and Belinda made the move to New York, I stayed and cheerfully moved in to live with Aunt Lucy. It was one of the happiest times of my life.

With me now living in Aunt Lucy's bungalow and Belinda far away in America, I could now put my sign – 'Sally's Room' – back onto the bedroom door and safely put my bride doll on display. Yes, OK I was 24, but these things mattered. This was home now, and I wanted it to feel like home, my home.

At 'home' Aunt Lucy would ask about the people I had met at my job in the local pub. I hadn't opted for further education, so had left school at 16 and, after working in a bar and washing up behind the scenes for a couple of years, quickly got the hang of pulling pints and serving drinks behind the counter, which I loved. I loved meeting people. Loved to people-watch and especially loved meeting single gorgeous men. Although she was not a fan of alcohol and initially frowned at my career choice, Aunt Lucy still appreciated the daily stories I told and couldn't wait for me to get back from a shift so that we could talk into the small hours of the morning. We were both night owls.

Aunt Lucy was by far the most patient person in the world, and I know how much she loved me, but I have made some stupid decisions since she passed away. I know she is in heaven, and I am sure that as she has been looking down at me over the last few years there would have been more than a few times when she would have banged her head against the nearest cloud and sighed, "Oh no Sally, not again."

It is very hard when you have spent your whole life looking for a certain type of man to make rational decisions when he seemingly appears over the horizon. But life has a habit of forcing you to grow up. Now I know it isn't all about me, because now it isn't just me.

NOTES FROM A PANDEMIC

Rainbows became quite a theme in the pandemic. Especially during the first lockdown when we couldn't leave the house for three full months apart from when we needed to go shopping for essentials or if we felt up to the allowed one hour of exercise a day.

People usually had one of two things in the window. Either a notice with the official lockdown motto 'Stay at home, Protect the NHS and Save Lives' or a picture of a rainbow. The rainbow became a sign of hope. Hope in a dark place.

Chapter Three

Aunt Lucy never had children, and I never asked why. Instead, she showered her love on Belinda and me, and even though Belinda wasn't her biological niece she treated her well and always tried to treat her fairly. There was never any doubt that she loved us both.

She also loved her one nephew, my cousin Roger. The only child of Aunt Charlotte, my father's younger sister. Roger, like Belinda, was ten years younger than me. He also enjoyed spending time with Aunt Lucy, as we all did. I think it was because of the amazing empathy she had and how she just seemed to know how everyone was feeling, usually before they did. And she always defended us all.

Aunt Lucy would not have a bad word said about any of us. When someone queried why the grown-up Roger was still unemployed and not pursuing a career, she responded that Roger knew what he was doing and when he was ready to work there would be people lining up to employ him. When it was suggested that Belinda was a hot-headed little madam and needed to be reined in a bit, she responded that Belinda was still finding her feet and would turn out just fine. And when it was rudely suggested that I didn't know what planet I was on and was always 'away with the fairies', she responded that I was perfect, no trouble at all and that there was nothing wrong with a good imagination.

She was like a mother tigress to us all, and I wouldn't want to be in the shoes of anyone who tried to harm her cubs.

Aunt Lucy loved us all, but it was me that she truly understood. We had a lot in common, were remarkably close, and never ran out of things to say to each other. Many of our conversations were made up nonsense, but we loved it. We had been like that for as long as I could remember. My move to the bungalow just made us closer.

Aunt Lucy liked me to go to church with her on a Sunday. I wasn't convinced about church. Some of the Bible readings seemed a little far-fetched to me but it was nice to be part of a church family. Everyone was so nice and as long as Aunt Lucy let me sleep in for the rest of the week, I was happy to get up early on a Sunday morning and go to church with her.

I could never really say 'no' to Aunt Lucy. She knew that I didn't quite get the whole church thing yet hoped that I would pick something up along the way. She believed there was only one way to heaven, and she wouldn't enjoy it very much if I didn't join her there one day.

We often had conversations about heaven and what it would look like. I queried the words of 'Amazing Grace', which suggested we would be singing for 'ten thousand years'. What an exhausting prospect that was. When I suggested that I would quite like an alternative of just slipping away and sleeping for ten thousand years she just laughed. She was a lady whose laugh lit up her whole face.

She had decided that she would have at least 50 years on me, and she would prepare a place for me in heaven and that we would enjoy an eternity together. She had a lovely picture hanging in the bungalow of what she perceived heaven to look like with streams, sapphire skies, and rainbows.

Aunt Lucy would have loved the rainbow symbol that emerged from the pandemic. She would have loved to see such a message of hope displayed so widely.

Another church-driven belief she tried to instil in me was good morals. High on her list was the need to respect my parents, as apparently it was biblically correct to honour your father and your mother. I wasn't sure if that was one of the Ten Commandments or if she made it up, but she insisted that I ring America on the first Saturday of every month. "There will be time before dinner to give your mum a ring Sally," she would say. "She will be pleased to know what you have been getting up to. Be sure to send my love to them all."

I didn't mind ringing Mum, and it was good to hear how they were getting on, but I rarely spoke to Belinda. She was never in and when I did ask after her the response was usually a standard, "You know what she is like… you know how hot headed she is."

It was always a struggle when Mum asked me how I was getting on as I wasn't a fan of talking about myself. And, as usual, when I did get going, I couldn't help making it into a somewhat embellished story. In response, I would get the usual, "That's not true though, is it?" It was just easier not to talk about myself.

Conversations were much easier with Aunt Lucy. Yes, she was a Christian and, by default, didn't like lies, but she recognised my stories were just me expressing myself and they made her laugh. She loved the fact I rambled about nonsense; she loved the fact I exaggerated, and she just loved our conversations together. We both did, and somehow, they usually managed to get back to the topic of men.

"See anyone hot in the pub tonight, Sally? Did you find a prospective prince?" Aunt Lucy genuinely believed one day I would meet the man of my dreams, and he would treat me the way I longed to be treated. She would always do my hair before bed, lovingly combing my black mass of locks and often tied it into plaits so that it would have a nice wavy effect in the morning. "Need to be ready for when you meet him lass," she would say.

Although she wanted to help me look pretty, she wasn't a fan of wasting money on looks. From time to time, I would get nail extensions and have these little diamond pieces put on, and she hated that. Natural beauty was one thing but throwing money away was quite another in her eyes. She didn't think debt was a good thing. Save up for what you want, don't get involved with credit cards. There was a time to be a daydreamer and a time to be a grownup as far as she was concerned.

I still wonder about heaven. I wonder whether you can actually sit on the clouds. I like to think they would be big and bouncy. Would you get to wear those little wings like the cherubs and suddenly be able to play a harp? I wonder if there are little windows in the clouds so you can look down on those you have left behind. I can only presume that isn't the case, because if Aunt Lucy had looked down and seen my alcohol consumption over the last few years, I am pretty sure there would have been a few large claps of thunder, and that hasn't happened yet.

I hope she understood why I took to drinking so much, that drink often helped me get through. When she was around it was easy to be happy, her joy was contagious. When she was gone, things got very bleak indeed.

NOTES FROM A PANDEMIC

As well as the rainbows, Aunt Lucy would have loved the fact so many people signed up to volunteer, a real testimony to the spirit of the 'great British public' pulling together. She would have been touched by the stories of medical staff that came out of retirement to help, and saddened by how many of them lost their lives by doing so.

Without a doubt she would have loved Captain Tom. Captain Tom was a 99-year-old gentleman who decided to do 100 lengths of his garden for his 100th birthday celebration to raise £1,000 for the NHS. She would have been turning the TV on every morning to cheer him on. She would have cheered when the money raised turned from thousands into millions. She would have cheered when the RAF did a birthday flypast for him and her cheering would have continued when he got to number one in the pop charts singing, 'You'll Never Walk Alone'. She would have cried like the rest of us when he too fell victim to Covid the year after this song was released.

The elderly got hit hard by the virus. They were just not strong enough to deal with it and quite early on it was announced that anyone aged 70 and over should stay at home and isolate. They were not even allowed to go shopping or have an hour's exercise like the rest of us. They were part of a special exemption group that needed extra shielding.

Many died in care homes as people were not aware you could be carrying the virus without feeling any symptoms. This was termed 'asymptomatic', and care home staff would innocently turn up for a shift without realising they were carriers. For that reason, it wasn't long before relatives were not allowed to visit their loved ones in the care home and, far worse, if their loved ones became ill and could not be saved, they were still unable to visit. They couldn't even say, "Goodbye."

Chapter Four

Fortunately, Aunt Lucy had been safely tucked away in heaven for a long time before the pandemic happened, as I am sure the stress of keeping her safe from the virus would have killed me.

I had ten wonderful years living with Aunt Lucy before her first transient ischemic attack (TIA) – or mini stroke – and during that time I got to know my cousin Roger much better. Up until moving into the bungalow I had never taken a lot of notice of him as being ten years younger than me and being a boy, we had little in common growing up. I didn't recognise him as a sweet kid as he kept very much to himself. Years later I found out that this was for good reason. Roughly the same age, Belinda was far too domineering for him. She used to boss him about and bite his arm if he didn't do what he was told when we were all together. He usually ended up sitting in a corner reading one of his books about boats.

From a very young age Roger decided he wanted to be in the Royal Navy. I was subsequently impressed to learn that he was as obsessed with the navy as I was with my wedding plans. During the time we spent together caring for Aunt Lucy I discovered that, whilst I had a treasured wedding portfolio, Roger had an equally treasured scrapbook about the navy, even down to specific ships he wanted to be on when he finally joined up.

He wasn't willing to look at my wedding portfolio and I wasn't interested in his ship scrapbook, but I recognised his commitment. I admired the way he had joined the Sea Cadets and worked himself up the ranks to a Sea Cadet Leader. Finally, having filled out many forms, passing a criminal check and sailing through a full medical, he was ready to live his dream and join the Royal Navy.

Physically, Roger really looked after himself. He went to the gym regularly, got plenty of sleep and ate the right food. In fact, he adored cooking and that was what he wanted to do in the navy. He wanted to be on the catering side. He wasn't bad to look at either, if you liked square men with cropped hair, and he had the same vaguely Mediterranean looks and olive skin as I had.

Roger spent a lot of time with Aunt Lucy after her first TIA. She struggled to stand long enough to cook, and yet there was always a meal waiting for me when I got home from work, which I knew had to be him. Aunt Lucy called him 'a diamond' and I had to secretly agree that he was. She wanted him to be married off almost as much as she wanted me married off. I think she secretly wanted to be a great aunty, and sooner rather than later.

By the third TIA, Aunt Lucy was getting quite weak so Roger would sit in with her until I got home, and then he would hand over care to me before going home to Aunt Charlotte's. He must have been shattered. He took her out on a Saturday in a wheelchair as well, as she insisted, I needed a break, though I didn't think I did. I loved spending time with her, and she could still make me laugh out loud, even as frail as she was. I wasn't allowed a break on Sunday as that was my turn to push the wheelchair, always to church, but I didn't mind. She wasn't a fan of me pushing the wheelchair as I wasn't very good at it, but it was a short distance, so we managed.

One Saturday when Aunt Lucy came home from a trip with Roger, she seemed very subdued. I asked what had happened, but all she said was she needed me to take her to the solicitor. She needed to hand the deeds of the bungalow over to me. She said Roger agreed with her decision and that she would make sure he and Belinda were OK.

According to her, this was to ensure I wasn't homeless when she was gone. Well, I suppose it made some sort of sense, but there was no rush was there? Apparently, there was a rush, and she needed to go on Monday. In fact, an appointment had already been made for Monday at 11 am, before my bar shift started, and she insisted we didn't need Roger, as he had enough to do.

I questioned this as I was notorious for always crashing her wheelchair into things, which was why I was only entrusted to do this on a Sunday, but she insisted that if she had a blindfold and bottle of brandy with her, she would be fine, making me laugh out loud again.

The next morning my steering was as bad as I had predicted. The bus driver had to get off and help me as he thought I was going to tip her out. I also kept bumping the footrest into the pavement. The third time I did this she let out a scream. "Save me someone! Sally, never take your driving test, promise me you will never take your driving test. Let's just pull in at the chemist, I need some seasick pills."

Eventually, we arrived and the first thing I noticed was that the solicitor was gorgeous. I asked if she had chosen him purposely, but apparently it was just a coincidence. He looked like everything my dream man should be. When all the papers were signed and sealed, he asked if there was anything else he could do for us. "Pretty sure our Sally would like to get you down the aisle," Aunt Lucy answered with a grin. I was mortified. She could be so embarrassing sometimes.

That was to be our last excursion. A few weeks later when I came home after a shift Roger ran past me in the doorway looking like he had been slapped across the face with a wet fish. I shouted after him, but he didn't stop, leaving me very confused.

I was not the only person confused that night. Aunt Lucy was muttering things that made no sense at all. "Belinda has hope. Look out for Roger. Mind your back, Sally."

Suddenly her face dropped, and she couldn't speak. This was not a TIA. It was a full-on stroke. I phoned for an ambulance, which arrived quickly. But while the ambulance crew were with us, she stopped breathing. They tried to resuscitate her, but she had gone.

I didn't cry at the time, I felt strangely peaceful. I knew she was at peace, which comforted me. But many tears came later.

During the pandemic people had been worried that "things will never be the same again." For me, the changes started the day Aunt Lucy died. She was the first in a long line of events that would change my life forever. My Aunt Lucy was gone, really gone. I knew that things would never be the same again.

NOTES FROM A PANDEMIC

There were times at the start of the pandemic where you needed to pinch yourself and ask if this was really happening, if normal would ever return, if things would ever be the same again.

The changes came quickly. Some changes were small but made a difference. There were limits on the amount of people you could see, and attendance was strictly limited at many events. These included football matches and, most upsetting, weddings, and funerals. Some people didn't mind having to cut back on the number of wedding guests, as it made the whole thing easier and cheaper, but funerals were a different matter.

When a loved one dies you want a chance to say farewell, and few people could. At first it was literally a case of a handful of people being allowed, sitting two metres apart, and no opportunity to hug and console each other.

By December 2020, the number of people allowed to attend a funeral had been upped to 30, which was far more generous but, for many, that still didn't seem enough. It must have been hard for people to decide who could and who could not attend a funeral. So many people lost loved ones that they could not say goodbye to.

Chapter Five

Aunt Lucy's funeral took place way before the pandemic, but there were still less than 30 people.

Aunt Charlotte and I represented the biological family. The rest were her much-loved church family.

Mum and Phil sent their apologies from New York. They said it was too hard for them to get away right now, there was lots going on. I assumed that referred to Phil's business. Belinda was not mentioned, but she didn't turn up and no apologies were sent – apologising was not her style. Roger wasn't there either, but at least Aunt Charlotte explained that he wanted to come but wasn't well.

I wasn't convinced. She was bright red when she said it and playing with her wedding ring. She looked uncomfortable. I didn't push her. This was her sister we were burying, and I could almost hear Aunt Lucy say, "She had her reasons for saying that lass." So, lass decided not to further any investigations, but it was devastating that I was the only one of her much-loved nephews and nieces that was able to attend.

I was also disappointed because I wanted to speak to Roger about the night she passed away. What on earth happened that made him run out of the house like that? Maybe he was scared, but it wasn't like him not to hang around and help.

He might be a navy geek, but he loved people and people loved him. I wanted to know what had caused him to act so out of character.

Aunt Lucy used to pride herself on the fact that he could make a screaming baby in a shopping trolley stop crying just by looking at it. He once held up a bus to rescue an injured pigeon. This wasn't someone who would purposely run out on an old lady in her hour of need. It didn't add up.

The devastation, disappointment and bitterness of the funeral soon turned into a spiral of depression and the low place I found myself in made me do some very weird things. This was to be the first of many 'bonkers' stages I would go through over the next few months.

During one such moment I decided that, as Aunt Lucy had given me this wonderful bungalow, I was going to make it into a shrine – a shrine without visitors. I kept my bedroom as it was, we had decorated that together. The rest of the house I painted dove grey and added pale grey carpets and white furniture. I chose a glass-top table and would shine it every morning before I had breakfast.

Aunt Lucy had given me some money in addition to the bungalow, which hadn't come through yet. Knowing it was on its way gave me the green light to go on a credit card spending spree, and I did.

New furniture in the house, new garden furniture outside the house, new pictures, new ornaments, new, new, new.

Another touch of insanity was my obsession with repeatedly reading my wedding day portfolio. I clearly remembered the day I had started my portfolio as a young Sally. Our teacher had said that during our long summer break we were to do an art project, and I had decided I would sketch every tiny detail of my wedding day. I remembered how frustrated Mum got when she wanted to take me out to enjoy the nice weather and I wouldn't come out of my room, obsessed with this project.

First, I had designed my own wedding dress. It was a long white silk dress that was straight until the bottom and then flared out slightly, it had tiny crystals on the bodice and a very long veil, also with tiny crystals. On my head would be a beautiful diamond tiara, which I would clearly be able to afford marrying a prince, so real diamonds wouldn't be an issue.

My engagement ring would be a white gold band with the biggest pink diamond ever and my wedding ring would be a single white gold band with three pink diamonds in the middle to match my engagement ring perfectly.

I made drawings of my wedding reception venue. I was to be married in the summer, when it was warm but, as I also loved Christmas, I wanted to have a Christmas-themed wedding! There was to be Christmas music and a fully decorated Christmas tree.

The wedding cake was to be a three-tier chocolate cake. Bottom tier milk chocolate, middle tier plain chocolate and the top tier white chocolate. I loved chocolate as well.

I had added to the sketches over the years, and in the midst of my temporary meltdown I had sketched a picture of a top table with an empty place right next to me, just where Aunt Lucy should have been sitting. I WOULD get married, and Aunt Lucy WOULD be part of that special day.

As well as spending too much time making the house into a shrine, spending too much time poring over my portfolio and obsessing over thoughts of weddings and wedding plans, I was also aware that I was drinking too much. I didn't think I was an alcoholic; in fact, I was pretty sure I wasn't, but a bottle of prosecco a night was becoming a bit of a ritual. Although I knew I should stop, I was low, I was sad, and I was depressed. Temporarily, I 'needed' that bottle of prosecco, it was my best friend and got me through the night.

My daily routine consisted of wake up, cry, tidy-up, cry, order something online, cry, go over wedding plans, cry, order some take away food, cry, drink some prosecco, then cry into my pillow until I'd finally drift off to sleep.

I hadn't been to work for weeks and was convinced I would have been sacked by now. I eventually decided to plough through my pile of unopened post, looking for the inevitable letter.

"Dear Sally, we regret to inform you that you are a crap employee, and we have sacked you."

I didn't find that letter. Instead, I found my credit card statement and was flabbergasted. How could they allow anyone to spend that much money in such a short time? Surely my bank should have been responsible enough to ring me each day and give me a daily tally? How would I ever be able to pay this back?

This was the type of kick up the backside that Aunt Lucy would give me if she was alive, and I knew I needed to act fast. First, I needed to beg forgiveness at the bar and go back to work. In fact, I probably needed to sign up for some overtime as well. I had a shower and rang the boss.

NOTES FROM A PANDEMIC

People got used to working from home after the pandemic. Initially they had been told to 'STAY AT HOME'. The deal was that if you stayed at home, protecting other people, and protecting the NHS then the government would pay you 80 per cent of your salary. Not a bad deal at all.

Gone were the days where you overslept and were late for work, running for a bus with a slice of Marmite on toast in your mouth, brushing your hair on the way. Suddenly, employers were finding everyone laptops and asking them to work from the safety of their home. Now, you could just set your alarm for ten minutes before a meeting, roll out of bed, put on a decent top if it was a video conference or just sit in your underwear if not.

Not everyone went back to the workplace on a full-time basis after 2020. What was there not to like about working from the comfort of your home, it worked for employees and employers alike.

Getting used to practical changes after the pandemic was easy. Moving on from losing loved ones and dealing with the anxiety triggered by the whole pandemic experience was harder.

Chapter Six

I knew that Aunt Lucy would leave a void nobody else could fill, but even I was shocked at how much it hurt. Fortunately, about a year after she died, I was finally managing to cope a bit more with the loss. This particular bonkers session was fading, and things were beginning to look up.

It took the mortgage deeds for the bungalow and the extra funds around ten months to come through, but when they did, my bank account was healthy again and I was able to become debt free and even put a healthy amount of money into a savings account. I was also getting good money from my new job.

The pub had been very kind. They liked me, my dry wit and my gentle sarcasm, which made the regulars laugh. I was good at my job, but going home to an empty house at night after the bustle and laughter of the pub was just too painful, so I decided to find myself another career.

The last part of Aunt Lucy's life had taught me that I enjoyed and was good at caring for people. I wasn't clinically qualified in any shape or form, but I liked the idea of being part of the caring community scenario. I decided to pursue this and soon landed a job as a receptionist at a local hospice. The hours were Monday to Friday, 9 am to 5 pm, but I often worked overtime in the evenings and sometimes at the weekend. It wasn't as if I had another life, and it kept me occupied – I had less time to think.

Many would say working on a hospice reception wasn't the happiest choice of job in the world, but it suited me, and I loved it. You would get tearful relatives who just needed to sit in reception for a little while with a nice cup of tea, you would get anxious partners who just needed a calming stroke of the arm on the way to the ward and you would get to receive the delivery of a vast amount of thank you letters, flowers and chocolates for the staff. I would obediently take them through to the staff room for the nurses and they would always insist I took a handful of edibles back to the reception with me. So yes, I was getting fat, but happily fat.

I had been speaking to Mum and Phil a lot during my low time and Mum wanted to fly over as she could tell I wasn't myself. She was always telling me to stop decorating the bungalow into the early hours, to stop spending money, but mainly to stop drinking. Many times, she had phoned just after my nightly bottle of prosecco, only to find I wasn't making any sense at all. She was worried about me.

During these conversations I had repeatedly asked her to speak to Belinda and Roger about how they felt about Aunt Lucy giving me the bungalow. She said Belinda was hard to track down these days, but she had spoken to Roger who said he had discussed it with Aunt Lucy and agreed it was the best thing to do. He and Belinda had been given a generous amount of money and I would be the only one who would be homeless. She and Phil could put things right with Belinda when it was their time to cross the threshold of the pearly gates but neither of them was in a rush.

I couldn't believe that my lovely, humble old Aunt who brought her clothes from charity shops could have this amount of money to share so generously and felt sad that she hadn't spent more on herself. I still hadn't seen Roger since that last episode with Aunt Lucy, but I spoke to him on the phone. There was something different about him and I had promised myself that I would go and visit him and Aunt Charlotte, but I never seemed to have the time. I was still working long hours, and, besides that, any free time was being spent planning the 'Big Event', which was happening in three months' time.

The Big Event was a wedding. Not any old wedding. It was my wedding. Yes, finally, on the wrong side of 30, Sally was getting married! Even better than that, my husband-to-be really was the husband of my dreams. He was gorgeous to look at, he was attentive and possessive and treated me like his most treasured possession. He wouldn't let me lift a finger and he loved me. He loved me just as a prince should love his princess. Suddenly, the 'happily ever after' I had dreamt about for as long as I could remember, was really going to happen.

The news of the wedding persuaded Mum I was actually coping, that I had support. I had a purpose, and my drunken binges were becoming fewer and fewer. So, rather than rush over now she decided she should save her visit until the big day.

It had been a quick decision to get married. I had only known Zak for six months, but I knew, and he knew, that we were made for each other. I couldn't believe how quickly my life had changed. One minute I was mourning my lovely aunt, the next I was in complete meltdown, and the next heaven suddenly sent me this gorgeous man. Well, I had no evidence it was heaven, I just hoped that somehow Aunt Lucy was involved. The only thing that I knew for sure was finally my life was going to change for the better. My dreams would come true.

Zak walked into my life the day he walked into the hospice reception area. I was already handling my life much better. I was keeping myself busy and busy suited me. I wasn't drinking nearly as much, I was eating better, sleeping better and really enjoying my new life as a receptionist. I had paid off my credit card and cut it into a million pieces. With my new positive outlook, I was on a mission – a 'looking for a man' mission. Feeling I needed all the help I could get I decided to pray.

Aunt Lucy spent a lot of her time praying. Sometimes she prayed with me and other times I would just hear her praying out loud in the kitchen. It always made me smile when I heard her pray. It was never starchy, more like she was speaking to her best friend. One evening walking back from work I thought I would give it a go.

She had often reminded me that when praying you are talking to God, not Father Christmas. He doesn't want a list of your wants, he knows them. God just wants you to talk to him, but if you throw in a few requests along the way that is fine as well. It was a lot to remember, especially when I only really wanted him to give me a husband, but I tried the chatting approach.

"God, it's me Sally. Hope you have had a good day. I made a few people happy today so tell Aunt Lucy I am getting there. Presumably, you see Aunt Lucy. There must be billions of people there. Do you even know what she looks like? Yes, of course you do, you are God. Just so you know I did enjoy learning about you on a Sunday when I took Aunt Lucy to church, and I know you answered prayers back in the days of the Bible, so hopefully you can answer my prayers now. I know you are not too old. I am looking for the perfect man, please can you have a chat with Aunt Lucy, she knows the details. Look her up and she will tell you. Do you think it will take a long time? Oh yes... Amen."

As it turns out it didn't take a long time at all. The following day my prayer was answered.

NOTES FROM A PANDEMIC

Sometimes when you are least expecting it, miracles happen.

When the pandemic started in 2020, we were told by various government figures and scientists that it was unlikely we would get a vaccination against this virus for at least two years. Nobody wanted to hear that. People were dying at such speed it was impossible to imagine that there would be enough people left to give the vaccination to by 2022, and it was terrifying.

Then at the beginning of December 2020, seemingly out of the blue, we got the news that a vaccine developed by the pharmaceutical company Pfizer had performed well in tests and had been given the 'all clear' by the government.

On 8th December 2020, a 90-year-old grandmother became the first person in the UK to receive the Pfizer vaccination. After that it was given out to as many people as possible at breakneck speed. The race was on – the vaccine versus the virus, along with its many, potentially more deadly, mutations.

So far, the vaccine was more than holding its own. It was a breakthrough in the war, and it was exciting. It was the best news ever for a scared and exhausted world.

It was a miracle.

Chapter Seven

I was on reception duty at the hospice when my own miracle occurred, and the man of my fantasies walked in. His name was Zak, and he was beyond handsome. I had spotted him before he entered the building but presumed that, like a lot of people, he was just using the car park and would then wander off. I honestly couldn't believe it when he walked in.

I was aware that my face was red, something it had a habit of doing at the wrong moment, so I assumed I was now the same colour as a pickled beetroot. I also had a habit of giggling insanely when I was embarrassed. The two together were a recipe for disaster. I instantly started fanning myself with a notebook.

"0h, my it's hot behind this desk." Giggle. "Is it hot outside?" Giggle. "No, of course it isn't, it's blowing a gale out there." Giggle.

Zak smiled at me, and time froze. He looked like my dad as I remembered him. He had thick, flowing dark hair with a long floppy fringe and the most gorgeous come-to-bed brown eyes. There was just enough stubble on his face to make him look manly, and to be honest, he made me quiver in all the right places.

"Hi, my name is Zak" he said. "I am here to see Mrs Greene."

I knew who Mrs Greene was. Her first name was Mary, and I had taken her some flowers earlier in the day. I pointed Zak in the direction of her room, and then put the 'Back in a minute' sign on my desk, as I scurried off to the staff room to adjust my makeup and make sure my hair was in position.

I could barely wait for his visit to be over so I could watch him walk past me and back to the car. Visits weren't usually long as this was a hospice and sadly these people were usually very unwell and got tired very quickly, so I knew I wouldn't have much of a wait for an opportunity to make a, hopefully better, impression. There was only one exit to the car park and that was past the reception desk, so there was no way Zak could escape without me noticing. And before I knew it, he was back. I gave him my best smile, and that was that. He had gone.

Fortunately, fate was on my side. When Zak tried to drive away, he found he had a puncture so had no choice but to sit in reception waiting for someone to come and replace his tyre, quietly listening to me giggling through various lame attempts at polite conversation. I was nervous and so I was babbling, telling him my name and age, all about my dad, all about Aunt Lucy and all about the bungalow. By the time the man from the garage came and rescued him almost an hour later, Zak had all the material needed to write my biography.

Zak wasn't signed up for roadside assistance and had looked uncomfortable when asked to pay for the tyre repair. "Oh, my," he said, "I have left my wallet at home. Do you think I could pop in and see Mary again?"

I told him that he didn't need to do that. Mary was probably sleeping now as his visit would have worn her out plus as I had more money than I knew what to do with, I could loan him the money. He was both relieved and grateful whilst, inwardly, I was excited. After all, if I lent him money, he would have to pay me back, right? By default, which meant I would see him again.

That encounter obviously broke the ice between us, and he left with a cheerful goodbye.

The following day he returned for another visit, and on the way back to the car park he stopped by reception. "What time do you finish work tomorrow, Sally?" he smilingly asked. "I would like to take you for a drink and thank you for saving my bacon yesterday."

And so, it began.

What did it feel like when Zak asked me out? It felt like a miracle. At last, it had happened. I was already falling in love, and it was with a guy who looked as perfect in real life as any of my imaginary husbands. I could only hope that he would learn to feel the same way about me.

On the Friday before we went out, I had popped in to see Mary, and there was another chap in there with her. I was taken aback as I hadn't been at reception when he arrived. He was a younger fellow with ginger hair, and he was stroking Mary's hair very gently. I didn't disturb them. I would ask Zak who it was later.

I had taken extra care of my appearance that morning and was hoping that Zak would notice how wavy my hair was as I had plaited it the night before to get that look that Aunt Lucy always said suited me so well. It wasn't easy plaiting your own hair and had taken hours, but it would be worth it if he noticed.

Before long Zak appeared. He smiled that smile, and I giggled back. I mentioned that Mary was not on her own and he looked a bit shocked.

"Oh, that's OK, Sally," he sighed. "I am not feeling great anyway and didn't want to pass anything on to you or to

Mary. Give me your mobile number and I will text you next week." I scribbled it down and he vanished.

Devastation immediately set in. Whether he was feeling ill or not, he certainly looked uncomfortable about that ginger kid being there. I wasn't very happy myself. That ginger kid had ruined this first date of mine, and choosing the side of negativity I decided there and then Zak would not be texting me. All that work on my plaits had been for nothing. It was soul destroying.

Mary Greene died that weekend. I felt sad for Mary, but I also felt sorry for myself, now there was no reason for Zak to ever return to the hospice. A couple of weeks later one of the clinical members of the end-of-life pathway team attended the funeral and said there was only a handful of people there and Zak wasn't one of them. That made me feel marginally better. Maybe he really was sick.

A month after the funeral I had accepted that my visions of Zak and me together had been just another nice daydream, when out of nowhere he sent me a text saying he wanted me to meet him at the Marina. I managed to play it cool and sent a very non-emotional response, "If you like," but inside I was dancing. This was real again; this was actually going to happen.

And happen it did. At the Marina I found out that Zak was five years younger than me, but he said it didn't matter. He said he was mature for his age and didn't want to date a young giggling kid, an older giggling woman would do just fine. He said he knew he could trust me, and I was everything he wanted in a woman. He thought I was naturally beautiful, he loved my hair, he loved my Mediterranean look, he just loved everything about me. Conversation came easily. Well, it did to me. He usually just smiled and listened. But like Aunt Lucy, he encouraged me to talk about my dreams.

And later on, he even looked at my wedding portfolio without mocking me.

My birthday was at the end of June and Zak took me back to the Marina, to the restaurant we had visited on our first date. It was there that he proposed to me, "Sally my giggling radish, you tick all the boxes for me," he said. "I love you. Will you marry me?" With that he reached into his pocket and pulled out a box which held an engagement ring.

I was surprised just how unlike the engagement ring in my portfolio it was. It was gold not white gold, and it was like a chunky wedding band with the smallest of diamonds in the middle of the band. It was definitely 'pre-loved', but Zak explained that he had chosen it as he felt it had brought a lot of happiness to someone once upon a time and he wanted that happiness to live on through us. He was right. Whoever owned it before had skinny fingers like me and it fitted perfectly, I loved it as much as I imagined the previous owner would have done on her engagement day. My response was instant. "Yes, I will marry you. Yes, yes, yes." And with that he moved into the bungalow. My happily ever after had begun.

NOTES FROM A PANDEMIC

For some, going through the pandemic taught them that you had to take chances and live for today. Life was short and they needed to make that bungee jump they had always talked about. Some were determined to jump on a plane to anywhere at all when the airports opened or take that Mediterranean cruise that had been on their wish list.

For others, it triggered anxiety and fear. Nothing like this had ever happened before and it was scary. Some people had been at home so long that they lost all confidence, feeling afraid to leave the house, get on a bus or, when the time came, to return to the carefree life they had lived before the virus came along.

We had been trained to keep two metres apart and for a long-time people jumped if someone passed them in the street, baulked if you tried to hug them and looked terrified if anyone sat next to them on public transport.

Somehow people became resistant to the concept of accepting things they didn't trust. They had already learned that they couldn't trust much of what the government said, and some people didn't trust what the scientists were saying about the vaccinations either. Why had the vaccinations been developed and given the OK so quickly, and what was really in them?

The pandemic had made a lot of people question everything.

Chapter Eight

Mum and Phil were certainly questioning everything and were not as ecstatic as I felt they should be. They knew this was my dream. It had always been, and yet they were so negative about the whole thing that it made me angry. Yes, I realised it was rushed and no, I probably didn't know as much about Zak as I should, but that would come later. All I knew was that he was drop-dead handsome and he adored me. I knew he adored me because he told me so every day.

They both agreed to come to the wedding. They would arrive a couple of weeks beforehand so they could get to meet Zak before the event. When I asked about Belinda, Mum said this was not the time to discuss Belinda, so I left it at that. This was my fantasy wedding, and I wasn't going to waste a second of it worrying about my half-sister. There would be plenty of time to catch up about Belinda afterwards.

Zak wasn't my first boyfriend; I had casually been through many boys, but that's what they were. They were boys – they were never gentlemen. All the boys I had dated had been good looking. They had to at least pass that test, but they didn't know how to behave or how to treat a lady. I had never met a gentleman, not until Zak. If we went out for a meal, Zak would pull the chair back for me, and I got to choose the wine. He did the shopping, he did the cleaning, he ran my bath, and in the bedroom, he was very attentive – it was all about me and my pleasure.

Mum and Phil needed to appreciate that I had been waiting for this all my life. Someone who doted on me, who treated me like a princess. They needed to be happy for me.

Zak wasn't perfect, he was stupidly forgetful, especially where his wallet was concerned. I was seriously tempted to buy him a handbag so he could hang it around his neck. The only other minor complaint was that although I had insisted that he read my wedding portfolio – often – I couldn't persuade him to wait until the following summer to get married. I had never even considered an autumn wedding, it was such a dull time of year, neither warm nor festive, but he was adamant that he couldn't wait another second to put a wedding ring on my finger. That aside, as far as I was concerned, he was 95 per cent perfect, which was a far higher percentage than I had come across in another man. I was 100 per cent content with that.

Zak was good at talking me into anything at all because I couldn't bear to lose him. He wanted to put his name on the bungalow deeds. I said he didn't need to as he would always be my husband and it would always be his home, but he got upset and I couldn't bear that. He explained that he realised how special the bungalow was to me and wanted to be an equal part of Aunt Lucy's legacy. Even though he never met her, he knew how much she wanted me to chase my dream and how special she was to me. I finally agreed and we arranged an appointment with a solicitor so that it would all be done and dusted by the time we were married.

The wedding dress of my portfolio apparently only existed in my head, but long white silk dresses which flared at the bottom were not hard to find. I found a shop that knew someone who was willing to hand sew some crystals around the bodice and the veil.

As the engagement ring was very different to the one, I had imagined, the wedding rings had to be different as well, but I ordered two gold bands with a pattern around the edges to make them stand out. They looked good. The cake was going to be a three-tiered chocolate cake as planned.

Everything was coming together very well indeed.

I tried to get Zak involved with the preparations, but he insisted he didn't need to. He had seen my portfolio; he knew what I wanted; he trusted me with everything. He had been thrilled with my choice of wedding rings and wedding cake. He loved chocolate. As for the wedding dress, he had seen the sketch and had read it was unlucky to see the dress before the wedding. Plus, he wanted it to be a surprise.

Turns out, the surprise would be all mine. Just over two weeks before the wedding, four days before Mum and Phil were due to board the plane in New York and three days before Zak and I were due at the solicitors, two police officers turned up at the door telling me that they wanted to speak to Zak in connection with fraud.

The fact that he immediately legged it out the back door, ran through the garden and tried to scramble over the back wall made it hard for me to believe that he was the innocent victim of some crazy misunderstanding. He didn't get far. He was caught and arrested, while I just stood there speechless.

Poor Mary Greene had been just one of a long list of people that Zak had conned out of money. When Mary had first started getting frailer, a local charity had been approached to provide someone to help walk her dog Tigger, and they had sent Zak around. He had faithfully walked little Tigger whilst she was ill. And he had also spent a considerable amount of time and effort trying to persuade her to sign her inheritance over to him.

I had been his latest target. He was a thief and a con artist, and I had made things easy for him, talking about my wealth, my hopes and dreams, and making it so ridiculously easy for him to promise me everything I dreamt of. All the while, scheming to take everything I owned. Poor thick Sally, in love with love; so, caught up with looking for a prince that she just couldn't see the wood for the trees.

Zak had conned many others, of course. Mary and I were not the only two, though I was by far the youngest. It was obvious to the investigators, and eventually to me, that the plan was to marry me, divorce me and then, automatically, the bungalow would be half his. I would then have to sell and turn half the proceeds over to him. That's what hurt the most, well to be more exact, that's what made me want to hurt him the most: the fact that he was willing to take away my Aunt Lucy's bungalow knowing how much it and she meant to me. He was not a Prince Charming. He was a toad. A toad of the vilest variety.

Fortunately, we had never made it to the solicitors to sign over the bungalow, but Zak had a free run on my bank account, and when I looked over the statements from those few months, he had really done serious damage to my savings. My reserve pot had kept the account topped up, so I was never alerted to a problem, but both the savings and the reserve accounts were looking very depleted. I wasn't financially ruined by any means, but I had lost a lot.

It wasn't losing the money that really affected me, it was losing my self-respect. Once again, I became a recluse. Mum and Phil still wanted to come but I declined their kind offer. The last thing I wanted was an 'I told you so' conversation, and I knew Mum would have her fixed sympathetic expression, something that I could do without. I think they must have spoken to Belinda and Roger and told them to give me a wide berth, as neither of them got in touch.

I couldn't afford to not work, so I went in every day and acted as if nothing untoward had happened. I simply told my colleagues that Zak and I had agreed to wait a while, something not that uncommon. It was a whopping great porker that I intended to eventually put right, but certainly not now.

I retreated into the job and remained professional. I needed to support people who were about to have their hearts broken. Mine was a self-inflicted heartbreak. People who were about to lose a loved one to an awful disease had no control over their heartbreak, making it even more cruel and undeserved.

In public I functioned as a normal respectable human being, but at the weekends I went back to being a crazy lady, scrubbing, cleaning and repainting the bungalow.

One night I woke up at 3 am, suddenly appalled by the fact I was still sleeping in a bed Zak and I had shared. Getting an axe from the garden shed I chopped it up. Although it felt very sensible at the time, I then had to sleep on the sofa until a new bed was available. Another night I panicked about the engagement ring, wondering if it had been stolen, whose it was and if they were looking for it. I put it up on the local community internet page, but nobody got in touch. I wouldn't wear it again but was reluctant to get rid of it in case it did belong to someone else. So, I just threw it into a drawer and closed that drawer forever.

No wedding cake was left, I made sure of that. I took some to work to share saying that it had been too late to cancel the order once we had made our decision and let the clerical, clinical and domestic staff enjoy it. I only took one layer into work though, which had left me two whole layers to consume on my own. A task that was easier than I had imagined. The wedding cake had taken its toll, the scales creaked and so did I.

Many nights I just stared at my wedding dress, now hanging up in my wardrobe. I had to believe that my wedding would eventually happen. Zak had taken away my self-respect, but he would not take away my hope for a fairy-tale wedding. Without hopes and dreams, what did I have left?

There was no rush. I decided that, for now, no man would cross this threshold. My bungalow was my place of safety. A place for me to revisit my routine of tears, takeaways, and, yes, prosecco.

I thought losing Aunt Lucy was the worst thing that would ever happen to me, but this hurt even more. This was humiliating, and I felt dirty, useless and stupid. I didn't think I would ever feel lower than I felt right then, but fate had many more curveballs to throw my way.

NOTES FROM A PANDEMIC

Some people actually enjoyed the lockdowns, particularly the first one. They enjoyed having 'time to themselves', especially those who had worked their socks off for years.

Many enjoyed being able to read all those books they had never had time to read or watch all those DVD boxsets they had never had time to watch or go for a solitary walk or bike ride. Some were able to spend valuable time with their children, play football with them, or just talk to them, whilst others were able to write some poetry or even have a go at writing that book that they felt was always inside them.

Some people took to being active, taking advantage of their one-hour exercise time slot by taking themselves on a long walk or a jog. Cycle lanes were set up all over the show, in a bid to get people who could not work from home to cycle or walk instead of taking public transport and risk spreading the virus further. This should have prompted more exercise, but what actually happened was that everyone brought a car and drove everywhere. Presumably, as there were less planes in the sky, the pollution impact would have levelled out somehow.

It was a good time for people to sort out their homes and garages, leading to piles of unwanted stuff outside houses with signs on them saying, 'Help yourself', 'Give me a good home' or 'Please... just take me'. This was mainly a knock-on effect due to the frustration of the charity shops and tips being closed.

For many, not everything about the pandemic was bad.

Chapter Nine

Not everything about almost marrying Zak had been bad.

If I hadn't met Zak, I wouldn't have had chance to buy my perfect wedding dress, try it on and finally look like a princess. At least I now owned my dream dress. It wasn't just a pencil drawing in a portfolio anymore, but an actual dress and it was even more beautiful in real life than it had been in my dreams. The same could be said for my gorgeous tiara.

If I hadn't met Zak then I wouldn't have met my new best friend, Dexter. It was Dexter, who turned out to be Mary Greene's son, who had unknowingly saved me from the fate of marrying Zak and, in turn, from having to give up my beloved bungalow.

I first actually met Dexter at Zak's trial, when we both had to give evidence against Mr Vile Toad. I recognised him right way as the ginger who had visited Mary in the hospice just before her passing, and I was surprised that he wasn't as young as I had thought he was at the time. He still appeared to be younger than me, but still looked much older than I remembered.

Dexter was quite good looking. Well, he was if that was your kind of good looking, but it wasn't mine. I wasn't really a fan of ginger hair and even less a fan of crew cuts. The combination was pretty alarming, but at least he didn't have a beard. I didn't warm to beards either. He had a lovely smile but really crooked teeth, and in my humble opinion needed to invest any inheritance he may be getting into some dentistry work to show off that smile more. He had really big muscles in his arms and his chest, which I would later learn was because he worked outside a lot and had a very physical job.

In many ways, he reminded me of Cousin Roger. Not just the haircut, but also the fact he seemed so very caring. I could tell he loved his Mum as much as Roger loved Aunt Charlotte. However, while Roger seemed to be drawn to the elderly and small children, Dexter was apparently drawn to dogs.

On the first day of the trial, Dexter and I went to the small coffee area in the court building. It felt awkward at first, but I eventually broke the ice and told him the bullet-point version of my sorry story of 'life with Zak'. I wanted to get it out of the way before he had to listen to me stutter and stammer on the witness stand. He looked sympathetic but said nothing. He didn't appear to judge me and just listened. Aunt Lucy would have liked that.

As the court case dragged on, we had plenty more coffees together and I was able to fill Dexter in on family dynamics, my job and other things that didn't involve Zak. I confided in him about the meltdown I had after Aunt Lucy's death and how I was 'marginally crazy' now but getting better. That, a little surprisingly, didn't seem to alarm him at all.

Dexter had very good listening skills, and I knew that whatever I waffled on about, for however long, he would really be interested in everything I had to say. He would listen intently, making sure he didn't interrupt and waited patiently for me to pause before he asked any questions. Sometimes it would take a while for that pause to happen, but he never looked bored.

He also made me smile. He could make light of any drama that was going on and had the ability to turn serious conversations around. If you had been panicking about something, you soon forgot what you were panicking about and felt instantly better. When he smiled, he smiled from the heart and when he laughed you found yourself laughing with him. Whenever he laughed it was with you and never at you.

He grinned when I eventually told him about my life-long hunt for a prince, my ideas on the ideal man and my perfect wedding day. A tale that included a detailed description of my wedding dress, tiara and wedding cake. When I told him about the Christmas-themed reception he laughed out loud, but somehow, I knew he wasn't being cruel, and we ended up laughing together.

"Aren't you missing something, Sal?" he asked. "Seriously, why not have a snow machine? If you are going to be doing a jig to 'Rockin' Around the Christmas Tree' in the summer, then a snow machine would finish it off nicely? Well, wouldn't it?"

Nobody had ever called me 'Sal' before.

It didn't take me long to realise that Dexter was a thoroughly decent guy. I got used to Zak standing in the dock, and although by the end of the trial he was looking tired and unkempt he still looked handsome. He showed no remorse, and I knew I should hate him. But it was hard. One day he glanced at me with such anger in his eyes that it scared me. Dexter who was sitting beside me noticed as well and just took my hand and gave it a reassuring squeeze.

NOTES FROM A PANDEMIC

There were a lot of people looking for support with their mental and emotional health during the pandemic. Constant negative news coverage just heightened the anxiety for those who had suffered mentally and emotionally in the past and so many others suddenly felt the need for help. People wanted to talk, to find ways to cope with their feelings of anxiety and fear. With many GP surgeries only speaking to people online or via the telephone, it was hard to have face-to-face conversations about coping strategies.

Loneliness was a serious issue. People were becoming isolated, and it wasn't long before animal rescue centres were inundated with people looking for a pet for company. Many of these poor pets would later suffer from separation anxiety, as some new owners returned to work after spending such a long time at home. Many more were abandoned when the cost of living rose, and people could no longer afford to keep them. Unwanted pets soon added to the list of innocent victims of the fallout of the pandemic.

Chapter Ten

The 'court coffee sessions' also gave me an opportunity to learn about Dexter. I was touched by what I heard. He and Mary had been completely innocent victims, they didn't deserve anything that had happened. They had not been stupid like me.

Dexter explained that it had only been himself and his mum, Mary, for quite a while. His mum and dad divorced when he was young, and although she remarried, that didn't work out either. Dexter and his mum were very alike, and both were crazy about dogs – especially rescue dogs. In fact, they dedicated a fair amount of their lives to supporting a Romanian dog rescue centre called Ruff 'n' Rescued. Mary did bookkeeping for a living which kept her quite busy, but she still found time to pick up phone calls and answer questions about the rescue centre and their related fundraising events. She also arranged appointments for people to have home visits, in order to check their homes and lifestyles were appropriate for a rescue dog.

I had queried what this meant, as in my mind coming into a warm house had to be better than sleeping on cold, wet streets. Surely, a home was a home? You couldn't be fussy. Who did these street dogs think they were?

Dexter explained that, in addition to checking the home was safe and dog-friendly, they had to ensure that the potential owner was not just getting the dog on a whim. That they genuinely wanted to look after them for the rest of that dog's days – they needed reassurance that the dog would have a 'forever home'. Their new dog also needed access to space whether it was a garden or park and ideally not be left on their own for longer than four hours. It all seemed a bit weird to me, I would never hurt a dog, but wasn't sure that I was convinced all this was really necessary. What next? A butler and bellpull?

Whilst his mum did the admin work, Dexter was more hands-on and regularly travelled to Romania when he could to help with the maintenance of the facilities. This could involve anything from helping to build a new enclosure, to repairing mesh fencing and putting summer canopies up to protect the dogs from the sun, to picking up poop and carrying large, heavy bags of dog food. He had his diploma in teaching English abroad, and had picked up a few words of Romanian, and as the local school close to the dog shelter knew him, he would often cover shifts when their regular teachers were sick or away. This helped to keep the funds coming in and pay for his food. He stayed in the home of one of the local rescue workers when he could. His name was Cristian and, although conversations didn't flow at the start, due to the language barrier they managed. Dexter's Romanian was improving, as was Cristian's English.

Mary had been diagnosed with lung cancer three years before she passed away. She had never smoked and, although she had part of her lung removed, the cancer quickly spread until the only treatment options became ones aimed at prolonging her life, rather than saving it. Dexter said that she was breathless at times but stayed active and otherwise managed to live a relatively normal life.

When they got a call saying Dexter was desperately needed in Romania due to severe flooding at the dog shelter, Dexter, with Mary's full support, decided that he had to go. On the surface, Mary was generally doing OK, and he would only be gone for a few weeks.

In addition, Mary and Dexter had a good neighbour they called Uncle Fred, who kept an eye on her whenever Dexter was away and updated him if Mary had any problems.

They lived in a humble ground-floor flat with a small garden, big enough for one dog. That dog was a Jack Russell called Tigger, who managed with just a back garden to exercise in but enjoyed regular visits to the park. As in the past, when Dexter was away, he arranged for a volunteer to help with Tigger. The volunteers came from a local charity, and this time when he phoned, they sent Zak. He had been before, and his mum liked him.

Dexter had been away for only two weeks when Uncle Fred started to notice that Mary seemed increasingly muddled. Then one day, she fell over, and Uncle Fred took her to A and E. There they discovered the cancer had now spread to her brain.

Dexter called his mum as soon as he heard from Uncle Fred. They spoke several times with Dexter insisting he would return immediately and Mary begging him to stay a bit longer and finish what he needed to do to help the dogs.

At that time Ruff 'n' Rescued were organising another 'happy van' – the nickname given to a van that transported the dogs who had a promise of a 'forever home' on their long journey from Romania to England. The van was scheduled to leave in seven days. It was agreed that Dexter would help prepare things for the journey and then accompany the dogs back to England. Mary was happy with that.

Unfortunately, Mary's health deteriorated much more rapidly than anyone anticipated which was how she ended up in the hospice. Dexter barely managed to make it home before she passed away.

Even before Mary was admitted to the hospice, Uncle Fred had rung Dexter to raise some concerns about Zak. Although Zak seemed to genuinely get on well with Tigger and walked and fed him regularly, a couple of things disturbed Fred. He once overheard Zak in the back garden telling Mary that he had phoned Dexter and begged him to come back but Dexter had said, "No." Something Uncle Fred knew to be untrue. Then he heard him trying to get her to sign some paperwork. He also heard Zak ask her for money from time to time.

Fred would always make an excuse to go over and intervene and tried warning Mary, but Mary liked Zak and wouldn't listen to anything negative being said about him. Mary said if there was anything dodgy about him then Tigger wouldn't like him – dogs were a good judge of people. Zak was good to Tigger and the dog adored him, which Mary took as confirmation she was right to trust Zak. When she was eventually taken to the hospice, it was Mary who asked Zak to travel with her in the ambulance and made him promise to visit her while Dexter was away. Zak, being the charmer that he was, played his role perfectly.

Later, following Mary's passing, when Dexter was clearing the house, he found an amended Will and Testament that Zak had clearly typed, leaving everything to himself. But thanks to one of Uncle Fred's timely interruptions, Mary had not had a chance to sign it. Bank statements also proved that when Zak was asking for the bankcard to get cash for little Tigger's dog food, he was taking out an extra £100 each time. He was a devious man who used his charm to con victims out of their money and more.

Mary wasn't the only victim. It was revealed in court that Zak had been working as a volunteer at many organisations for about ten years, and in that time, he had conned many elderly people. He took advantage of the fact they were confused and forgetful and would charm women and men into giving him their bankcards. Apparently, one elderly man had even been convinced that Zak had taken his World War Two medals but, when confronted, Zak had pretended to be deeply offended by the accusation.

Since his arrest it was proved he had indeed taken the medals and sold them on.

I, of course, was the youngest victim and I think everyone in the courtroom was amazed at how easy I had made it for him to rip me off. Nobody in the courtroom seemed to understand why I thought giving him my bankcard so early on in our relationship was such a good idea. My explanation, "But I liked him to do the shopping. I liked not having to lift a finger" seemed to be frowned upon. I made no eye contact with anyone. I knew I had been stupid.

Zak's long-term plan had been to get his name on my bungalow deeds, and he almost did that. The appointment had been made and it seemed a logical next move. After all we were going to be happily married, weren't we? Fortunately, because Dexter reported his findings immediately to the police, they intervened before that happened. I still had my bungalow plus a tiny bit of pride left.

During our coffee chats Dexter tried to persuade me to get a rescue dog for company. He thought it would be a good distraction to have someone else to focus on and showed me photos of dogs that had been rescued from the awful local Romanian authority dog pounds and were now living in some of the private dog shelters he had helped to build while waiting for their forever homes.

He didn't sell the idea very well. When he showed me a video, meant to demonstrate how content the dogs were in their new kennels and how friendly they were, all I could focus on was the fact these dogs were licking the humans all over their faces. Lick, lick, lick. Yuk, yuk, yuk. No flipping dog was ever going to lick me, no matter how awfully they had been treated or whatever part of Europe they came from.

Our coffee sessions were a good distraction from the trauma of the trial and were to continue long after it ended. We just got on very well and Dexter became my new soulmate.

Zak was given a jail sentence of five years for fraud and embezzlement. At first, I was shocked, as it was a much longer sentence than I expected him to get. But he had conned a lot of people. When the judge summed up Zak's past convictions, I found myself wishing he would get more! What an unpleasant scumbag my 'perfect man' had turned out to be.

At the time, five years seemed a long way off, but jail sentences often end up being shorter. On reflection, it would have been much better for me if he had been put away for a lot longer.

Chapter Eleven

One year after Zak was sentenced things were beginning to look up. I was thinking less and less about him and the dream wedding that wasn't to be.

I had got rid of everything that reminded me of Zak and the bungalow was becoming less shrine-like now. I no longer vacuumed, scrubbed and polished like an obsessed person. I still did housework, as I loved my bungalow, but I was far more relaxed about it. So relaxed, I even let Dexter visit from time to time, if he took his shoes off, and he was absolutely not allowed to bring Tigger into the house.

Dexter was now living alone in the flat he had shared with his mum, and I used to visit him and Tigger there. Something that just made me even more determined to never have a dog in my bungalow. There was dog hair everywhere, and the whole flat smelled of dog.

Although I didn't feel the same bond that Dexter and his mother had with dogs, I was beginning to enjoy taking Tigger to the local park with Dexter and was getting quite attached to him. I loved seeing him making new friends and frolicking away with the other dogs. It was a dog's life for sure; eat, sleep, go for nice walks and play with your friends. I had assumed because Tigger lived with Dexter's mum that he was an old dog but no, he was in the prime of his life.

Dexter said Tigger had arrived just before his mum was diagnosed with her lung cancer and was only meant to be a foster dog whilst he waited for his 'forever home'. That was something else they both did, take in rescue dogs and train them before they moved on. Some of these dogs didn't know they were meant to go to the toilet outside, others were scared of leads, as they had been restrained and they didn't know how to associate them with having a good time, and some were nervous of stairs. It sounded like hard work to me, but at least it explained the smell. It was likely much toilet training took place on those old carpets.

Apparently, Tigger was different. This small dog that looked like a Jack Russell had arrived knowing how to 'ask' to go outside when he needed to. He would sit when you put the lead on and although he enjoyed being let off the lead and having a good run from time to time, he seemed to manage with just a couple of short walks which at the time Mary was able to give him. He also managed with just a sniff around the garden. Even though he had been found on the streets, it had been presumed he hadn't been there for long and had probably had a good home before that. Soon Mary became very attached to Tigger, and they decided that he would be a good companion whilst Dexter was on his trips.

Dexter and I spent so much time together that people understandably began to think we were a couple, which made us both laugh. When people enquired, Dexter would reply, "People always confuse us as a couple, don't they Mum?" which usually got him a swift kick in the shin from me. I would say, "No, he's my little brother." That, in a nutshell, was how I saw him, my little brother, good to hang out with and always making me laugh. The trouble was that in many ways he was more grown up than me. He had replaced Aunt Lucy as my voice of reason.

Although I was no longer obsessed about my dream wedding, I still wanted it to happen. Possibly even more now I had the wedding dress hanging in the closet at home. I still dreamt about what my prince would look like and, unfortunately, he looked nothing like Dexter. I was curious to know what Dexter would look like with straight teeth and long hair and even offered to pay for him to get his teeth straightened which he laughed at and enquired as to why I wasn't in the queue when God gave out tact.

Unfortunately, although Zak was a toad, he was visually still the man of my dreams, and when I was flicking through the online dating websites, I couldn't help trying to find someone who looked just like him. Alas, men with those looks were rarely single or straight. It was one evening when I was at home checking who was on offer that I got a call from Mum, which rocked my relatively happy boat.

Mum and I had been in regular contact since the Zak thing. She had been as kind and supportive during the hearing, as she had been when he was first arrested, never saying anything negative, apart from "Thank God" when he was sent down. She seemed genuinely heartbroken that I was going through this and appreciated the fact that this chap Dexter who was going through his own heartbreak had been good enough to support me as well.

Most of the time we talked about Dexter, Tigger and my job at the hospice. She often told me how proud Phil and she were about the way I had managed to come through my second bout of depression and just get on with it. I wasn't sure why she was so proud and wasn't convinced there had been any other option.

One thing we rarely talked about was my sister, but on this particular evening Belinda was definitely on her agenda.

"Sally, you remember I said I would fill you in on what Belinda had been up to after the Big Event? I need to tell you something I should have told you a long time ago. Please don't be cross with me. Belinda could do with some support right now. Could you speak to her?"

"Yes of course I can; put her on the phone."

It was then that the big confession came out. Well, I thought it was a big confession at the time, but it was small compared to what I was to learn over the next few months.

"Sally, Belinda has been back in England for a while."

"Has she? How long?"

"Five years, Sally."

That was the last conversation I had with Mum for many weeks.

I was angry, really angry.

Aunt Lucy had passed away three years ago. Had nobody told Belinda Aunt Lucy was ill? If not, why not? surely people realised that Aunt Lucy loved having visitors. She loved Roger's regular visits and would have loved seeing Belinda as well.

There was something very wrong with this whole set up and I had lots of questions that I needed answered, but nothing would make me pick up the phone and ring Mum. What the hell had happened that had made her just leave America and move to England, and why had nobody told me?

Why was she not at the funeral? When I announced that I was getting married why had nobody bothered telling me she was over here?

As well as feeling angry, I felt vulnerable, confused and I felt I wanted to shout at someone, so I phoned Dexter and ranted about the phone call and exactly what I thought about it. I declared that I was renouncing my family and washing my hands of them, and then finally paused for breath so that he could speak.

I knew it was coming. Mr Positive would never stand for this kind of aggression and resentment.

"Belinda might need you, Sal. Think about it. Something has happened that has triggered your mum into telling you after all this time. She needs you to reach out to Belinda. Oh, and Sal... I am going back to Romania. There has been more flooding, worse this time. They need volunteers to build an emergency shelter. Uncle Fred is having Tigger for me. I will be gone for at least three months."

I was not very lady-like in my response. With no element of a princess in my behaviour or language.

"No, I swear word do not want to reach out to my sister."

"No, I swear word do not want to talk to my mother."

"And I certainly don't swear word need you to just vanish out of my life just now."

Nobody at the hospice knew what was going on. There was nobody that I felt close enough to tell, so I just focused on doing a good job whilst I was there and then went home. I continued to be professional, and I worked hard but I didn't fancy taking on any evening, weekend or bank holiday shifts anymore. Evenings, weekends and bank holidays were now my official time to live like a pig, eat takeaways and drink. These were things I looked forward to.

Working at the hospice ensured that I didn't open any bottles of booze until 7 pm which, in my mind, meant I didn't have a drinking problem and was a woman in control. This was the third 'feeling sorry for myself' session in as many years. It was beginning to become a habit. It was a habit I needed to break eventually, but there was no rush.

Blatantly ignoring irritating text messages from Mum and the voicemails that Dexter insisted on leaving on my mobile, I was determined to isolate myself. The only people I could trust were me, myself and I. All three of us were striving to be happy together.

NOTES FROM A PANDEMIC

Lockdown was serious business and people had to get used to their own company during the pandemic. The United Kingdom had three lockdowns, but the first one was the most damaging, as nobody really understood the virus which was all very new and scary.

A long time before the first lockdown was announced scientists were warning the over 70s that they were vulnerable and should stay at home. Then another announcement was made about some people being in the perceived 'at risk' categories. These were the people who couldn't leave the house, not even to exercise.

Although wonderful people signed up to volunteer and do such tasks as fetch prescriptions and shop for the vulnerable and at risk, these good deeds didn't stop the loneliness.

Medical experts recognised this and in June 2020 another phrase was introduced: the 'bubble'. If you had nobody, then you could select a limited number of people from another household who could visit you – your bubble. They could take you shopping, give you something to get up for in the morning and provide the company you craved so much.

Isolation was no fun.

Chapter Twelve

I was starting to feel isolated now and going to work once a day just wasn't enough anymore. Plus, takeaways were getting boring, and my stomach was beginning to burn with all the alcohol I had been drinking.

I missed people in the evening, I missed Dexter. I had almost picked up his calls a few times and was beginning to cave, which Dexter seemed to be able to sense. His voicemails were making me laugh so much it hurt my stomach, even more than the acid.

"Sal, it's me, your favourite guy. Do you miss me?"

"Did you want me to tell you how many times I got kissed by a dog today, He was huge, his breath smelt of bottom and he just kept licking me. Lick, lick, lick."

"You shouldn't let Zak put you off your dream wedding you know. Thought any more about getting a snow machine for your reception?"

"About your wedding reception, I would be honoured to be your Santa Claus. I could grow a nice long ginger beard. I know how much you like ginger and beards."

"You're caving in Sal; I know you are. Any day now you are going to pick up that phone."

I picked it up the following day, and it was so good to

hear his voice that I was happy to listen to him ramble on about dogs for the whole conversation, while I said nothing.

The next day I got a text to say that Mum was coming over. She would be getting a taxi from the airport to my place, unless I had an issue with that, in which case she would book into a hotel. She would be here for three weeks and was looking forward to seeing me. She needed to fill me in on what had been going on.

She hoped during those three weeks she would also get to see Belinda and maybe have a meal with both her daughters.

I texted her back to say I would be waiting for her, and of course she could stay with me, I wanted to hear what she had to say. I needed some answers.

That night when Dexter rang, I told him the news about Mum coming over, and he was over the moon.

"You are lucky to still have your Mum Sal, enjoy your time with her and hold that tongue of yours. If you feel like you are going to kick off just ring me or text."

"Are you still coming home in May, Dexter?"

"Why? Oh, you do miss me?"

"In your dreams."

"OK see you in five years' time then... Byyyeeee."

As usual, I switched my phone off laughing. That was all I needed from Dexter back then, a buddy to talk to, to exchange stories with, to make me laugh. As time went on, I was going to need to lean on my buddy a whole lot more.

NOTES FROM A PANDEMIC

One of the things missing in 2020 was laughter. The hairdressers were closed, most of the offices were closed, or if they were open people were separated by distance or glass screens. The restaurants, cinemas, theatres, and pubs were closed. Places people went to socialise and to laugh.

The scientists told us there would be a 'new normal', where we would learn to live with the virus.

They promised, that, in time, for most of us, the virus would become more of an inconvenience than a risk.

That was a promise we hoped they could keep.

Chapter Thirteen

Mum arrived and stayed for the promised three weeks. It was lovely to see her, and the time went by quickly. The first couple of days she was a bit jetlagged and out of it, but once she had worked out which way up she was, it was time to talk about Belinda.

Apparently, Belinda loved America and settled in quickly. She went to art college where she made friends with like-minded people who followed their own fashion by making their own clothes and dyeing their hair all different colours. Her friendship group all had piercings in various places, not just in their ears, but they were nice enough girls. Belinda seemed to settle down at home as well and Mum and Phil thought this was the answer. They had simply not invested enough time trying to understand her quirky way, and life was good for a while.

Then things changed and she got in with the wrong crowd, namely a girl called Alice. Apparently, Alice had zero respect for anyone or anything at all and she had been known to steal from her parents, shoplift and swear at teachers, to list just a few of her unattractive traits. Alice drank to excess and took drugs openly. It wasn't long before this rebellious behaviour stirred something inside my half-sister and the old Belinda raised her ugly head.

When challenged, Belinda became very protective of Alice and told Mum and Phil that she hadn't ever changed. She had taken drugs with the other group as well, just more discreetly, and had shoplifted since the day they landed in America. The jury was out as to whether this was true or not, but life inside the house was sometimes becoming unbearable.

Phil had a really bad time of it, as she would try to make him feel like a bad person, accusing him of lying or misunderstanding what she said. If anything went wrong, she would blame him for taking her away from England, which she apparently 'loved', and to America, which she now apparently 'hated'. She was convincing, and she made him feel dreadful.

After college, Belinda didn't know what she wanted to do, so she just did nothing and, every so often, would vanish. She wasn't a drug addict by any means, but seemed to enjoy smoking weed socially, and as she had no income coming in would then steal things to pay for the weed, and anything else that she couldn't afford, and then vanish before anyone could confront her. When she eventually disappeared again, it wasn't really a huge shock and it wasn't until Phil got his credit card statement showing a flight from New York to Heathrow Airport, plus accommodation at a hotel near Oxford Street, that they realised she had flown back to the United Kingdom. Phil cancelled the credit card. They thought she would ring but had heard nothing.

Roger had phoned Mum the morning Zak was arrested to tell her that Belinda was in trouble again. Belinda and Roger had apparently been in touch with each other. Mum was not sure what he meant by 'again'. She tried to get more information out of him, but the discussion turned to Zak's arrest. Roger said he would cope with it, and not to worry me as I had enough going on.

However, he had phoned again recently to say that enough was enough. He and Aunt Charlotte could no longer handle things and someone else needed to take responsibility for Belinda. It was someone else's turn. Roger needed to join the navy now before he got too old, and Aunt Charlotte needed our support as it was all too much at her age.

Mum was as confused as me. It was a bit like reading a second-hand Agatha Christie book where somebody had torn out some very important pages. She knew Belinda was in England. She had been for a while. But why was Roger involved and how?

The only way to get to the bottom of this was to go and visit Roger and Aunt Charlotte. They were pleased to hear from us and invited us over that day.

It was lovely to see Aunt Charlotte again, but she looked old. I had last seen her at the funeral, which didn't seem that long ago, but now she looked haggard and drawn. She offered Mum and me a cup of tea, which we happily accepted. We were sitting around the table making polite conversation when Roger arrived with a very pretty little girl in tow. Her hair was a lighter brown than mine and someone had put it into very sweet bunches. Her eyes were hazel, and she had the longest eyelashes I had ever seen. She looked shy and had a small toy white dog held tightly in her hand. Roger sat down and she sat on his lap.

I felt a pang of jealousy. Roger had finally cracked it. Not only had he got himself a partner but got her pregnant as well and become a dad. I wondered how this was going to help him chase his dream of joining the navy, and if this was why he was so tetchy about Belinda. Was Belinda staying here as well?

As everyone was looking awkward and nobody was speaking, I decided to break the ice.

"Oh, my goodness Roger, well done. She is adorable. What's her name?"

"Hope."

"How old is she?"

"Five."

Hope buried her head in Roger's chest without saying a word, and Aunt Charlotte suggested that a nap might be in order. With that, Roger silently ruffled his daughter's hair picked her up and carried her upstairs.

It wasn't long before he was back downstairs. He looked at Mum before nervously announcing.

"Congratulations, Aunty Grace. You are a grandma."

I was outraged.

"No way! ... you and Belinda? That is disgusting, don't you know that you can have a two-headed child if you have sex with your cousin?"

"Oh, shut up Sally," Roger replied. "Hope is nothing to do with me. She is all Belinda's handy work. Belinda and a guy named Jez."

NOTES FROM A PANDEMIC

There were times during the pandemic when we sat watching the TV in utter disbelief. Disbelief at the speed the virus took hold, the amount of people in hospital and how poorly they were. And disbelief and sadness at how many of them didn't make it.

We hoped the United Kingdom would be spared from this awful virus, that somehow, we would be the secluded untouched nation, but that was not to be. We had not prepared very well, our hospitals had neither enough staff nor personal protection equipment in place. There was no track and trace for many months, or the facilities to check if people had the virus or not.

The prime minister had warned us that people would lose their lives to this virus, but we were still stunned by how many did.

Chapter Fourteen

Utter disbelief is what Mum and I felt when we heard the story of Belinda and Hope. We sat and listened in stunned silence.

Belinda had turned up at Aunt Charlotte's house when Hope was a baby. She had begged Aunt Charlotte to put them both up, and despite Roger telling her it wasn't a good idea Aunt Charlotte had said yes. She loved children and neither she nor Roger could consider homelessness as an option. By the time they worked out what a nightmare scenario this was, and how unreliable Belinda's maternal skills were, Aunt Lucy had already had one TIA, and they didn't feel they could burden me with Belinda and Hope in addition to caring for Aunt Lucy. Belinda had made them promise not to say anything to her mum or dad, so the two of them decided they had made their bed, and now had to lie in it. They had to just manage.

He said Belinda blew hot and cold. One minute she was a dream, the perfect mum, teaching Hope how to make jam tarts and doing hand paintings and things, and then it was almost like she got bored. She would go out in the evenings and sometimes not come back until the next day. Sometimes she'd stay away even longer.

When Belinda heard about Aunt Lucy being ill, she asked Roger if she could take Hope to the bungalow to cheer her up. She was going through a very sweet and stable stage at the time, appreciating everything Roger and Aunt Charlotte were doing for her and Hope. Roger knew Aunt Lucy would fall instantly in love with Hope, so he agreed.

Aunt Lucy was thrilled, and Hope sat on her lap in the wheelchair. Then Belinda suddenly started kicking off about the fact she knew Aunt Lucy was going to die soon and she needed her own home to raise her child, and she thought that Aunt Lucy should leave the bungalow to her and Hope. Aunt Lucy tried to explain that would make me homeless and then Belinda started yelling about the fact that, "It is always about Sally. What Sally wants, Sally gets, and it isn't fair," with a few swear words thrown in for good measure.

That, I concluded, must have been just before Aunt Lucy asked me to take her to the solicitor.

She met Belinda one more time after that when Belinda managed to persuade Roger that she wanted to say sorry, so again he took them to the bungalow to visit. She shoved Hope on her lap again trying to send her on another guilt trip about making Hope homeless, and that Aunt Lucy should be 'ashamed of herself'. Then she picked up Hope and stomped out.

Rogers eyes welled up and he looked at me and Mum. "I am so sorry; I should never have taken her to see Aunt Lucy. I honestly think that is what caused that last big stroke."

He explained that Aunt Lucy hadn't had the stroke when he left, but she wasn't right. He just felt he needed to get back home and make sure his Mum and Hope were OK, so he ran off as soon as he saw me returning home. As it happened, they were fine, and Belinda was singing nursery rhymes with Hope and acting as if nothing had happened. Because of this he felt too embarrassed to attend the funeral. He felt he had failed Aunt Lucy and me, and it was not his place to attend.

He wanted to give me enough time to grieve and then share the burden of Belinda and Hope, only to find out that I was going to be getting married to Zak. Then came the court case, delaying the inevitable conversation again. Six months after that, Belinda left.

Mum asked Roger to define what he meant by "Belinda left."

"She left, Aunty Grace. She left me and Mum with Hope, and she was gone for months. She came back for Christmas, all apologetic and full of regrets and things have been settled since then. But she has started staying out late again and I have been accepted into the navy. If I don't go now, it will be too late, and Mum is too old for this responsibility."

I listened gobsmacked as Mum and Roger discussed the solution to this disaster. Apparently, that solution was me! I was being discussed as if I were anywhere but in the same room.

Supposedly, I would give up my job and Mum and Roger would make up the lost money so that I would always be available to take and to pick up Hope from school. Me going to work part time wouldn't be an option, as there would be school holidays to cover. My 'new job' would be to pick Hope up from school and take her back to Aunt Charlotte's for her evening meal and bedtime, which was Roger's current role, as Belinda had a job that didn't finish until 6 pm.

Meanwhile Mum and Phil would investigate moving back to England. "It is our problem not yours, or Roger's, Sally. We will move back... but it will take time."

I absolutely agreed with one of those statements at least. This was not my problem and all I wanted to do was to hit the 'opt out' button.

Not able to find the opt out button, I came up with an alternative – that I continue to work in the job I loved, whilst Belinda looked after her own child. Were there not after-school clubs and things? Did other single parents not manage? Eyes rolled and Roger explained that it wasn't that simple. It was as if Belinda had two personalities and Hope needed the security of knowing that there would always be someone at the school gates, always be someone to put her to bed. She needed security, consistency and order. This included me being on standby if Belinda were to vanish again.

"Think about it," said Mum.

"Think about it," said Roger.

What was there to think about? The answer was 'no', a big fat no. This was not going to happen.

The following evening Mum decided to go back to Aunt Charlotte's to try and catch Belinda, but I chose to ring Dexter. I wasn't in the mood to speak to Belinda yet. I was still trying to get my head around what a selfish brat she was.

I had warned Dexter by text that I had a story to tell and that he was not to talk whilst I told it and keep any questions until the end. So, I expected him to be quiet – but not this quiet. Once I had finished rambling about my visit to Aunt Charlotte's house Dexter was silent.

"You can talk now."

"I don't know what to say."

More silence.

I knew what he should be saying. He should be saying, "Sally that is too much responsibility for you. This is down to one person, Belinda, and if she cannot raise her own child that is not your problem."

Only he didn't.

First, he said, "That poor little girl," and then he said, "What an amazing person Roger is putting his life on hold for his cousin's little girl. I would like to shake his hand and buy him a pint."

I couldn't disagree with that statement. I would like to buy him a few pints and match every one of them with a large wine for myself and, yes, Roger was incredible. Aunt Lucy often told me how big a heart he had, and now I had witnessed that for myself.

I made sure I was in bed before Mum came home. I knew nobody would be on my side. Nobody would want to know my feelings and fears about being thrown into a situation that I had no control over. I knew that many people would love the opportunity of being paid to stay at home, who wouldn't? But what did I know about children? Nothing is what I knew about children. I had no experience at all and yet suddenly I was expected to be a live-in nanny.

That night I found it hard to sleep. I needed Aunt Lucy, and I needed alcohol. I couldn't risk waking Mum up tiptoeing to the fridge, so with neither Aunt Lucy nor alcohol available I watched Mary Poppins on my laptop. If this was going to happen, I needed all the tips I could get.

NOTES FROM A PANDEMIC

There were no schools open during the first lockdown and this brought a whole new respect for teachers and what they did. It was hard for untrained parents to take the role of a teacher and persuade children to do their online homework. It was hard to explain to children that their daily exercise had to be limited to an hour.

The children looked forward to daily online exercise classes with someone called Joe Wicks. Called 'PE with Joe', it was shown daily on YouTube and was aimed at helping kids stay active during lockdown. As well as encouraging them to be physically active, he boosted their mental health as well with his uplifting messages.

People were counting the days until lockdown was over. Parents were counting the days until their children went back to school.

Chapter Fifteen

It took Dexter two days to persuade me to agree, in principle, to look after Hope, and it took Mum another three days on top of that to persuade me to see Belinda.

The only reason I gave into Dexter was because he managed to persuade me that I should look at it like a sabbatical. Someone was going to be paying me to have a nice long holiday, and if I got bored or didn't like it a few months down the line, then at least I could say I had tried. If my current job was no longer available, then Dexter said there were other similar admin posts within the care sector I could apply for, and it might be nice to do something different and work somewhere else which didn't hold memories of Zak. I had mentioned to Dexter before how I had jumped a few times when the dark-haired postman had walked into reception with a parcel, so that was a clever move on his part.

Dexter promised to help me entertain Hope when he was around and wasn't in Romania or doing his teaching online. If she liked dogs, then we could take Tigger on nice walks. He also suggested in my free time, when she was at school, I could try writing a children's book and put my active imagination to good use. A Princess Named Sally or some such title. They were all good ideas, hard to argue with. But he knew that.

He also tried to re-promote his 'good idea' of me getting a dog. This so-called good idea was not a good idea at all, and I quickly rejected it. I wasn't ready to have my cream-coloured carpets covered in little muddy doggie footprints, or have my settee covered in dog hair. It was my bungalow, my refuge, and it was still very precious to me. For that reason, I would definitely not be entertaining my new niece anywhere other than outside in the fresh air or at Aunt Charlotte's house.

The only reason I had agreed to see Belinda was that I was ready to give her a piece of my mind, and I only agreed to do it if I could meet her on my own without the fear of Mum holding me back. I would feel uncomfortable saying what I had to say when Mum was around. Only when I felt that I had got things off my chest with Belinda could I focus on getting to know Hope.

I arranged to meet Belinda at the local pub. My vivid imagination and I had already decided what she was going to look like; the witch from Snow White, dressed in black with this big dark cloud surrounding her and dramatic music as she walked through the door. I imagined her having many piercings on her ears, a stud on her tongue and a large hoop at the front of her nose like a bull. She would have tattoos all over her face including a 666 tattoo on her forehead.

When she arrived, she didn't look like that at all. She looked quite beautiful. Yes, a lot more makeup than I could have put on, and I had no idea how long it would take her to remove that lot at night, but the few earrings she wore were acceptable silver studs and the tattoos Mum mentioned before must have been hidden on her torso as I could not see any evidence of them at all. No 666 on her forehead and no hoop in her nose either.

She did not have the same olive skin as me, as Phil was very blond and her natural light brown hair colouring was now dyed platinum blonde, almost white. It didn't look wrong though. Her hair had been cut very short with sticky out bits on the top which made her look like a pixie. She was tiny like a pixie as well. Why had I never noticed she looked like a pixie before? Whether she was a pixie or not, she was Belinda. My little sister. I didn't feel the need to embrace her at all, but she made me feel warmer inside than I had expected.

I did give her a piece of my mind which she took on the chin, yawning and glancing at her phone. She wasn't listening and didn't care, but it made me feel better and after that the conversation flowed easily. I had taken on board what Roger had said about Belinda's conversation with Aunt Lucy and that she had a problem with me having the bungalow, but she didn't talk about the bungalow and neither did I. There was no bitterness, and as I had absolutely no intention of inviting either Belinda or Hope to my home… ever… I didn't think this would be an issue, so decided to leave the past in the past. We seemed to get on well.

Belinda was working in a local tattoo parlour, which suited her. It was a Monday to Friday job that started at 10 am and ended at 6 pm and, according to Belinda, she would come straight home "if nothing is happening," so couldn't understand what all the fuss was about and why I was being asked to step in as some kind of babysitting bodyguard. The way she said, "If nothing is happening," certainly helped open my eyes as to why I was being asked.

Two things struck me as strange during that first meeting. Firstly, she didn't ask me anything about myself. It was as if these years had slipped by, and she literally didn't care what had happened to me. Secondly, that she couldn't understand why anyone would be upset about her disappearing for so long. When I pushed her on the subject, I was told that "shit happens." She really was a loose cannon.

Without a doubt she loved Hope and enjoyed talking about how her little girl was turning out. She was proud of the fact that Hope enjoyed, and was good at, drawing and cooking. She clearly had Belinda's creative streak which made Belinda happy.

NOTES FROM A PANDEMIC

There were things that happened in the pandemic which were not OK. It was not OK that people were lonely and isolated, that they could only get phone calls from their GPs, and no face-to-face appointments.

It was not OK the amount of queuing that the elderly had to do, whether waiting in the cold for their Covid vaccinations or queuing outside shops as part of the safety system put in place to avoid overcrowding. People could no longer sit together in buses, in a bid to avoid transmitting the virus, which meant less seats for the elderly who often had to stand for the whole journey.

It was not OK that there was no food left on the shelves for nurses after their long shifts on the Covid wards. People became greedy, they wanted to make sure their cupboards were full, often with little thought for others.

Nobody hugged or shook hands anymore.

This 'new normal' as it was called seemed cold and impersonal and was not OK. The 'new normal' wasn't normal at all.

Chapter Sixteen

Some of the things Belinda assumed were normal just weren't normal at all. A normal person would not have even contemplated that a mother abandoning a child was acceptable. She assumed that, as Roger and Aunt Charlotte loved Hope, they would have enjoyed that whole idea of spending quality time with her daughter. When I queried how she thought this would affect Hope, she couldn't see that would be an issue either. She thought the opposite, that it would help Hope in the future by helping her become more independent. She didn't need a mother around all the time, she could still get what she wanted, possibly even more with Aunt Charlotte doting on her every whim.

The week before Mum went back to America, she and I spent a lot of time with Hope, Roger, Belinda and Aunt Charlotte, getting to know Hope and getting to know her routine. I suddenly felt scared about Mum going back. I didn't want her to go, but she promised she would be back. She hoped that she and Phil would return in time to spend Christmas with us and assured me that they would be putting their house on the market as soon as she got back.

I said goodbye to Mum as she got in the taxi to the airport and felt very alone. She had gone, Roger was finally joining the navy and Dexter wasn't back for a couple of months. Everyone was leaving, everyone was running away, and I wanted to run away with them – only I had nowhere to go. So, I didn't.

Roger had already got the qualifications that he needed to join having acquired them a long time ago. You could tell he was both excited and nervous. He worried about being too old and not gelling with the others on the ship. Aunt Charlotte did what every good mother should and tried to be happy for him, but you could tell how much she would miss him. She couldn't break down in front of Hope. She was very brave.

Belinda took the first week of term off so we could pick Hope up from school together, which I initially thought would be a weird thing to do but it was quite nice. I had zero experience with small children and was desperate to be a good auntie. I had hoped she would introduce me to some of the other parents, but she didn't seem to know any of them. The only notable words she muttered that whole week at the school gates were, "I hope they don't think we are a couple of lesbians."

I thought it was going well and was beginning to learn the routine. You waved at Hope as she came out of the school building, you put your hand in your bag and pulled out her favourite toy dog and a lollipop and then you chatted all the way home, asking her about her day. At this point she chose whether to answer you or just ignore you. When you got home you were to give her a glass of orange juice and a packet of crisps and put on her favourite TV show, whilst you prepared dinner.

I was beginning to feel I was cut out for this auntie business, until Belinda went back to work, and it was down to me to do the school run on my own. As soon as Hope came out, I waved at her but instead of waving back she just burst into tears screaming, "I don't want to go with her." That 'her' would be me then, how embarrassing.

The classroom assistant recognised me and brought her over to me, but Hope just hung onto her leg and screamed even louder, "Where is Roger, where is my Mummy, I don't want to go home with her."

I pulled Hope away from the assistant's leg, smiling awkwardly at the onlookers. Her screaming was getting louder, and I was aware that my grip on her tiny hand was getting tighter. I hoped her fingers didn't fall off. She managed to scream all the way home and then when the door was opened, she ran into Aunt Charlotte's arms and instantly stopped crying, turning to look at me as if I was the evilest person ever put on this earth. This was far more stressful than I had imagined. I had not signed up for this. I was ready to hand in my notice.

A couple of days after that Belinda asked if I could take Hope into school as well so that she could go into work early. She was being trained on how to pierce someone's nipples apparently. As soon as we left the house Hope started to cry and as soon as she was safely in the hands of the classroom assistant she stopped. I decided that if Belinda vanished again, I would join Roger in the navy, this was not going at all well. That Mary Poppins film had not covered this. Julie Andrews had not had this grief.

Belinda and I had got into another routine of going out for a drink on a Thursday night before I went back to the bungalow, leaving Aunt Charlotte in charge of putting Hope to bed, which she didn't mind at all. We had to compromise on the places we went as she was hellbent on taking me nightclubbing and that wasn't going to happen. I was quite excited about a quiet restaurant and a few drinks, but she wasn't keen on that. We ended up going to mutually agreed upon pubs.

I hoped Aunt Lucy could see us. I never really understood heaven. It seemed a bit far-fetched to me – a zillion believers all singing and praising God, each in their own language, and yet understanding each other. All with wings and halos. I still hoped heaven had windows like an aeroplane and that Aunt Lucy, now healed and free of her wheelchair, would be able to look out from time to time and see me. She would like this Thursday evening's view of Belinda and I together getting on so well. I could hear her now. "Well done girls, well done."

It was during one of these sessions that Belinda started telling me about Hope's dad, this Jez guy who had no interest in his little girl. Apparently, they didn't terminate the pregnancy as Jez was desperate for a son to share his interest in biking, but when Hope wasn't a son, he wasn't interested.

The poor kid wasn't named for quite a few weeks, but the word 'hope' kept coming up, so Belinda thought it made sense. Initially she would 'hope' Jez changed his mind. Then Jez would say, "I 'hope' you don't think I will change my mind." Finally, she got a text from Mum saying, "I am worried about you and 'hope' you are OK."

She decided Aunt Lucy would probably prefer the name Hope to Bellatrix, which was the name she really wanted. Hope would have a desirably religious ring, rather than Bellatrix, who I only knew as a particularly nasty witch, and so Hope was named.

Belinda still wasn't particularly interested in my life, but she did seem quite fascinated about Zak. She knew I had been virtually ditched at the altar. Roger and Aunt Charlotte told her that. What she didn't know was the circumstances, and once I told her, she just wanted me to relive the story over and over again.

She was not interested in the wedding dress, the venue, the cake or any of the frills. All she wanted to hear about was the part where the police officers turned up at the door. How it felt to find out I had been thick and that he had never loved me at all. She wanted to know if I had learnt anything about not being "so f***ing stupid" about love going forward.

Having told her that he was serving his time at a prison in Lewes, East Sussex, she asked me if I wrote to Zak, followed quickly by had I visited Zak, followed by an outrageous suggestion that we visit him together and make a day of it. She liked Lewes, as it apparently had some quirky antique shops.

Dexter was still away but very faithful in ringing me every evening, so I decided after that particularly weird conversation I would make it my business to fill him in with all the details during his phone call.

I didn't stop for breath, just rambled on, "She said... then she said... and why did she think I would write to the man... does she think I have a screw loose?"

Eventually, I paused for breath. "So," I asked. "What do you think?"

"I think I would like to tell you about my day" he said, and irritatingly he did.

"Dexter, are you drunk? You are lisping."

"Drunk. I am too busy to be drunk."

Dexter's theory was that Belinda was one of those people who thought about themselves constantly, with little or no empathy for others. She would not have stopped and considered for one minute what it would have been like for me caring for Aunt Lucy, or how traumatic her passing was. He thought it was unlikely she would have been excited when she heard I was getting married, and her happy place would have been hearing the wedding was cancelled. Hearing stories about Zak breaking my heart would make her think that everything was how it should be, in a 'I had it coming' kind of way.

He felt Belinda was a loose cannon and asked how she was with Hope.

I had to admit that apart from her thinking it was OK to not come home after work whenever she felt like it, she was a very good mum to Hope. She enjoyed making and baking with her daughter and was actually very patient with her. Aunt Charlotte was never called upon when Hope needed anything in the night. That was all down to Belinda and Aunt Charlotte would often find Hope in Belinda's bed in the morning.

Dexter seemed relieved. "Just focus on little Hope, she must really miss Roger. You are looking after her on your own tomorrow, aren't you?"

Yes, I was. Aunt Charlotte was going on a coach trip. The local community group ran a group for the over 50s, and Roger had persuaded her that since I was around, she should take advantage of one of the free trips that were on offer. Tomorrow she was going to a garden centre for a cream tea, though by the way Aunt Charlotte was talking, you would think it was a Mediterranean cruise. She was dead excited.

Like Roger, I felt pleased for Aunt Charlotte, though the trip was from 2 pm until 6 pm, which gave me three hours on my own with Hope after the school run, and I wasn't sure I was ready for this baptism of fire.

"Dexter I am dreading it. Hope hates me."

"Stop being so melodramatic. She doesn't hate you; she just needs to get to know you better. First her Mum was there and then she wasn't, and then Roger was there and now he isn't. She is probably a bit nervous about Aunt Charlotte vanishing in a puff of smoke as well. She must really miss Roger."

He had a point, she hadn't appeared to be hysterical when Roger left, but you never know. Maybe there were separation anxieties going on, she did seem to have a lot of nightmares and was still wetting the bed from time to time, another good reason she would never stay in my bungalow.

"Dexter you are definitely lisping."

"I am just tired, Sal. I don't sit around stroking dogs all day, there is a lot of work to do, it's no walk in the park. Give little Hope space tomorrow. Let her come to you. Put the TV on in the background and do some colouring or something. She will soon join in. You can do this; you can make her trust you."

He ended the conversation by saying that he wouldn't be readily available for a while as he needed to help in another part of Romania and then, just like that, he was gone. Once again, I felt alone.

As I pondered on his advice, I realised how much I missed Aunt Lucy. Or was it Dexter I missed these days? That disturbing thought made me open a bottle of prosecco and close the curtains. I intended to drink enough to make me sleep. This was not going to be one of Aunt Lucy's kind of evenings, she didn't need to watch.

NOTES FROM A PANDEMIC

One thing the great British public had to learn during the pandemic was 'trust'. Whether you liked it or not, you had to trust the scientists and you had to trust the government.

When the government told you to keep two metres apart and then changed that overnight to 1.5 metres, you just had to trust that they knew what they were talking about. When they told you to wear masks on public transport, and then suddenly told you it is was no longer necessary, you had to trust what they were saying was correct. When they said it was much safer to meet people outside than inside and you found yourself sitting outside a café drinking what was once a hot drink whilst frozen to the marrow, then you had to trust that really was the right thing to do.

Chapter Seventeen

Hope needed to trust me, and I understood that, but I honestly didn't know how to make that happen.

My first hour alone in the house with Hope started badly. She didn't cry anymore when I picked her up from school. She seemed to accept it would be me and not Roger, but she certainly never appeared happy to see me. She didn't hold my hand on the way home and although I chatted enough for us both she never joined in. She just walked ahead of me in silence ensuring I knew that her intention was to get back to Aunt Charlotte quickly so she could just ignore me again.

When we got home that day and she found the house empty and it really was just me and her, that her worse nightmare had been confirmed, she just cried. First there were a few tears, then the tears turned to sobs and then the sobs just got louder.

I carried on with the after-school routine. I pretended I hadn't noticed she was upset and put on her favourite TV channel, whilst handing her an orange juice and a packet of crisps. That calmed her down for a whole ten minutes until she remembered she hated me and then she began to cry again. I found myself Googling, 'how long can a child cry for?'. I had never thought about tears before. Would they eventually run out? Would she die of dehydration? Should

I ring Dexter in the hope he would pick up or should I just ring 111 and ask for medical advice?

Inside my head I was talking to Aunt Lucy. She would know what to do, she was good with kids right? She helped drag us up OK, didn't she? "Aunt Lucy help me. I might murder Hope otherwise and then I will end up in jail with Zak. How would that help this small child?"

I don't know if Aunt Lucy transmitted me a good idea or if I did it all by myself, but I risked life and limb by taking Hope's small toy dog from her hand. The shock that I was evil enough to take her toy made her stop crying and she just stared at me as I attempted to play an imaginary game with her favourite cuddly toy.

"Oh, please don't be sad little dog, Hope isn't ill she is just sad. Let's help her not be sad. Would you like a new kennel?"

I ran upstairs and started rummaging through some wardrobes. In Roger's room was a shoe box with some posh black patent leather shoes in. This would do... he wouldn't mind... all in a good cause and why would someone in the navy need patent leather shoes anyway? A bit of dust wouldn't hurt them. I placed the shoes gently on the wardrobe floor and took the shoe box downstairs.

I picked a lovely pink colour from the felt tip box, which got the desired effect.

"No, not pink Aunt Sally, he is a boy dog."

That was music to my ears. Not only did she speak, but she knew who I was. I was Aunt Sally. Hooray for Aunt Sally. Victory was mine, eat your heart out Julie Andrews.

This was a huge turning point in our relationship. We had found our connection; my niece and I had incredibly active imaginations. This much-loved dog, who apparently had no name, had saved the day and for the next few hours his reward was us making him many more lovely things. This included: one silver bowl, courtesy of a piece of cooking foil wrapped around a lid from one of Roger's deodorant sprays, a nice lead made out of a pair of shoe laces from Roger's patent leather shoes (which I intended to replace), and we were in the process of cooking him some small bones, actually bits of pasta, when I was suddenly aware that Aunt Charlotte was back and laughing at me.

"Well lass, I was a bit worried that I was late back, but you two don't seem to have noticed. Now the wee dog is sorted for food should we feed Hope?"

Ooops. I had forgotten that bit.

Belinda came back from work moments later unimpressed that there was no food for either her or Hope, and equally unimpressed with the game we were playing.

"For God's sake, Sally, I don't want her to turn into a liar like you. Quit the imagination thing."

I couldn't have been happier. A good imagination, in my mind, is a gift. Aunt Lucy had it, I had it and now Hope had it. It was being passed down the family tree and it was wonderful.

As time went on Hope and I became closer. Our imagination went right off the scales of weird and we started to appreciate and enjoy each other more and more. The fantasy thing was here to stay.

Chapter Eighteen

By autumn, my relationship with Hope was going from strength to strength. My interaction with her small toy dog had taught her not just to trust me, but to enjoy my company as well. School pick-ups were now a positive event where she would see me, wave to me and then hold my hand and chat all the way home.

Hope's imagination was fantastic, and she was dog crazy. She had a little dog encyclopaedia which told you everything you needed and didn't need to know about dogs, and she seemed to recognise every breed. One day while passing a white lump of fur on legs she excitedly pointed and said, "Look Aunt Sally, a Pomapoo." To which I replied, "A poma what?"

I told Hope about my friend Dexter who was away working with dogs and was able to show her some photos on the internet of Ruff 'n' Rescued and other animal rescue centres. She was fascinated, and we spent the autumn half-term making dog shelters out of cardboard boxes, which resulted in me then having to take her shopping to buy a few more small toy dogs that needed to be rescued and placed in our shelters. I knew I had been conned, but it saved having to fork out for half-term trips out, and was much warmer staying in. Although all the dogs had names her original dog, the special one that Roger had brought her, remained nameless.

Something else we had in common was our enjoyment of Christmas and the anticipation of the magic that came with the season. When she returned to school after October half-term, they went straight into Christmas preparations which included colouring cards, making stained-glass effect nativity scenes and discussing the Christmas concert.

Hope was going to be a Christmas mouse in the school production. Well, that was a new one. I wondered what Aunt Lucy would make of that. Mary, Joseph, Baby Jesus, with the shepherds, the wise men... and the Christmas mouse!

I tried to get Belinda enthusiastic about the concert and get her to engage in the conversations and preparations, but she seemed distracted. Aunt Charlotte had said she often went out when Hope was in bed and often didn't come back on a Friday night. Our Thursday nights were also getting cancelled at the last minute, which wasn't the end of the world, but the fact she wasn't planning on making her own daughter a mouse outfit was beginning to grate on my nervous system. I had made a personal pact to whine, moan, and nag until she did.

"Belinda, you make loads of your own clothes and Hope's clothes. You are good at making things, you are gifted, you can make anything out of anything. Can you not just bring yourself to make a mouse outfit. How hard can it be?"

"If it is that easy, then you do it."

"We both know I have never been good at needlework, or cooking or making anything at all, come to think of it. OK I am the useless sister. Can you just do it. It would make Hope so happy."

"I am not like you and Aunt Lucy, Sally. I haven't got a religion. I am not into Christmas or Easter, or any of that crap."

"I am not asking you to become a born-again Christian. I am asking you to make a mouse outfit for your daughter."

"Whatever."

"Well, the school has given us six weeks' notice, so the whatever needs to happen soon."

Lots happened during those six weeks.

First there was Aunt Charlotte, who got knocked over by a young lad on a skateboard whilst she was putting the recycling out. Fortunately, it happened after tea, and although Belinda was late back, I was still there, and I was able to ring the ambulance. As she was stretchered into the ambulance, she made me promise to ring Roger and make sure he knew that it was not the young man's fault, and she should have been looking where she was going. The longer I spent with Aunt Charlotte the clearer it became how alike she and Aunt Lucy were. They were angels. No wonder God wanted Aunt Lucy back. I hoped he wasn't in a rush for Aunt Charlotte, as I wanted to get to know her more.

It didn't take the hospital long to work out that, yes, she had indeed broken her hip and that she needed to have an operation. Roger didn't need to ask me to move into the house, especially after what Aunt Charlotte had disclosed about Belinda and her evening antics. I packed my bags and set myself up in Aunt Charlotte's spare bedroom.

I was still able to pop into the bungalow when Hope was at school, so I still had a few hours of sanity, but I missed my evenings there and now had to get used to changing sheets when Hope wet the bed, which was getting less frequent, but still happened. The longer I was there the less Belinda came home and when she did come home, she had a man with her. Sorting out Hope at night was fast becoming my job. Nobody said so, it just happened.

I was not sure if there was a rule about her bringing men into the house, as before Aunt Charlotte went into hospital, I had never seen a man in there apart from Roger. I wasn't a fan of this man, and I was even less impressed when Belinda said, "Sally, this is Jez."

Jez was every bit as vile as I had imagined. He was a large man in width as well as height with long dark matted hair, which was often in a ponytail. I wasn't sure if there were things moving around in his hair, or if that was just me presuming there should be, but it made me scratch my own head.

He was always in jeans and wore long boots, presumably because he rode a motorbike. But they rattled when he walked, and they made him even heavier on his feet than he already was. Every time he was near Belinda he felt the need to squeeze some part of her body, usually her butt, and Belinda would respond by sticking her tongue out and wiggling it around and around in some weird but suggestive way. She was always covered in love bites.

I desperately wanted to speak to her alone without Jez but that was never going to happen as he became a permanent feature. I was pretty sure that Hope didn't like him, which was something else we had in common. I was convinced she had no idea that this was her father, as he was not at all warm towards her, and she seemed to jump every time he came near her. I hoped that was because he was like a bull in a china shop, rather than because she feared him. He was always banging into the poor kid, just ploughing through her like she wasn't there, and he didn't seem to care.

Belinda did everything in her power to get rid of me. At first the requests were polite.

"Sally, I am so grateful for all the help you have given me and Hope but I have Jez now so we can probably manage between us."

"I am sure you can manage as well, but you don't need to because I am staying put."

Then the angrier side of Belinda started coming out.

"Jez is here now Sally, we don't need your [swear word] help anymore, so [swear word] go back to your [swear word] bungalow."

Where was Dexter when I needed him?

Well, I wish I knew.

NOTES FROM A PANDEMIC

Without a doubt mobile phones and computers were a godsend in the lockdowns. Things would have been very different if the pandemic had happened in a time when there was no email and when the natural way to correspond was with pen and paper. Imagine a pandemic with no mobiles and people having to queue up to use a nearby payphone, having to feed money into it whilst worrying about who used it before you.

Social media saved many people from going stir crazy, and modern forms of electronic communication could be used to contact family and friends for video chats and online quizzes on platforms such as Zoom, WhatsApp and Facebook Messenger.

Video links provided a small but welcome relief to families with elderly relatives in a care home, or those who had to say their 'goodbyes' to people in hospitals.

Chapter Nineteen

During that rough time when Aunt Charlotte was in hospital and Belinda was becoming even more weird, I would have accepted any communication from Dexter through any social network platform. I would have accepted a text, a Zoom call, a telegram, or message via a carrier pigeon if it came to it. However, there was no news from Dexter, and it was making me grind my teeth so much they were beginning to hurt.

Dexter's 'disappearance' was making me cross. I appreciated that he had said he would be offline for a while, but that had been weeks ago, and he should really have been back in England by now. He should have been walking Tigger, and he should have been back sitting here, on this sofa next to me, helping me work all this out and keeping me sane.

I was pretty sure that he had gone and put his hand up to volunteer to do something saintly again. But what about me? He was honestly going to make someone a rubbish husband one day. What was the woman he married meant to do whilst he travelled around Europe rescuing dogs and just going missing whenever he felt like it?

As well as feeling cross and frustrated, part of me was getting worried. The difference between a person without an active imagination being worried about a missing person and a person with an active imagination being worried about a missing person is that the latter tends to come up with their own, sometimes crazy, theories.

I found myself questioning that lisp that he swore wasn't there. It absolutely was there, so why was he lying? Had he turned into an alcoholic? He didn't drink a lot of alcohol in the UK, but maybe it was something he did in Romania. Did he secretly lead a double life? Is that why he kept going back?

Had he started taking drugs? Had a Romanian dealer given him a dodgy bag of weed and he was now lying in a coma in a Romanian ditch being licked by rabid dogs? And nobody had noticed.

He mentioned travelling to a different part of Romania. What if his van had been hijacked by some local terrorists? What if he was being held hostage and they were cutting his limbs off one by one and feeding them to his beloved dogs?

I had phoned him hundreds of times by now and got the same, "I cannot take your call right now, please leave a message." I had left many messages. Some I had sobbed through, begging him to respond, while other messages were just downright unlady like. I knew Aunt Lucy wouldn't like my language these days. I blamed Belinda for that. I had picked up all kinds of words and expressions I had never even heard of before. When I told her about Dexter, she had called him a 'dickwit'. What was that? I had no idea, but it ended up at the end of one of my messages anyway.

Finally, I had a good idea and rang the dog shelter. He had spent most of his adult life working for Ruff 'n' Rescued, so if anyone knew where Dexter was then surely, they would. I got through on the second ring, which was exciting, then remembered I didn't speak Romanian, and nobody understood a word I was saying. Considerably less exciting, so I hung up. This went on for far longer than it should with me ringing and hoping that the next person to answer would say in a posh English voice, "Good morning, Ruff 'n' Rescued. How may I help you?"

That didn't happen. I couldn't understand the people who picked up the phones, and the people picking up the phones certainly didn't understand me.

In the end, desperation swept over me, and I yelled, "ENGLISH!" down the receiver. There was silence, but the person at the other end didn't hang up, which was positive, and within minutes I spoke to what sounded like a young female whose English was far better than my Romanian.

She apologised. She said she was sorry, but nobody called Mr Greene worked there. Perhaps I was confused?

Yes, I was very confused. I left it at that, thanked her and hung up.

Was I actually confused, or had I been conned? Something I had already proven myself susceptible to. Why had Dexter lied? Why had he told me he was working for Ruff 'n' Rescued' when he wasn't?

Was he having an affair? OK, so we were not in a relationship, so it would hardly have been an affair, but why did he lie about his name? Was he working for MI5? Was I now at risk for being involved with a special agent?

I phoned Mum, who was understandably less interested in Dexter and more in Belinda. I had kept her up to date with Belinda and her antics, and she expressed disappointment that I hadn't taken Hope back with me to live in the bungalow, which would have been further away from Jez and nicer for her.

I, in turn, had taken the opportunity to remind her that my love for Hope didn't stretch that far, and as much as I adored the child, bedwetting in the bungalow was not for me. Hope was a messy little madam who had the ability to spread the contents of a jam sandwich over the entire bungalow in less than five minutes. No, I just wasn't ready for that kind of commitment.

The telephone conversation ended with Mum trying to persuade me to think about it, whilst also explaining that she and Phil couldn't come over at Christmas. It was disappointing, but I understood. It had been impossible to tie up a business and sell the house within that timeframe, and a Christmas visit would delay things even more.

I hung up muttering to myself. That was so typical. My best friend was missing, possibly being fed to dogs as we spoke, but nobody cared. All anyone cared about was Belinda. It was always about Belinda. Plus, I missed Aunt Lucy so much it hurt.

I had been to the cemetery a lot recently. Aunt Lucy had been buried in the same cemetery as Dad, so I used to visit them both. With Dad I just looked at the photo on his headstone and laid some flowers, telling him that I loved him and would endeavour to make him proud. With Aunt Lucy I had full-on conversations. I updated her about Hope, how like me she was and so, by default, how like Aunt Lucy she was. I told her about Aunt Charlotte and her insistence that we shouldn't attack anyone passing by on a skateboard, as none of what happened was anybody's fault but her own.

As Christmas was fast approaching, I decided to take a couple of miniature Christmas trees to the cemetery. Dad's was already decorated and I was halfway through decorating Aunt Lucy's when my mobile phone vibrated. Hoping it was

Dexter I immediately looked at the message, only to find it was my local parcel delivery company telling me my parcel was eight stops away. Not quite the same as hearing from Dexter, but I finished the tree quickly and headed back to the bungalow, barely able to contain my excitement. I knew what the delivery was. It was Hope's Christmas present. I had ordered her something that I knew she – OK, we both – would enjoy.

One of the best-selling toys at that time was the Sylvanian Family. Somebody, who was now probably very rich, had come up with the idea of a doll's house, but one that wasn't for dolls. It was for tiny toy animals. You brought their house first, which cost a small fortune by itself, and then brought a 'family' for the house. A badger family, a fox family or, in my case, a dog family. There were a few dog families to choose from, and I had brought three. Well, she was my niece, and she did like dogs, and we could have hours of fun in our imaginary world with this thing. I couldn't wait for her to open it. I was buzzing.

I had spoken to Belinda, and she had gone along with the suggestion that one dog family would be from Father Christmas. Another of the dog families would be her gift to Hope, leaving me with what was left. Basically, I would pay for it all, and she certainly didn't argue with me about that. I had tried to get Roger involved, but he said if he had to choose a small toy family, then it would have to be the badger family. So, I ignored him and told him to arrange his own gift.

I promised myself that I would be grown up when the doorbell rang. I would open the door in a casual way and sign for the parcel without making eye contact with the delivery man. Then I would calmly have a cup of tea before ripping the paper off. However, when the doorbell did ring,

I found myself running towards the door shouting, "Give me the house, give me the house!"

I flung open the door, and there was Dexter.

"What house?" he asked.

NOTES FROM A PANDEMIC

Delivery people were among the few who weren't locked down. Delivery people, medical staff, bus drivers, those in the care industry and a few others were classed as 'essential' workers. People started to look forward to seeing their postman or woman, and receiving a letter or package became exciting.

Places like Amazon that sold electronics and toys as well as books and movies did very well. The shops were closed, and people spent far too much time just spending money online, because they could. Even that was different though. Neighbours could no longer take in parcels and items being dumped behind dustbins became another 'new normal'.

Until we could shake hands again, hug again and invite people into our homes again our postmen and women would become our best friends.

Chapter Twenty

Dexter and I were both surprised. I was surprised because I wasn't expecting him, and he was surprised when I threw my arms around his neck and wouldn't let go. It was such a relief to see him. Eventually he was able to prise himself free and we just stared at each other. He looked so different. His hair had grown for a start, and it suited him. Being longer it seemed far less ginger, and there were some dark highlights going on in there. He looked quite fit, more alive somehow. This laying concrete business was obviously good for him.

Then I suddenly remembered to be angry.

"Where have you been, anyway? Not Romania, that's for sure!"

"And how, Miss Marple, did you reach that conclusion?"

"I tried to reach you when you went off radar. I even called Ruff 'n' Rescued and they had never heard of anyone named Mr Greene."

"Neither have I. Who is he? Would I like him?"

He smiled as he explained that his Mum had remarried. Her second husband's name had been Greene, not his. He had never been Dexter Greene.

"If you are going to start accusing me of things, then you need to get your facts right. If you had said 'Dexter' everyone would have known who you were banging on about. Why were you checking up on me anyway? Surprised you didn't think I worked for MI5."

"Don't be stupid!"

Dexter sat quietly as I caught him up on all that had been happening while he'd been away. The good, the bad and, mostly, the ugly. He was as relieved as everyone else that I was staying at the house during the evening and if he had thought Hope should stay at the bungalow, he didn't mention it. He was proud of the way I had "embraced the unknown". I shut up long enough for him to fill me in on what he had been up to. He had a picture of one of the newly finished shelters which really did look impressive.

The delivery arrived whilst we had been talking and we opened the Sylvanian house together. I could tell it was wasted on him and that he didn't share Hope and my common link when it came to lively imaginations. I couldn't wait for him to meet her. They would bond over dogs for sure. He would know what a doodlepoodle was.

Dexter did look good but was looking tired – and he was definitely lisping.

"Dexter what's wrong with your mouth… Oh my God, it's a brace you have gone and got yourself a brace. No wonder you were lisping."

"I bet you convinced yourself I was a drug-taking alcoholic."

"Now you are being totally ridiculous."

This man knew me eerily well but at least he didn't mention Romanian terrorists. Instead, he excused himself so he could go home and spend time with Uncle Fred and Tigger before a much-needed nap. Poor man had been travelling over 48 hours to deliver his small furry passengers to their very excited new mummies and daddies, where they could start getting used to their 'forever homes'.

His appearance had provided me with another conundrum. Why had he spent so much time making himself look more like my ideal man and less like a dork? Surely not... no, don't over think this. He was just growing up, giving himself a new look, maybe spending some of his mum's money – spare funds which he never had before. Yes, that would be it. Phew! Dexter was my best friend; I couldn't think beyond that.

Things had suddenly started to go very well indeed. Dexter was home, Aunt Charlotte was getting better, Mum was disappointed about not coming over for Christmas, but she seemed OK out there. Roger was settled into navy life and even Belinda seemed to be in a good place right now. In fact, the last couple of times I had seen her she talked about the Christmas mouse outfit she was making.

Christmas magic had also entered the bungalow, although I was getting a bit worried about the amount of money I had been spending online for Christmas goodies. In my opinion, ordering online was far too easy. Before you had time to talk yourself out of anything you had hit that 'buy now' button and it was game over. My purchases included far too many lights. If a Boeing 747 didn't inadvertently land in the garden it would be a miracle.

I was genuinely excited that I would be able to see Christmas through a child's eyes once again this year. Hope and I walked the streets in the evenings before bed just taking in and wowing over the Christmas lights. We purposely didn't walk past the bungalow, and I felt a bit mean. Maybe next year she could help me decorate the outside... and the inside. I was getting there.

I presumed her excitement about Father Christmas had come from living with Roger and Aunt Charlotte, as Belinda didn't seem to have the same inbuilt enthusiasm about Christmas traditions. She was really excited about the upcoming visit from Father Christmas and so was I. I knew what the bearded fat man in the long red coat was going to bring and I was buzzing with excitement.

Hope was thrilled when Belinda agreed to come with me to the Christmas play. Whatever my reservations were, there was no doubt that Hope loved her mummy, and it turned out to be a fantastic evening. Belinda and I both laughed at the scene in front of us. Mary, Joseph, Jesus, a donkey and over 20 Christmas mice. "Bloody hell," muttered Belinda. "Didn't they have pest control in Bethlehem?" We laughed our way through the play.

Nobody in the school hall that evening knew what was coming. A few months from then it would be announced that we were in a pandemic; a year on we would be told that Christmas, at least as most of us knew it, was 'cancelled'.

Would we have believed anyone if they had told us that, though? If the school headmistress had stood in the front of the hall and said, "Ladies and gentlemen, I need to tell you that there will be no Christmas next year, due to a pandemic that will kill thousands of people – a Christmas concert would be too big a risk, so we won't be having one," most of us would have thought it was a sick joke.

But this was Christmas 2019, and things were still very normal. Well, as normal as a nativity scene with Christmas mice running around can be anyway. After the play, the three of us went for a walk around the streets looking at Christmas lights before going home and video calling Mum and Phil. We arranged that we would all meet up online on Christmas evening to open some presents together. Christmas was coming together nicely. I was looking forward to it and hoping I could fit in a Christmas walk with Dexter and Tigger.

Well before Christmas I had asked Belinda if I could pick Hope up from school sometimes with my friend Dexter, as he had a little dog that Hope would love. She clearly thought it was hysterical that I had a boyfriend that I was calling a 'friend'. By then I had given up explaining to onlookers that Dexter and I were just friends, and if others wanted to make up their own version, then we were both fine with that.

Belinda didn't mind. It was Dexter who had suggested that Hope might find it complicated having another male 'friend' introduced to her life, but my sister couldn't see what all the fuss was about. "Don't be so old-fashioned Sally. All of Hope's friends' mums sleep around, sometimes with the opposite sex, sometimes with the same sex. She will get over it."

There was nothing to 'get over' as we were not sleeping with each other, or anyone else for that matter. Hope loved the days when Dexter joined us after school, and she was able to run around the park with Tigger. Sometimes Dexter couldn't make it, and I would pick up Tigger from Uncle Fred's and then Hope and I would take him back afterwards. Uncle Fred loved this special time with Hope and appreciated our company. He would often have a piece of cake waiting for us.

I felt proud about the way Hope interacted with Uncle Fred. She really did have a very caring nature. I also felt proud about the fact I could now pick up doggy poop without gagging. I still didn't want a dog, despite Dexter constantly trying to persuade me, but I was beginning to understand why people enjoyed the companionship of man's best friend.

Belinda, meanwhile, was still in a very good place and had even taken to cooking the evening meal, a loose term for the ready-meals she put into the microwave, but we still appreciated it. Neither Belinda or I enjoyed cooking, and I worried that Hope was not getting the correct dose of vitamins from what we were feeding her. I knew that both Aunt Lucy and Aunt Charlotte would frown upon what we put in front of that poor little girl at times which is why I had opted to pay for her to have a proper school lunch. That aside, Hope was happy, I was happy, and Belinda was, at least for now, happy as well.

As nice as it all was, I still missed my bungalow and my popping in when Hope was at school didn't give me enough time to be alone with my own thoughts. Aunt Charlotte's recovery had been slow, and she was now in a rehab unit while they fitted some bits and pieces to the house to make things easier for her. These included a ramp at the front of the house and some special accessories in the bathroom, such as grab handles and toilet seat raisers.

I was beginning to get a weird feeling that I may be here a lot longer than expected.

Back then I thought that moving into Aunt Charlotte's house and giving up the independence of my bungalow was a big deal, but there were far bigger deals to come.

NOTES FROM A PANDEMIC

One of the biggest shocks from the pandemic was when Prime Minister Boris Johnson contracted Covid himself, highlighting the fact that this virus didn't care who it brought down.

Many people spotted him looking a bit green around the gills during one of the press briefings and then we were told that he had Covid, but not to panic. When he ended up in intensive care, the Government could no longer hide the severity. It took him a long time to recover.

Whether you voted for him or not nobody wanted him to die. Everyone suddenly felt very close to him and wanted him to make it.

He soon lost that popularity again when, in December 2020, another variant of the virus sent the infection figures sky high and Boris had to cancel Christmas as we knew it with instructions that we were only allowed to meet people from up to three households, and only on Christmas day itself. From Boxing Day, as the clock struck midnight another lockdown would be imposed.

Everyone soon forgot how ill he had been in the spring, and he soon became known as 'the Grinch who stole Christmas'.

Chapter Twenty-one

Christmas Day 2019 was lovey. Hope loved her gift from Santa. She was almost as excited as me when she opened it, and we spent all morning playing whilst Belinda made our Christmas lunch of bacon butties and mince pies. In the afternoon we visited Aunt Charlotte and took her some mince pies and other gifts. We had planned a very special Christmas present with her rehabilitation home's manager which was a video link with Roger, and she could not be happier. I wasn't sure what made me smile the most, seeing her face light up at the sight of Roger or seeing the impact Hope made on her and the other residents. Hope was a natural at making people happy and this was a very special time indeed.

On the way back from visiting Aunt Charlotte Hope asked if we could take Tigger for a Christmas walk. Belinda opted out, not being a fan of either fresh air or dogs, so, after confirming with Dexter it was OK, we went our separate ways. Belinda went home, warning me I only had a couple of hours before our online video call with Mum and Phil, leaving Hope and me to bring Christmas cheer to Dexter and Uncle Fred.

Dexter and Uncle Fred had shared a turkey roast, pulled a couple of Christmas crackers and had settled down to relax in front of the TV but they seemed pleased by our interruption.

Uncle Fred needed a post-lunch nap and Dexter needed to get some fresh air.

I had never been out on Christmas Day before, not even with Aunt Lucy. Aunt Lucy and I had our own routine, which had included watching the Queen's speech, followed by back-to-back Christmas movies and other easy-to-watch festive entertainment on the TV. It was lovely to be out. Children were playing on their new cycles and scooters whilst a couple of grownups were bravely trying out new roller skates. Everybody was full of Christmas magic. The weather was bright but cold, it all felt quite magical and before we knew it our time was up. We had to say goodbye to Dexter so not to rock Belinda's happy place by being late.

As we said our goodbyes, he pulled a small parcel out of his pocket and placed it in my hand.

"Merry Christmas, Sal."

After the video call and when Hope was in bed, Belinda and I cracked open a second bottle of prosecco to celebrate a successful day. We had been doing a lot of that lately and I wondered if things were OK between her and Jez. He hadn't been around for almost a month now and she was in most evenings. I didn't want to ruin Christmas by bringing the 'Jez' conversation up, but she seemed happy to bring the 'Zak' conversation up. We once again ran through how I felt when the police turned up at the doorstep, had I reflected on how stupid I had been. And a new question for Christmas day; would I do it again? Her theory was that if Zak knocked on the door right now, I would fall instantly in love, forgive him for everything he had done and allow him to rip me off again.

"He is the man of your dreams, Sally... why wouldn't you?"

Well, whether he had been the man of my dreams or not, I wasn't going to dwell on it tonight, so I made my excuses and went to bed. Actually, they weren't excuses at all, I was exhausted. I had been childlike in my excitement all day and it was beginning to catch up with me. I planned to 'sleep like a baby'.

That was an Aunt Lucy expression, though I was never sure where it came from as it never made sense when babies didn't sleep, they cried all night and wet the bed, and I certainly didn't plan on doing either of those things. I giggled to myself. Oh my, I was so funny when I was drunk.

I kept myself awake giggling at my hysterical sense of humour and then remembered my present from Dexter so jumped out of bed quickly, grabbed it and ripped the wrapping paper off.

The giggling stopped and I was gobsmacked at how breathtakingly beautiful and thoughtful his gift was.

A Walt Disney-themed snow globe featuring Sleeping Beauty. It had a palace as a background, and if you shook it, snowflakes came down.

Dexter knew I loved winter scenes; he knew I loved princesses, and he knew I loved the magic of Disney. It was perfect. I hadn't had anything as beautiful or as thoughtful as that since my bride Barbie doll, and I knew I wouldn't let Belinda anywhere near it. I would treasure it forever.

I found myself thinking about Dexter, and the thought that he had put into that perfect gift. He knew me so well, almost as well as Aunt Lucy had known me. Such a shame he was ten years younger than me, had far too much energy and looked nothing like my dream man.

Who knows? He could quite possibly have been the one.

Dexter was the last person I thought of as I drifted off to sleep. Merry Christmas Dexter, hope next year is perfect for you. You deserve it.

NOTES FROM A PANDEMIC

It was obvious quite early on in 2020 that it was NOT going to be a good year. As much as we, the great British public, were trying to bury our heads in the sand and assume that this awful coronavirus was not going to touch us, early indications suggested that it was already in the country. Presumably we, like the rest of the world, were paying the price for travelling by air and boat. This virus, whatever it was, was spreading quickly.

People soon became afraid of the unknown. A 'super spreader' – another new phrase to learn that year – had contracted the virus abroad and was spreading it quickly. Once he, poor man, was in hospital, everyone thought it would all be OK, and the spreading would stop. But it wasn't OK. It would be a long time before anything was OK. We could all see how quickly the virus was spreading, and things were spiralling out of control.

Chapter Twenty-two

Christmas had been perfect, but things were now definitely getting wobbly again and they were things I had no control over. Unfortunately, although Aunt Charlotte had been back home for a while, she was now back in the care home for assessment to see if living at home again was a reality. It transpired that she was much harder to deal with than Aunt Lucy. Aunt Lucy had not been mobile, and she had stayed put. Aunt Charlotte, on the other hand kept moving around… and falling. She didn't seem to understand that she could no longer cook for Belinda, Hope and me. She didn't understand she had to wait for someone to help her before she tried to move.

Roger had been home for a couple of weeks, thinking he could sort it out, but he couldn't. In fact, it was worse if anything, as she just wanted to please him; bake his favourite cake, make his bed, run his bath and be the mother for him that she had always been. For now, a care home was the safest and kindest option, as she and Hope were often in tears. It was so heartbreaking to watch.

Belinda eventually confessed that she and Jez had split up and she seemed much happier. She did ask me to cover the weekends a few times as she was seeing someone who lived out of the area but when I asked about him, she just said it was complicated, and it wasn't practical for it to become serious when he lived so far away. We left it at that. The main thing was she was so much happier without Jez. I had even heard her singing in the shower, which was unheard of. She was also trying to convince me to move out as she, 'honestly was in control now, and she and Hope didn't need me hanging around'. Plus, she presumed I would rather be at my bungalow. She wasn't wrong.

In the end, the compromise was that she would stay put for the weekends and I would spend Saturdays and Sundays in my bungalow. I would leave Hope with Belinda when she got home from work on a Friday and then pick her up from school on the Monday. We could sort school holidays out nearer the time.

Although it felt safe, I decided against telling Mum, Roger, whose leave was now over, or Dexter. I was a grownup, and this was my decision. Belinda was doing OK, and it felt right.

The first Friday night I felt a bit like a naughty teenager, and I could hear Aunt Lucy saying, "If it feels wrong lass, then it is wrong." This is called 'guilt', I believe. However, I chose to ignore 'guilt' and instead ordered a chicken and mushroom Balti and cracked open a bottle of wine. This evening was going to be all about me. It was much needed, and it felt good.

Sadly, this self-indulgence didn't last long, and it was Dexter who discovered my guilty secret soon after. It was a Monday, and we had both picked up Hope with Tigger. Dexter and I had been watching them both messing around with the ball. A new game called 'ready steady go' where Hope said "ready, steady, go" threw the ball and they both chased it. One laughing and one barking.

It was a cold day, so we decided to get a hot chocolate from the café and, as it was dog friendly, we sat inside to warm our hands and paws. Dexter asked Hope if she had thought of a special name for her dog yet. She looked thoughtful.

"No."

"It has to have a name. You can't just call it dog."

"He doesn't need a name; he just knows he is my dog. Hope's dog. If I say 'I love you' he knows I am speaking to him."

Dexter smiled. I loved his smile, even with the new brace, it was always from the heart and never artificial.

Hope continued to make her point. "When my Mummy says she loves me she doesn't say 'I love you Hope'. She says, 'I love you' and I know she is talking to me."

I suddenly felt the need to join in the conversation and took advantage of this opportunity that had been thrust at me "Does your Mummy often say she loves you Hope?"

"Yes of course, because she does. She says that even when she isn't quite with it, that it doesn't mean she doesn't love me. It just means she can't think of the words."

I smiled. "When she has too much to drink you mean?"

"Yes, yesterday her and that man had too much to drink, and they started smoking those smelly cigarettes. I asked Mummy for a drink of water, but she couldn't get me one, so I got some juice out of the fridge instead. Can we go home now, I want to watch my program?"

I knew that I was red, and I guessed it wasn't a light red either. I knew this was a real 'red hot chili pepper' tone, and I felt I was slightly heated as well.

Dexter looked at me and I knew what was coming.

"You're still staying at the house, right?"

That evening when Hope was in bed and Belinda had gone out I video-called Dexter and told him my guilty secret.

I was honest with him, that I had only been going back to the bungalow for the last two weekends, but I had enjoyed it and was feeling mentally more in control. I told him that I thought Jez was off the scene and Belinda had a new man. She had said she could handle things. She had said she could look after Hope. Now I knew that she had lied to me.

Saying it out loud helped me to believe what I was saying, not that Dexter doubted me or called me a liar. That wasn't his style, and he knew I was telling the truth. He also knew that Hope couldn't stay alone with Belinda at the weekends. We both now knew that.

I promised to speak to Belinda the next day. I clearly wasn't very good at being a grownup and making my own decisions. I should have listened to guilt and taken my responsibilities more seriously. Aunt Lucy was right even when she wasn't around, and it sucked.

NOTES FROM A PANDEMIC

People took the first national lockdown very seriously, as they feared the unknown. By the time the third one came people were becoming more relaxed. The vaccination was out, the elderly and the at-risk had, by now, received their jabs. People started to make up their own rules, at least as far as bubbles and social gatherings were concerned.

People were fed up now. Nobody expected the virus to last the year, nobody expected Christmas to be cancelled and they certainly didn't want the new year to be starting with a lockdown.

Did it really matter if they met more than three families Christmas day? Could they not party New Year's Eve if the doors were open?

People were beginning to get more complacent, and rules were being broken.

Chapter Twenty-three

I asked Belinda if Dexter could pick Hope up from school the next day and take her back to Uncle Fred's so we could talk, and she was fine with it. She acted like she expected me to ask, like she knew what was coming.

She flicked through her phone and listened to me ramble without any eye contact or interest in what I was saying and when she eventually looked up, she just said out loud what she was thinking. She wasn't at all sorry and had no idea what the fuss was about.

Yes, Jez had been coming over. She had a life at the end of the day. She worked hard to be a good Mum during the week and spending time with Jez at the weekend, getting drunk and stoned was her way of relaxing. It was safer for Hope to have someone in the house, if she was a bad mother she would go out and leave her home alone, which she would never do. She hadn't realised Hope needed water, but she knew where the tap was, and she probably enjoyed the juice more than water anyway.

The whole conversation was shocking, but it was me I was most disappointed in. She had lied to me about Jez not being around and I had naively fallen for it. While we were growing up, I was the one who got branded a liar, even though, as far as I could remember, I hadn't told a lie in my life. Yes, I had an active imagination and yes, I could exaggerate and yes, I could write a good story, but I had never told an outright and blatant lie. She had told me Jez was out of the picture. She had told me that she was better off without him. She told me she could look after Hope. She told me she had a new man.

I was hurt. I felt cheated, I felt guilty but most of all I felt angry. I was shaking with anger and, irritatingly, the anger made me tearful. I blubbered as I yelled.

"You lied to me Belinda. How can I ever trust you again? You lied about Jez, you lied about your new man, and you lied about being able to look after Hope. I should report you to social services."

"Yes, but you won't will you Sally, because you have no bloody spine. You will worry about Roger, about Aunt Charlotte and about Hope. You will worry about ruining her happy ever after. She is doing OK as she is, and you know it. I am a good mum, I'm just not good at doing it all the time. There's nothing wrong with that. What's the alternative? You would rather she went into care?"

No of course I wouldn't.

She concluded by saying that she had told Jez all about her new man, and yes, there was a new man. Jez thought it was a fantastic arrangement. Jez wasn't her boyfriend, he was a 'friend with benefits' and wasn't upset about her seeing other men.

I left a message for Roger to ring when he was allowed, and he phoned later that week. He said yes, Belinda did smoke weed. He smelt it on her clothes, and she had come in stoned a few times, but she had never smoked it in front of Hope. He suggested that maybe I should have Hope stay at the bungalow at the weekends with me. That way I could enjoy the bungalow with Hope and Belinda could enjoy her lifestyle. He admitted this is what had worried him about going away. Apparently, this is what Belinda did. One day she was the perfect mum taking her responsibility seriously and the next day it was all about her.

Everyone thought that me having Hope at the bungalow at weekends was the only solution. Uncle Fred, Dexter and Mum and Phil, when they were told, all thought it was a good idea. I had no doubt if I had phoned Boris Johnson or the queen, they would have thought it was a good idea as well. I stupidly hoped that Belinda would try and talk me out of having Hope at the bungalow, that she would have a flashback of the fact she felt bitter about the bungalow or something but that didn't happen. It was just another happy-ever-after ending I had got completely wrong. My bungalow was about to be introduced to bedwetting and jam-covered furniture.

A decision was made on Wednesday night that Hope should stay with me that following weekend, which gave me, Dexter and Uncle Fred just Thursday and Friday to turn Aunt Lucy's old room into a room for Hope. Nobody asked Uncle Fred to help, he was getting frail now, but he wanted to pitch in. He said he was "dapper with a paintbrush" and managed to do his part.

Aunt Lucy's room was still a bit of a shrine and hadn't been touched since the day she died. Yes, the sheets had been changed and it was clean, but her jewellery box was still open, her hairbrush still in front of her mirror on the dressing table, her commode was obviously empty but still in the corner of the room as were many unopened bags of panty liners.

We decided between us to keep the bed until a new one could be purchased but the furniture, commode and liners

Dexter would take to the tip, and we would start again with Hope choosing her own bits and pieces. Dexter did the tip-run while Uncle Fred helped me wrap Aunt Lucy's personal possessions in tissue paper and lovingly place them into some storage boxes to be put into the attic. Maybe one day I would feel ready to sort through and give things to a charity shop but not now. This was hurting a lot more than I wanted it to and I wasn't ready to get rid of anything else anytime soon.

Dexter came back from the tip-run with some fish and chips for lunch and I took the opportunity to take myself into the back garden for a private cry while they laid the table. It wasn't long before Dexter found me, and he just held me as I sobbed into his shirt. I sobbed and sobbed and sobbed until his shirt was covered in tears and snot, and he let me. He said nothing, there was nothing he could say.

When we went back in Uncle Fred looked surprised and had eaten most of the chips. This was to be the first time we would notice his memory was fading, and the last time we would leave him unattended with our food.

For many weekends after this Dexter and Uncle Fred helped Hope to decorate her new bedroom. She decided she wanted the room to be painted dark purple and dark blue. The accessories were all from the Walt Disney film Frozen. She had a Frozen duvet cover, a Frozen pillowcase set, a Frozen waste bin, and a Frozen table lamp. And it transpired that Uncle Fred really was dapper with the old paintbrush.

Dexter asked if he could bring Tigger over while they decorated so he wasn't home alone, and I didn't feel I was able to say no in the circumstances. Yes, Tigger was a small smelly creature, but I was pretty sure being houseproud was going to go out the window very soon. Goodbye clean carpets, goodbye pristine settee, goodbye sanity. Yes, Tigger was welcome.

I decided that in public I could sacrifice my home comforts, but when I was on my own there were certain things that were staying. Nights in with prosecco were staying and parading around the house in my wedding dress was another secret, sad, pleasure that was staying as well.

The wedding dress was now in my own bedroom with the wardrobe door carefully locked. People could take away my Aunt Lucy's room, they could take away my weekend freedom and they could take away my clean house, but nobody could take away my hopes and my dreams. Nobody could take away my still-strong longing to meet my prince. I knew he was out there somewhere. Without a doubt having Hope at the weekends and living in squalor was going to make things more complicated, but I would find Mr Perfect and I would have my dream wedding.

Aunt Lucy had believed in my dream. She believed that there would be a wedding, and I was going to make sure it happened and there absolutely would be a spare place for her laid at the top table. That was one happy ending I was determined would happen.

Thoughts of my dream wedding cheered me up a lot. It was also nice to have a project in the winter. I never really liked winter, as I was neither a fan of the dark nights or the cold weather. The fact Christmas was approaching kept you going during autumn, but as soon as the last Christmas light came down it was just dreary, cold and dark. It felt like we were all just hanging around waiting for Spring to happen. With all the decorating and clearing going on, there wasn't much hanging around going on this year and there always seemed to be something to do.

Away from the bungalow something else was happening this winter as well. There was a new virus. I had only managed to catch a glimpse of the headlines, but this virus, which started in China, was spreading through other parts of the world. I reassured myself that it wouldn't come to England and if it did, it wouldn't spread as quickly as the other parts of the world. England wasn't overcrowded like some of these countries. We had large spaces, parks and beaches. There was no way it would spread in the same way.

This evening's news hour suggested that there were indeed cases in England, but the prime minister was telling us not to panic and to just wash our hands thoroughly every time we came in from the shops. It was suggested that singing 'Happy Birthday' twice over whilst washing your hands would do the trick. Seemed a bit hard to believe, but he was the prime minister so presumably he could be trusted.

I reached for my wine and wondered how many glasses Boris Johnson would be having tonight. He was voted in to get us out of Europe and I was pretty sure he didn't sign up for this.

Was this something a prime minister would automatically know how to deal with?

I raised my glass "Cheers Boris, good luck."

NOTES FROM A PANDEMIC

A lot of mistakes were made in the United Kingdom at the beginning of the pandemic which wasted a lot of time. We had tried many solutions: putting people carrying the virus into isolation, even putting people returning from China in separate 'isolation hotels'.

The prime minister initially seemed reluctant to instigate a lockdown and instead promoted two controversial ideas. The first was called 'herd immunity', which meant we would be allowed to endure the virus to develop protection against the disease through our bodies' natural immune responses. It was later suggested that this delay had cost us a lot of time and, more importantly, lives.

The second was the idea of washing your hands vigorously while singing 'Happy Birthday' twice over.

Meanwhile, while we were singing 'Happy Birthday' hopefully, other nations were essentially locking their countries down. Many people here were suspecting that we would eventually start paying attention to the rest of the world and a national lockdown would soon be announced. These rumours spread quickly and before long the shelves in the supermarket were bare. It started with a shortage of toilet rolls and paracetamol, and then soon everything ran out.

The government announced that there was nothing to worry about, there was no need to 'panic-buy', but that is exactly what everyone was doing. They were panicking.

Chapter Twenty-four

My bungalow was now officially a tip. People were beginning to panic-buy as they were expecting a lockdown to happen any minute and so we, like everyone else, had been grabbing toilet rolls 'just in case', which meant piles of toilet rolls now joined the piles of dirty laundry and the piles of Hope's toys.

Positively, Hope had stopped wetting the bed at night, which was something, but the bungalow was becoming a bit of a free-for-all. Dexter and Tigger were becoming regular visitors. Neither of them wiped their feet and the bungalow smelt of dog.

I still had sole responsibility for Hope at the weekends and sometimes I did feel I was doing a wonderful job. All those clothes to wash, a million toys to put away, and homework to be done in time for school on a Monday.

Hope seemed unfazed about the comings and goings of her mother and the change in routine at the weekend. Upheaval was something she had needed to get used to from an early age, and Roger and Aunt Charlotte had done everything they could to keep her life stable, with a routine. I loved the fact that she prayed at the end of each day. That, I presumed, was Aunt Charlotte, as Aunt Lucy had instilled that into myself, Roger and Belinda. Not that it took in all three cases.

One thing I didn't love about Hope was her hissy fits. When you said 'No' to Hope she kicked off. She could go from first gear to fifth gear in minutes, and sometimes screamed so much she ended up gasping to get her breath back. I had a genuine fear that the kid would get so wound up she would explode one day, but I tried to be strong and not give in during every anger episode.

My proudest achievement was that I could now cook a roast dinner, which I did every Sunday. It wasn't rocket-science, most of the joints of meat from the supermarket had instructions on them. Occasionally, Dexter and Uncle Fred would join us, which was lovely, particularly for Uncle Fred. It got him out of the house, and he often insisted on paying for the joint of meat.

Part of me enjoyed my achievements, but another part of me felt exhausted. I craved 'me time'. I wanted to just lay on the bed and dream, I wanted to try on my wedding dress, look at my wedding portfolio and keep my dream alive. I wanted to be me.

Everybody was telling me how well I was doing; they were blown away with how I was embracing having Hope at the weekend; they were impressed that I had suddenly advanced from takeaways and beans on toast to cooking a roast. Even Belinda was sending regular texts congratulating me on how well I was doing, so it was a very confusing time.

I wanted times where I was doing nothing, and yet I was quite enjoying all the praise I was getting. It was nice to be told I was doing well. What was it Aunt Lucy used to say about pride before a fall?

That fall was about to happen. If I thought this stage of my life was weird, the prime minister was about to make a speech that would make it even weirder.

NOTES FROM A PANDEMIC

On Monday 23rd March 2020 the prime minister made this sombre announcement.

"From this evening, I must give the British people a very simple instruction: you must stay at home. Because the critical thing we must do is stop the disease spreading between households.

"That is why people will only be allowed to leave their home for the following very limited purposes: shopping for basic necessities, as infrequently as possible; one form of exercise a day – for example, a run, a walk, or a cycle, alone or with members of your household; any medical need, to provide care or to help a vulnerable person; and travelling to and from work, but only where this is absolutely necessary and cannot be done from home.

"That's all. These are the only reasons you should leave your home. You should not be meeting friends. If your friends ask you to meet, you should say 'No'. You should not be meeting family members who do not live in your home. You should not be going shopping except for essentials like food and medicine. And you should do this as little as you can. And use food delivery services where you can.

"If you don't follow the rules the police will have the powers to enforce them, including through fines and dispersing gatherings.

"To ensure compliance with the government's instruction to stay at home, we will immediately: close all shops selling non-essential goods, including clothing and electronic stores, and other premises including libraries, playgrounds and outdoor gyms and places of worship; stop all gatherings of more than two people in public, excluding people you live with; and stop all social events, including weddings, baptisms, and other ceremonies, but excluding funerals.

"Parks will remain open for exercise, but gatherings will be dispersed."

Chapter Twenty-five

I couldn't believe what I had just heard, this must have been what it was like all those years ago when people were listening to Winston Churchill on the radio talking about the start of World War Two.

This was really happening. We, the United Kingdom; the place of the stiff upper lip where disasters never happened, where we never got our toes wet in a tsunami, or our homes shaken in an earthquake, were about to have our world turned upside down. The virus had actually reached our country. There was nothing special about us. Like the rest of the world, we were going to have to change our routines, stick to the rules and face whatever was coming. This was now officially being called a global pandemic. Nowhere in the world was safe and I was regretting my bad taste in film selection at Christmas, when I watched a movie called Pandemic which now only magnified the fear.

I phoned Mum as soon as the announcement was made, and she confirmed that the chances of her and Phil coming over any time soon were very slight. The risk of not being able to get back were too high. Mum thought the 'novelty' of the virus would soon blow over. All these rules would be lifted and then she and Phil could come over and seriously look at the housing market, which was currently closed.

I hoped Aunt Charlotte would be safe in her care home and was grateful we didn't have to worry about her. People over 70 were, without a doubt, the most vulnerable, and the most likely to die. They just were not strong enough to fight this awful disease.

Surely, Hope would need to go back home to Belinda now. Belinda wasn't working, the schools were closed, she was not allowed to see Jez and unless she was growing it in the greenhouse, she wouldn't be able to get her hands on any weed either.

Well, that was another 'nice try, Sally' that didn't come to pass, as nobody wanted me to send Hope home. To a chorus of, "Of course Belinda will break the rules," "Jez will be there every night you know that," and "Really, Sal?" it was decided that yes, Hope and I were going to be locked in together. It was me that was going to become her teacher and have to entertain her somehow, and I knew that wouldn't be easy. What the heck was I going to do without Tigger and Dexter? No, I didn't know either.

Dexter assured me it was going to be OK. At least we could have an hour's exercise, some countries couldn't even do that. Hope would be able to see other people walking dogs in the park, even if just from a distance. We could do a little project together, a kind of 'I-spy' with the different dog breeds we saw while out. Dexter could do a quiz online for us to join in. Things could be worse.

He was right, we were allowed to exercise, and we were allowed to do essential shopping. I hoped that prosecco fell under the list of 'essential products', because I was going to be running out very quickly.

Chapter Twenty-six

The first part of lockdown lasted until May, and teaching Hope was as awful as I suspected. She had absolutely no respect for me as a teacher and I had absolutely no inclination to push her into something she didn't want to do. I mean it wasn't as if she was doing any life-changing exams, not at her age.

Dexter tried to persuade me to get a routine going, which kind of helped, but somehow both the routine and schoolwork got forgotten somewhere during the day and we would both get bored and start watching Disney films, which was so much more fun.

The alarm went off at 8 am and we staggered around in our pyjamas – another thing we had in common, we were not morning people. Some chap called Joe Wicks was doing free online fitness classes every morning for children and parents to keep fit while self-isolating. It came on late morning which killed a few minutes, and it was fun. In my mind that counted as a lesson as Hope did PE at school. I could then confidently say we did at least one lesson a day.

I then decided to stoop to a new low level – bribery. It worked. If Hope did one hour worth of schoolwork after lunch, then she got to dress up. We both did. This counted as 'drama'.

That part of the day was far more than drama and dressing up, it was our special time of day, a time for us to bond. I had shown Hope my wedding dress quite early on during lockdown as something to do, and she obviously wanted to dress up as well, so I ordered her some children's dressing up clothes: princess dresses, bridesmaid dresses and one beautiful kiddies' wedding dress. The one thing you could count on during lockdown was the delivery man, and ours was beginning to look especially tired. I made a mental note to give him a huge Christmas tip.

Most days I would wear the wedding dress, and she would wear whatever she felt like wearing. It was fun and it killed a few more hours in the day. Sometimes I would be a bride and she would be a bridesmaid, other times we were both beautiful brides. One day she decided that she wasn't going to dress up but just make me, "look beautiful." I laughed at myself in the mirror. So much lipstick on my lips, my teeth and my cheeks. We both laughed. We did so much laughing that sometimes it was me that was at risk of wetting myself. Our jaws ached with laughter.

On another occasion, Hope persuaded me to order an adult 'Jasmine' costume. Jasmine was the Princess in Aladdin and Hope thought I looked just like her with my long black hair. It was a sweet thing for her to say, but I wondered if this was going a step too far, and if this was now borderline weird. It probably was, but she was having a fantastic time and so was I, so I decided it was harmless fun.

We spoke to a lot of people via video which was lovely, and it wasn't long before Belinda got to hear about our dressing up as brides in the afternoon. I was listening from the kitchen when, to my horror, I heard Belinda say, "You need to ask Aunt Sally to tell you the story of her fairytale wedding Hope. Ask her how it all went wrong. I think Aunt

Sally might like it if you coloured the dress in red. Red is her favourite colour."

While Hope was still on the call I went into the bedroom and locked the wardrobe door. I put the key high up on the top of the wardrobe, where even I couldn't get it without the stepladder and the stepladder was then locked in the shed. I was sure that Hope wouldn't do it as an evil act, but she may well now think that red was my favourite colour. Nothing wrong with the colour. It just wasn't a wedding day colour. I had forgotten how cruel Belinda could be.

Once the call was finished the questions started to come.

"Were you going to get married Aunt Sally?"

"Does it matter?"

"Well kind of."

"One day I met someone that I thought I would marry. He was my handsome prince, but he went away."

"Oh no, that is so sad. Is he coming back?"

"No, but I am hoping one day I am going to meet another prince, and we will have a fairytale wedding. Then I will get, my wedding dress dry cleaned."

"I will help you, Aunt Sally. When Covid has gone away, and the rainbows come down I will help you find a prince, and then you will be Princess Aunt Sally. Just like Princess Meghan."

When she was old enough for grownup discussions I would share my feelings about Princess Meghan, who married an actual prince and then seemed surprised that she had to perform princess-like duties. But now was not the time.

Hope and I also painted rainbows. Lots of people did. One day we went to the beach and picked up some flat pebbles, which we painted rainbows on, and put them on the driveway for people to help themselves to. We were pleased to see the delivery man take one, turn around smile and wave. Oh good, we hadn't broken him. The rainbow was the sign of hope and lots of people, including us, had large rainbows in their windows.

We tried to go for a walk in the park and do some shopping once a day and often had to queue outside the shop. More and more people were wearing masks and trying to stand two metres apart – another instruction from the government based on advice from scientists.

I tried not to become obsessed with the news, but there was a press conference on every day at 5pm with a different person heading it up each day. I would discreetly put it on in the background.

Care homes were often mentioned, and I was worried about Aunt Charlotte, as was Roger, who called the home regularly for updates. I was worried about the virus boarding Roger's ship as well, as it was almost impossible to stay more than two metres apart. There were already cases of the virus on cruise-liners and all people could do was hope for the best and wait it out. Roger said you needed to get off the boat for it to get onto the boat, and he felt confident he would be OK.

We had plenty of online time with Dexter as well, and Hope would always insist that he lifted Tigger up high enough for us to enjoy for the first five minutes. We would then run through the list of lessons we had done. He was quite impressed and said we should count art as well because of the good job we were doing with the rainbows and that we could incorporate maths through shopping. Good call.

Sometimes he would have a quiz ready that Hope was always going to win, as it was about television programs or children's story books that she knew far more about than me.

One quiz I almost won until Dexter came up with the final question.

"In My Little Pony is Twilight Sparkle a boy or a girl?"

Hope shouted out, "Girl!" and won again.

If this lockdown went on much longer, I could get a job lecturing on My Little Pony characters. All was not lost.

Chapter Twenty-seven

I hadn't realised how isolated I had started to feel until May, when it was announced on the 5 pm news update that we could now meet one person outside of the house. I shouted "Yippee!" and started jumping up and down on the sofa. It wasn't long before Hope appeared from the bedroom wanting to know what the noise was about. When I told her she was soon jumping up and down with me.

Our yippee soon upgraded to clapping, then cheering, then jumping off the sofa and linking arms and dancing around in circles before finally jumping on the bed. With so many rules having to be adhered to in the outside world I had given up on being houseproud. Yes, jumping on the sofa and the bed were now officially allowed.

As we bounced, I was yelling like a mad person "Yippee, yahoo Hope, we can meet one other person outside from Monday."

She bounced higher than me, yelling back, "Yippee, we can meet Dexter."

I stopped bouncing and sat down, pulling her down next to me, not just because of what she said, but because I was also beginning to feel sick. "What about Mummy?"

"We can see Mummy on Tuesday, and then on Wednesday we can find you another prince. Would finding another prince make you happy?"

Bless her heart. Just her saying that made me happy.

The weather had been glorious since March. It was a real blessing, and soon people were meeting in parks sitting on picnic blankets. The suggestion was that people didn't share food, and most people were adhering to that, getting their own packed lunch out and just enjoying the moment, the freedom, the gift of meeting someone else.

Like many other people, Hope, Dexter, Uncle Fred and I soon started stretching the rules.

It was only a little tweak to the rules, but we just had to involve Uncle Fred. We had three picnic blankets in his back garden, two metres apart and shouted at each other across the lawn. It was fun, it was fantastic. We only did this in the privacy of Uncle Fred's garden though. In public we behaved. I was terrified there might be some kind of Covid policeman watching our every move and certainly didn't want to find myself locked in a prison cell, now I knew how horrid being locked in anywhere was.

Understandably, the care homes were still very strict. The poor manager looked tired and terrified. She seemed pleased to see Hope though, and we were allowed to sit in the garden and wave to Aunt Charlotte through the window. Hope would show her a picture through the window and then post it through the letterbox. Sometimes Aunt Charlotte had tears in her eyes. You could tell it was all too much for her, and it was heartbreaking to watch.

We saw a lot of Belinda as well, though she never once asked for her little girl back, and her little girl didn't once ask to go back. It was strange in a way, but then there were times I had preferred Aunt Lucy's company to my mum's, so tried not to make too much out of it. As long as everyone was content, safe and alive then it had to be the right thing, and it eliminated the anxiety about Hope spreading the virus between the two homes.

Most of the time I was content as well. There was still plenty of time to watch Disney movies and stroke my wedding dress, and now I could see Dexter outside as well as online. But there were times when I was starting to feel sorry for myself again. I didn't like being single, this had never been my dream. And I wasn't getting any younger. This darned virus was getting in the way of my happy ever after, but things were beginning to get back to normal. I just had to be patient.

Soon it was announced that we could meet 30 people outside the house and six people inside. This was such a relief and would make things so much more bearable. Another announcement authorised people to go back to work if they couldn't work from home. Public transport was now opening up again, but many people were too scared to use it. It was strange to see empty buses, the drivers wearing masks and sometimes medical gloves and looking terrified. But clearly not as terrified as the public who were quite obviously still avoiding any type of public transport.

People who had nobody, were being encouraged to 'bubble up' with other families and could now be included in social activities inside and outside of their homes. Slowly but surely things were getting back to normal.

The children going back to school was a huge relief to parents, children and possibly teachers as well. Many teachers must have been mortified by the quality of homework being sent in. Even then, things had to be put in place. There were one-way systems for dropping off and picking up your child, there were Covid tests on arrival and so much hand gel. Everybody's hands were sore from applying hand gel and I was amazed how many times Hope actually managed to rub her eyes after applying it. The children were also put into bubbles and could only talk to and play with the children within their bubble. If one of the children within the bubble got Covid or anyone from their house got Covid then the whole bubble had to stay at home. This happened twice with Hope, and I was relieved I didn't work.

Hope became a victim of 'the bubble' and on her first day back at school was in tears as she had been put into the green bubble and she hated green. Far worse she had been separated from Olivia who, apparently, was her best friend, even though this was the first time I had ever heard her name mentioned. In between sobs I was told, "We can't even talk to each other outside." It was tough for children, for the elderly, for the lonely. It was tough for everyone, and I vowed to never forget how rough this time was for so many.

Dexter was allowed in the house now, so the Disney videos stopped and, instead, he and Hope spent ages keeping up to date with the happenings at Ruff 'n' Rescued. Hope had been asked to do a project for school and she decided she was going to follow one dog on its journey from the shelter in Romania, across Europe in the 'happy van', until it was handed over to its new 'humans' in England. It kept them both quiet, Tigger as well, who stared at the laptop screen with them and seemed to know exactly what was going on. This gave me the green light to sneak into the bedroom and read some good old-fashioned romance novels.

The trouble with them looking at all the dogs who needed rehoming meant that Hope wanted to rehome them all, and she was constantly nagging me for a dog. I was constantly refusing to get her one. I wasn't houseproud now, so that wasn't the issue, but my life seemed full enough without adding a rescue dog to the chaos.

Everyone was talking about their 'new normal' and how they missed their 'old normal'. I wasn't sure I wanted a 'new normal' or my 'old normal'. I just wanted my 'dream normal'. It was hard to be smiley all the time, but having Hope around gave me something to get out of bed for in the morning and stopped me revisiting that downward spiral of despair. She was my little ray of sunshine.

One day when I was laying on the bed daydreaming, I heard her and Dexter discussing her toy dog's name.

"Dexter, I have thought of a name for my toy dog."

"Really? Wow, that is very exciting. What is dog called now?"

"Prince. Aunt Sally was going to marry a prince, but he went away. I thought she might like another prince in the house."

I heard Dexter laugh. "That is great Hope, just great."

I enjoyed the innocence of a child's mind, I enjoyed hearing Dexter laugh, and things would probably have been great if I had just accepted life the way it was. Me, Hope, Dexter, Tigger... and Prince. But life has a way of throwing curveballs, and one was about to be thrown my way.

Chapter Twenty-eight

A round the time that things started to 'open up' I received my first email from Zak. At first, I thought it was a fake as I found it in my spam folder. It just said, "I love you" and wasn't signed by Zak or anyone else. I didn't recognise the email address, and I didn't even consider Zak, as in our short time of courting I hadn't remembered us ever emailing each other. As I was in the middle of booking a bowling lane for Hope's birthday, I didn't take a lot of notice. I certainly didn't worry about it. I just deleted it without giving it a second thought.

Hope's birthday was 4th July, which was the date the Government had given us for everything to open up. Somehow, we were going from very few places being allowed to open, to everyone being allowed to open, which I wasn't sure about. This included hairdressers, beauticians, nonessential shops and the whole of the hospitality sector.

If I was going to book a bowling lane then I needed to get in quickly. I had tried to persuade Hope that it might be nice to take a group of friends bowling to help her celebrate, as this I hoped would take her mind off wanting a dog. Instead of being grateful she had thrown herself onto the floor kicking, screaming and having a mighty fine tantrum. "I don't want to go bowling. I want a dog."

I wondered if they taught you about temper tantrums at antenatal class, or whether they focused on labour pains alone, thinking that was all you needed to know to be a mother. Surely it should be compulsory for mothers and babysitters to know that tantrums would inevitably happen. There should be a warning statement and some training given.

I didn't know much about raising children, but one thing I did know was that you shouldn't give in, so when this particular tantrum, like many tantrums before was taking place, I just took myself to my bedroom, put some music on and some headphones in. What Hope didn't realise was I was beginning to change my mind about a dog, but I wanted to make sure that when I told her, it was absolutely clear that my decision had nothing to do with her spoilt brat tantrums and that the dog would be mine not hers. Unfortunately, there was never enough time between tantrums for this conversation to take place.

It was Dexter who had persuaded me. The two of us had been talking about the world returning to normal, which had prompted us to talk about Belinda and the possibility of her becoming 'some kind of normal'. If that happened and she decided that actually she DID want to be a full-time mum and DID want it to work out with Hope, then I felt I would be isolated and lonely. It would take me time to adjust. That gave Dexter the green light to really sell the idea of a rescue dog to me. Something that was mine, that would need me as much as I needed it. Since then, I had been looking at his work website. I had promised myself that if it was going to happen then it needed to be a dog that didn't shed its hair. Something like a Bichon Frise, a small, white, non-shedding dog that was compact enough to pick up and carry if things got out of hand. Yes, that was it, a Bichon Frise. But I wasn't sure how realistic that idea was. They were street dogs at the end of the day. Would a pedigree lady Bichon just happen upon a pedigree male Bichon in a Romanian forest somewhere just to perform what came naturally and make my ideal dog happen? It was unlikely.

I went to the cemetery and asked Aunt Lucy to ask God for a sign. Presumably I didn't need to pray to him now as they just hung out together in heaven. Even if they were singing for a thousand years there must be a coffee break or something in between for them to chat, even in heaven you would get a dry mouth. Heaven seemed a very mysterious place. It was best not to think about it too much.

The cemetery was the ideal place to remind Aunt Lucy how much I missed her and how I now understood why she spent so much time with her nephew and nieces. Why she spoilt us so. There was absolutely a special bond between me and Hope despite her hissy fits and I needed something to fill the hole she was going to leave if she went home. If Aunt Lucy and God thought a dog was a good idea, then I needed to find a small, non-shedding dog, preferably a purebred Bichon Frise, with an appropriate name. The name would be the sign. Maybe Hugh, as I still had the hots for Hugh Grant, might be appropriate. I left this prayer request in the safe hands of Aunt Lucy and headed for home.

I hadn't told Dexter that I was caving in and actively looking on the Ruff 'n' Rescued website, but then I hadn't told Dexter about the emails I was getting from Zak either. It was now clear that the first one that had come through wasn't a fake, it was very much from Zak. He was signing his messages now. I had no idea I had even given him my email address though, on reflection, there were a lot of comings and goings with the solicitors about the deeds of the bungalow, so I must have copied him in.

These emails were now coming daily, and although I hadn't responded I hadn't deleted them either. I was reading them. Zak was no longer in prison, he had been let out early, for good behaviour and he was desperate to see me. He wanted to explain that it wasn't how it looked. The police and the judge had got it all wrong. Didn't he deserve ten minutes of my time just to set the record straight? He promised that after his explanation if I didn't want to see him again then he would just walk away.

I would be happy for him to walk away right now, without the ten minutes. I decided that, as I had zero feelings for him, reading the emails wasn't going to hurt me or anyone else. Besides I had a dog to find.

When Hope's birthday finally came, she was as good as gold. She did not mention getting a dog once and we had a really nice day. She was thrilled with the present I had brought her, which was two more families for her Sylvanian house, and Belinda had picked her up from school with me with another surprise, a new scooter. And not just any scooter. This one had Elsa from Frozen on it. All her friends gathered around to have a look, and all took a turn on it as we travelled by foot to the bowling alley.

Belinda didn't intend to come bowling with us, but she did, and she enjoyed herself. She was going through another 'stable' stage. She mentioned having a new fella, who was different to anyone else she had ever met. It was the one she had been travelling to see and it transpires that they were getting on really well. She asked me if I had found anyone and if I had caved in and was now dating that dork, Dexter. A bit weird that she was asking about me, but I responded with a polite "No." I had been so focused on getting a dog I hadn't really been trying very hard to look for anyone, dork or not.

Belinda was spending the weekend with her new guy, so we continued the birthday celebrations with Dexter and Tigger on the Saturday, and that is when I decided to disclose my dog secret to them both. "Good behaviour should be rewarded." That is what Aunt Lucy would say.

Dexter was there when Hope asked if we could watch a film, and I said that I had a much better idea. I thought they should both get out the laptop and help me find my perfect dog. First there was silence and then Hope burst into tears before running around the bungalow shouting, "Yes, yes, yes!" whilst Tigger ran after her barking. It was chaos. Finally, she hugged me and told me that I was the best aunty in the world. Then she hugged Dexter saying he was the best uncle. Ooops.

I told them both my specifications and warned that it could take a while as I wanted to be sure I was choosing a dog that was perfect for me. They were both happy with that, still stunned that I was actually looking. Hope then used my phone to text Mum, Roger and Belinda to tell them about the good news before going to bed early as she wanted the next day to come quickly so she could check the internet for my perfect dog. Dexter smiled and joined me for a nightcap of the fizzy variety.

Dexter had been staying in the evenings when Hope went to bed, and I looked forward to it. He always went home at the end of the evening, but we got on well. He was my soulmate. Someone I could tell anything to. Anything, but not everything. How could I tell him about Zak's emails? What was stopping me? I wasn't responding, just reading them. No harm. That is what my head said, but my heart knew I was beginning to look forward to them. Zak was clever, he knew exactly what I wanted to hear. I wanted to hear that I was special, that I was loved, that he would look after me. I knew I was slowly losing this battle.

That was clearly why I hadn't told Dexter. I didn't want to hear him warn me about doing something stupid, especially when I knew he would be absolutely right.

Chapter Twenty-nine

I had enjoyed my summer with Hope, Dexter, Tigger and, yes, Belinda. Even Roger had managed to squeeze in some more leave.

Roger had stumbled across Belinda's new boyfriend, Mark, when he arrived home a day earlier than expected. It was just before bedtime and Belinda had been cross that he had not called her with his new plans. Once Roger had pointed out that, actually, this was his home, and he could come and go as he wanted, he had introduced himself to Mark who he described as "nothing like the usual freaks she brings home". Mark was smart, handsome and well-mannered and Roger was so impressed that he had turned a blind eye when Mark stepped out of Belinda's bedroom the following morning. He was both disappointed and frustrated when Mark said something had come up and he had to go, which left Roger with a sour-faced Belinda for the rest of his leave.

It was obviously early days and Roger asked me to review things again if, and when, Hope moved back. For now, he was happy with the situation and we both were excited about the prospect that this new chap might teach Belinda some good manners, if nothing else.

I asked Belinda a few times if I could meet Mark and was told quite bluntly that I should be focusing on my own love life not hers. Well, I couldn't argue with that though, clearly, she had forgotten that me having Hope wasn't the perfect situation for my finding anyone soon. Then just as I was about to approach the subject of 'two hands being better than one' and that she might like to have her little girl back so I could focus fully on my own love life, it was announced that due to a rising number of new Covid cases we were about to have a 'circuit breaker'. Another new term we were going to have to get used to and work out the meaning of.

Apparently, just as an electric circuit breaker is designed to protect an electrical circuit from damage caused by too much electrical current passing through, this circuit breaker would be designed to protect us from the damage caused by too many Covid cases. This would then prevent us from having to have a proper lockdown which, if it did occur, would be for a much longer time. The circuit breaker would be in effect from the beginning of November until the start of December. Then, or so the plan stated, life would return to normal, Santa's helpers in the North Pole could continue to make toys for the children and Christmas festivities would commence in the usual fashion.

The circuit breaker seemed to trigger a domino effect of shocks for me, though none of them were electric ones.

The announcement was the first of these shocks. Was I the only one seeing life through rose-tinted spectacles? Was I the only one who thought that now things had started to open the virus had gone away? Were we not now all going to live happily ever after with no more mention of the word lockdown? Clearly not.

The second shock was that Belinda asked to have Hope back for the half-term week and the two weeks afterwards. This tied in with the circuit breaker as the tattoo parlour would be shut and she thought she would spend some quality time with her making and baking. Probably not the big deal I was making of it, after all she was Hope's mother, but I had plans for half-term and none of those plans included me being locked down on my own. She said Mark was going 'up North' to visit and bubble up with his parents and she would enjoy the company.

I phoned Roger and he said, "Why not? You could do with a break Sally... be selfish for once."

I didn't want a break. I had made plans for Hope and me during this half-term, and I wanted to be selfish on my terms.

The third shock was Dexter telling me that his next trip to Romania was now planned, and he was leaving in two days' time and would be gone a while. Well, of course he would. This wasn't the first time he had left me home alone; his timing sucked.

The reason for him going was that the weather had turned very cold and there was a lot of maintenance work needing to be done. Positively, Ruff 'n' Rescued had been doing a lot of home checks and at least one 'happy van' was going to be coming over. The United Kingdom was due to exit the EU by the end of December and nobody knew how that would affect regulations concerning the transportation of dogs, and so the charity was keen to get as many dogs out of Romania as they could.

On the happy side of the board, and in an exciting twist, 'my dog' was one of those being fast-tracked out of Romania.

We had stumbled across my perfect dog at the end of August. Well, Hope had. I had been on the phone ordering pizza for the three of us when I heard the familiar sound of chaos coming from the lounge. When I peeped in, Dexter and Hope were jumping up and down on the settee chanting, "Yes, yes, yes." Even Tigger looked confused, and he and I just watched until they finally stopped.

Hope showed me the laptop. One small white male dog – possibly a Bichon Frise – had been found at the side of the road. I questioned the fact a purebred Bichon Frise would be found on the streets of Romania, but that is exactly what he looked like. He had already been taken to the vet to be looked over and was estimated to be four years old.

The way it worked over there was that the person who found the dog got to name them, and the lady concerned had named this little guy Prince. OK it wasn't Hugh, but even I had to admit that this was a sign, a very big illuminated in flashing lights, kind of sign.

Dexter said Prince would be snapped up and before I could object, he was on the phone to the rescue centre. Everyone there was thrilled that their main man, Dexter, was going to take the dog and, just like that, it was done. I had finally found my Prince. In fact, I could potentially be living with two Princes if you counted the little scraggy toy that Hope still carried around with her. Fantastic. All I needed now was a real human Prince. That would be the icing on the cake.

When October half-term came it was clear that Hope didn't want to stay at Belinda's house for three weeks any more than I wanted her to go, but Belinda and Roger were adamant that Belinda needed to take responsibility for her child, and I needed a break. As I watched Belinda drag her into the house mid hissy fit, I was tempted to join in, but I knew she would be OK. We both knew the next time Dexter walked through the front door he would have Prince in his arms. With Belinda onboard with the whole dog thing, we decided that Hope could track him online on his journey and Dexter promised there would be lots of photos for her to look at.

The final and nastiest shock of all was losing Aunt Charlotte. As sad as it was for us, it was a lovely way to go. She passed away in her sleep which made it nicer for everyone and we were able to tell Hope that she had just closed her eyes in her bed and when she opened them again, she was in heaven.

Belinda and I broke the news to Hope together, and although she cried, she summed it up beautifully.

"I am crying because I will miss her, but she must be so happy. Just imagine going to sleep and waking up in heaven. I have seen Aunt Lucy's picture. There are rainbows, flowers, turquoise lakes, and bunny rabbits. Aunt Lucy and her will be together for always." I hadn't seen any bunny rabbits on the picture, but it seemed a lovely idea.

It was decided that the funeral would be after the circuit breaker, which would be marginally more normal and give Roger time to sort out his compassionate leave.

Before I could take everything in, I was on my own again. Hope was gone, Dexter was gone, Aunt Charlotte was gone and all that was left was me and my wedding dress. The worst thing about being on your own is it gives you too much time to think, too many temptations to ease the boredom, temptations like takeaways and alcohol and too many opportunities to make wrong decisions.

I was about to make one of the biggest of the many wrong decisions of my life.

Chapter Thirty

Hope had only been with Belinda for a few days when I started feeling sorry for myself. I was lonely.

I remembered Aunt Lucy telling me that if I ever felt sorry for myself then I was losing the battle and should pull my socks up immediately, so not to begin a downward spiral of negativity, despair and depression.

I wasn't wearing socks but having been on that downward spiral more than once I decided that online shopping for bits and pieces for Prince should keep me occupied and take the focus off myself, so got my laptop out and started the ordering process.

It was quite nice being able to make my own decisions about my own dog without anyone interfering or telling me I was spending too much, which I clearly was. I decided that red would suit a white dog and brought him a red collar, a red lead, a red drinking bowl and some red toys to play with. I brought him a lovely bed which would stay in my room. If he didn't snore it would be nice to have some company in the bedroom. Not the company I really wanted in the bedroom, but it was a start. I was looking forward to introducing him to Tigger and being able to take him on some nice long walks with Dexter and Hope.

I had also been getting some fantastic photos of Prince from Hope. Presumably, that was why Dexter was so quiet. He was busy sending Hope updates. I was fine with that though, and I was glad she was enjoying herself. A few of them showed Dexter and Prince together and I hoped Dexter wasn't introducing him to bad habits. I didn't want my dog to lick my face every time he felt like it.

Seeing close-up photos of Prince highlighted the fact that he absolutely wasn't a Bichon Frise. Yes, he had the same white curly poodle-like coat, but he had almost fox-like features. According to Hope this was because he was crossed with a terrier. Then she went on to say that terriers always had their nose to the floor sniffing for food and they ate anything, even if it was bad for their tummies. Oh great, another reason why he shouldn't lick my face, who knew where that tongue had been.

The evenings in the bungalow were the worst as Hope went to bed so much earlier than me and Belinda didn't exactly encourage communication, so I had nobody to text or chat to. I figured quite quickly that the best way of coping with loneliness was going back to my old ways of washing down a good takeaway with a bottle of prosecco. And somewhere during that bleak time I started responding to Zak's messages.

My replies were short and sharp, but I was responding, and I knew I shouldn't be. If I had enough alcohol inside me, I could sleep afterwards, but once I got up, I felt guilty knowing how much it would hurt Dexter if he knew.

By the end of the first week, I was really struggling with my emotions. I was so confused. I was as sure as I could be that Dexter didn't want a relationship with me, even though part of me was beginning to wish that we were more than just friends, which was strange. I had never felt like that about Dexter before. Dexter was stable, he was good with Hope, he was kind, and I knew he thought the world of me as a friend, but he didn't love me.

Now that his teeth and hair were sorted, Dexter was actually very good looking. The downside of Dexter was that he didn't know how to treat a woman. Ask all those women who worked with him at Ruff 'n' Rescued. I had often seen photos of women mixing cement and pushing wheelbarrows whilst Dexter leant on a shovel smiling at them.

Then there was Zak, who knew exactly how to treat a woman. He bought flowers, he did the cooking, he made you feel like you were the only person in the universe. He was good looking, he was fit, and he knew me. He knew my hopes and my dreams and seemingly still wanted to make them a reality.

According to his emails he never wanted to take my bungalow from me. I was the turning point in his life, he had found love and was honestly going to change, but then the police caught up with him due to his previous crimes.

He said he had been visited by a local church while in prison and had become a born-again Christian. He wanted to eventually reach out to the families of his victims to say how sorry he was. However, for now he just wanted to apologise to me and prove that nothing about his feelings for me had changed. He still wanted to treat me like a princess. He wanted to see me walk down the aisle in the dress of my dreams. He still wanted to be my husband, my prince.

Belinda contacted me after the first week of her time with Hope to say how well it was going and that she and Roger had decided that after the circuit breaker and Aunt Charlotte's funeral Hope should start going back to her at the weekends. She knew that when the dog arrived Hope wouldn't want to be with her full time, and she knew that I would still want my space, so this seemed a good compromise.

She was desperate to know about what I was doing with all my spare time. What did she think I was doing? She had Hope and Dexter was away. Nothing is what I was doing, a big fat nothing. Well, that wasn't completely true. I was reading Zak's emails but now was not the time to tell her that. She would love it, and I didn't need her encouragement.

I kept reading the emails.

"Come on Sally, think about it, nobody else could run you a bath the way I did."

He wasn't wrong. Nobody had even tried.

Meanwhile in the outside world it was the beginning of December, and nobody was convinced this circuit breaker had worked. The number of people infected by the virus was growing if anything.

People had started putting their Christmas lights up mid-November trying to convince themselves that this mini lockdown of ours really was going to work and Christmas really would happen. Even though it was plain to see that the new strain of the virus was spreading at a terrifying rate, the government was still encouraging us to make our Christmas plans. Up to three households would be allowed to meet up between 23rd and 27th of December. People believed this promise and were encouraged. They could finally drive to and visit loved ones during the holidays even if those loved ones lived in a different tier.

The concept of 'tiers' was something else we were now hearing a lot about. The tiers ranged from tiers 1 to 4 with 1 being medium alert, 2 being high alert, 3 being watch out and tier 4 meant you were in big trouble and had to stay at home. For this allocated Christmas period the promise was that unless you were in tier 4, in which case you would wave goodbye to Christmas anyway, then you could actually visit people in different tiers.

When the circuit breaker was over it became clear that people were not sticking rigidly to the rules anymore. They seemed disillusioned and bored of rules. I had decided to allow myself two bubbles. The Belinda and Hope bubble and the Dexter and Uncle Fred bubble, once Dexter returned, which would be very soon now.

Roger was given two weeks' compassionate leave which seemed to go by quickly, but he enjoyed his time with us. He was somehow talked into playing Sylvanian families and had managed to order a badger family. I was not impressed with the addition of this new non-dog family, but Hope didn't seem to mind, she was just pleased to have Roger home. The time went quickly but Roger reassured Hope that his proper annual leave was only a couple of months away and that they could play again then.

The funeral was lovely. Well, as lovely as a funeral can be. It was a very small family affair but very special and we had all done her proud. The vicar used Hope's description of heaven having rainbows, flowers, turquoise lakes and bunny rabbits. When Roger made his own tribute to his mum, Hope held his hand during every word he said. It was an emotional and yet extremely special time for us all.

After the funeral the new routine started, with me having Hope weekdays only and it was going well.

Hope and I had plenty of time when we were together to look forward to seeing Dexter and get stupidly excited about the new dog he was bringing back with him. Even Belinda seemed to be content as she was obviously in love, though still very cloak and dagger about it all. Whenever a meet up with Mark was suggested, she would use Covid as an excuse, "What about the virus?"

If anyone else had said that it would have made sense, but from Belinda it made no sense at all. She never put a mask on, she made it ultra clear she would never have a vaccination, and she thought the world was overreacting over this 'heavy cold' everyone was getting. I wasn't sure why she didn't want to show him off if he was as perfect as Roger kept telling me he was. But I wasn't sure about most things Belinda did. I was now more convinced than ever that Mark was a married man. Dating someone who already had a wife and family wasn't something that would have played on Belinda's conscience. I wasn't even sure she had a conscience.

Then one day I stupidly told Belinda about Zak's emails. She was quite smug, didn't seem shocked at all, and then proceeded to give me advice, which was not to feel guilty about the ginger kid and just take the dog and cut him out of my life. Her advice was typical of the cold, unfeeling human being that she was.

Her advice that I hadn't asked for continued to come through via text that evening. "Sally, you are into all this Jesus and born-again stuff, you know about forgiveness and all that crap, Zak is the man for you."

I was impressed she had absorbed so much information in so much detail, but the born-again stuff wasn't the issue, the issue was the Dexter stuff. And I couldn't understand why she thought something that hard could be so easy. Zak conned Dexter's much-loved mother, why would he delight in the fact I was contacting him?

The 'ginger kid' returned the following week, just after things opened up again after the four-week circuit breaker, so before long I had forgotten all about Belinda and her crazy ideas about Zak.

The 'happy van' with Dexter and Prince on board arrived on a Tuesday, but all arriving dogs needed to spend a couple of days in quarantine in an English kennel to ensure they were all well enough to travel onto their new homes. Hope and I had to be patient until Thursday and I managed to persuade Belinda that it would save another hissy fit if Hope stayed for this particular weekend.

"This weekend only, Sally. I have plans for weekends and you aren't screwing them up."

Whatever. I had plans for my weekends as well and those plans were going to involve Dexter, Hope and my new dog.

Chapter Thirty-one

December was a mixed bag. The month started out promisingly with the announcement of the approval of a vaccination against the virus. This was a miracle, as we had originally been told it would take two years. The vaccination was given out at breakneck speed and the race was on; virus verses immunity, but the virus already had a head start.

Boris Johnson was chuffed with himself and started to gain popularity again. At least he did until Saturday 19th December when he addressed the nation to announce that Christmas was 'cancelled'.

Everyone started calling him 'the Grinch who stole Christmas'.

Christmas wasn't really cancelled. Not even Boris was that powerful. But it did mean that we could now only meet members of our household and support bubbles. The promised opportunity to drive long distances to visit family and friends in other areas was withdrawn, and from Boxing Day we were back into full lockdown.

Prince's four paws were over the threshold well before Christmas Day and, as Belinda, Hope and I were officially bubbled, there was no reason we could not continue with our plans of Belinda having Hope at the weekends.

From the time Prince arrived he was a wonderful distraction from what was going on in the world. Dexter brought him in on a Thursday evening, just over a week before Christmas. He had briefed Hope and I about how to behave. We were to ignore the dog and just talk to Dexter, pretend the dog wasn't in the room, sit quietly and not to stroke him unless he came to us. That would work for me as I was still nervous, but I wasn't sure how that would work with Hope and was wondering about sellotaping her arms together. No Sellotape was needed on her arms which were very still, and she obediently didn't move as requested, but we couldn't keep her mouth shut. She was getting louder and louder.

"He is too cute. Look at his dark brown button eyes and his little nose. Oh, Uncle Dexter, he is perfect."

I didn't think his nose was little at all. In fact, the more I looked at him, the more I thought this dog was really a fox wearing a white poodle coat. And I certainly wasn't convinced he was perfect either, considering the number of times he was cocking his leg on my furniture. What I did know was that I was stuck with him, and he was stuck with me, as there was no way I was going to persuade either Dexter or Hope that I had changed my mind. I guessed doggo and I would have to get used to each other.

The first night I asked Dexter if he would mind sleeping on the sofa which, of course, he didn't. I worried that the dog would pine for him all night if he went home, as he seemed to go to Dexter for safety. They had already formed a bond. I put Prince in his bed in my room but left the door open and, needless, to say when I got up in the night the bed was empty. I could just see, by the light of the lamppost outside, Dexter sleeping on his back with Prince lying on his chest, nose nestled in his neck. I wasn't sure I wanted Prince to get into that habit, since this was to be a 'no-dog-on-the-bed' bungalow. I didn't want to wake Dexter either, so watched them sleeping for a few minutes before going back to bed.

I wasn't sure what Prince would do when Dexter went home, and I knew exactly how the pooch felt. The bungalow felt better with Dexter in it, more calm, more relaxed. Seeing him sleeping on the sofa just made me feel that I wanted him – Dexter that was, not Prince – in the bed with me. He was strong, of a similar build to my dad. I couldn't imagine anywhere safer than his arms. Help! I needed to splash some cold water on my face and get some sleep.

I woke again that night and was greeted by an unpleasant breath smell. If that was Dexter then my vision of him in the bed needed to be revisited. It was disgusting! It wasn't Dexter, though. Somehow Prince had found his way back into my room and was currently snoring his dog breath straight into my face. I didn't want to wake him, but I didn't want to smell him either, so very carefully turned around so that we were sleeping back-to-back. It was quite nice actually. I soon dozed back off with a smile on my face. I had promised myself I would one day sleep with a prince. Well, there you go. It had happened.

From then on Prince slept on his bed during the day and with me during the night, Dexter pointed out that he was definitely 'my dog' and he was. If I went to the kitchen, he came along, if I went to the loo, he followed me. There were many times when it was just Prince and me, and I had to do the business with my knickers around my ankles and the door open so he could see me. This was just how it was going to be: another 'new normal'.

Prince walked well on a lead, so Hope and I took him to visit Uncle Fred and Dexter on Christmas morning.

We introduced him to Tigger, and it was clearly the best Christmas present Tigger had ever received. We all laughed at them chasing each other around the garden, first one way and then the other. We left Prince there while we went to visit Belinda. It made sense for us to all be at her house as Boxing Day fell on a Saturday, so we exchanged gifts before a video chat with Mum and Phil. Mark was nowhere to be seen but as Belinda was in a good mood I presumed things were going well.

I wondered as I waved goodbye to them both what the New Year would have in store for us all. Belinda seemed to be heading for a good New Year with her new man, whereas I had a new dog and the clearing up that went with him. I also had two men, neither of which were mine, but they both made me happy, one face-to-face and the other via email. I wondered what the next 12 months would bring. I wondered what I would be doing a year from now.

Chapter Thirty-two

It was the middle of January when I started seeing Zak.
His emails had been getting longer, my replies had been
getting longer. I convinced myself that this was Belinda's
fault for taking Hope at the weekend and leaving me with
too much time on my hands, though it was probably more to
do with the fact I had zero willpower.

My meetings with Dexter were all outside as he was
'shielding' Uncle Fred. We talked about Hope, Tigger and
Prince, we enjoyed each other's company, he knew me
better than anyone, often better than I knew myself, and we
laughed a lot.

With Zak it was different. We talked about me. About
how I was different to anybody he had ever met, about how
I deserved the wedding of my dreams, about how he wanted
to put right all the hurt he had caused me, about how much
he loved me, a love beyond anything he had ever experienced
before. He didn't know me as well as Dexter, but he knew me
well enough to know what I wanted to hear.

With Hope not around at the weekends it was just too
easy. I still picked Hope up from school on a Friday for
consistency as, presumably Belinda would eventually
be allowed to go back to work in her tattoo parlour, but I
didn't need to stay long and by the time I got back, Zak was

already there. When I brought Hope back to the bungalow on Monday, Zak was gone.

I sometimes met Dexter to walk the dogs at the weekend so he wouldn't become suspicious, but Zak didn't mind that. It was almost as if he got the Dexter and me thing. He knew he existed, knew that he wasn't my type and was just a friend. I also think he thought that after what he had done to Mary, he kind of owed it to Dexter to allow him to continue be my friend. Zak just did the housework whilst I was out, and it all smelt so lovely when I came back home. A combination of bleach, polish and whatever he decided to put in my bath.

Zak wasn't technically in either of my 'bubbles' and we knew we were breaking the Covid gathering rules, but it seemed everyone was. More and more people were making up their own rules. People were done with rules, especially now they had either received or were getting close to receiving their vaccinations. That was a good thing as people were less fearful than before.

I had no choice but to let Zak in the first time he knocked the door. It was out of the blue and I wasn't expecting it, so my first reaction was to shut the door in his face. Unfortunately, I did it with such force that he ended up with a bloody nose. We were both shocked and I couldn't just leave him there dripping in blood. But as I held an icepack on the bridge of his nose, I was shouting at him. It was a combination of apologising and venting pure anger, because I couldn't really work out if I was sorry I had done it, or if he had it coming.

As I mopped the blood off the floor, I was still shouting at him, listing all the allegations against him that had been read out in court and highlighting just how awful it had been for me the day the police knocked on my door. One moment I was screaming, the next I was crying. Poor Prince just vanished under the bed. I knew Dexter would be furious with me as dogs were reactive to their surroundings and I knew the poor little dog had already gone through so much, but the lid had come off and I was hysterical.

During his following visits I had been more stroppy than angry and let him talk about being in jail and how the prison chaplain had listened and talked to him regularly. He had gone through his list of convictions with the chaplain and had been told God had forgiven him. He said that had meant a lot to him, he could live with that, but if I forgave him, it would be even better.

I wasn't sure if I had forgiven him or not, but I liked having him around and it soon became a weekend ritual. I knew deep down that it wasn't right as that horrid guilt feeling had returned. I didn't feel I could tell Mum or Dexter, and that added to my feeling that it couldn't be right. I also hated the fact that Prince took himself under the bed every time Zak arrived. That was my fault, he now saw Zak as someone negative.

For some reason I told Belinda about Zak's return quite early on. I had to tell someone. I knew she would be ecstatic as she always became weirdly excited when I talked about me and Zak which I didn't understand. Usually, she was at her happiest when I was at my lowest, but if I was happy and Zak was around then suddenly that was OK.

"Ha, didn't take him long to get your knickers off, did it Sally?"

Trust her to just presume the worst, though she wasn't wrong. It actually hadn't taken him long at all. Wouldn't the chaplain have talked to him about not bonking until one was married? Pretty sure Aunt Lucy wouldn't approve at all.

I couldn't help but think of Dexter. Not once had he tried to get my knickers off, or even talk about doing it. Once or twice, he had held my hand, and it was lovely, but he had never tried to force himself upon me. I was pretty sure I knew which one Aunt Lucy would be steering me towards.

Eventually I told Mum, knowing I would break the news more gently than Belinda would.

"A leopard can't change its spots, Sally."

Poor leopard. I bet it would love to change its spots if it could. Anyway, Zak was no leopard and, in fact, had changed his spots. Still, I knew there was no point arguing with Mum, she had made up her mind and we would just have to agree to disagree. I knew Dexter wouldn't be thrilled either, but I wasn't ready to have the conversation with him. He was my soulmate, my friend, and having secrets felt wrong, but I wasn't ready to upset anyone else.

Boris Johnson wasn't the only person who was confused.

Chapter Thirty-three

2021 had started badly, with no evidence that the latest lockdown was having any effect at all in reducing the numbers of people coming down with the latest strain of the virus, and the NHS was on its knees trying to deal with new infections. Eventually, the shocking news was announced that we had now exceeded 100,000 Covid-related deaths. Captain Tom Moore who had worked so hard to raise money for the NHS, was one of those who succumbed, and his death was announced in February.

Coverage of ambulances queuing outside of the hospitals and exhausted hospital staff walking around like zombies made the news even harder to watch at times.

I was exhausted as well, but mine was a different kind of exhaustion. An exhaustion that can only come by leading a double life; a double life that was spiralling out of control very quickly. It was hard keeping up the pretence, keeping up the lies. Considering that all my life everyone thought I was a liar, it was ironic that I really couldn't do this lying business at all and had trouble imagining how anyone could live like that.

I wasn't really lying to Dexter, I told myself. It wasn't as if he had asked if I was seeing Zak and I had said 'no', but it was deceitful, it was wrong, and I knew it was wrong because this darned guilt was making me feel physically sick.

Dexter knew something was up, he just didn't know what. Something had changed between us. Me. I wasn't talking as much. I was neither good at acting nor deliberately lying. I felt two-faced and ashamed. We both enjoyed walking the dogs and we both enjoyed our time with Hope, but we both knew things weren't the same.

Roger was due home on leave soon and although I hadn't told him about Zak, I wasn't sure how much contact he had with Mum or Belinda. Maybe he knew already. If he did know we were seeing each other, he would be shocked enough. But if he knew we were already talking about engagement and marriage?!? I couldn't get my head around how quickly this was moving, so why would he?

I spent a lot of time at the cemetery making the three graves look nice. It was a pleasant place to walk Prince, our special place where we could just be us. I spent time at Dad's grave and Aunt Charlotte's grave, but it was still Aunt Lucy's grave I spent the most time at. I would speak to her as I cleaned her gravestone and often thought how wonderful it would be if during one of these sessions Aunt Lucy would audibly 'speak' to me.

"Now lass, this is what you have to do."

She would tell me to be wise. She was always telling me that. She loved telling me Bible stories and from an early age would tell me about the wisdom of King Solomon. I was neither Solomon or a king and I knew I wasn't being wise. I was letting my heart rule my head and there was absolutely nothing I could do about it.

I would marry Zak, he was the man of my dreams, even though he had made mistakes, for which he was truly sorry. This would be my dream wedding. Yet I knew guilt wasn't the only thing slowing me down, there was also a small amount of doubt, and certain things weren't adding up.

Although Zak was always going on about being a born-again Christian, he really didn't have a clue about the Bible. When I mentioned King Solomon and wisdom he had asked if Solomon was one of the Jesus team?

I presumed he meant one of his disciples, rather than a football team Jesus played for on a Saturday.

I asked which verse in the Bible had persuaded him to change his life if it was the Old or the New Testament and he smiled in a way that suggested he didn't even know there were testaments in the Bible or what was I talking about.

Another thing Aunt Lucy talked about was forgiveness, especially when it came to Belinda. I knelt beside the grave, ignoring the fact Prince was cocking his leg on my beautifully placed flowers. Maybe if I got closer, I would have a better chance of hearing what she had to say.

"So, it is right then that I forgive Zak? It is right that I give him another chance?"

She didn't respond.

"What was it the church used to say about guilt, Aunt Lucy? Though shalt not feel guilty. So, I shouldn't feel guilty about not telling Dexter, right?"

Thinking about Dexter made me feel guilty, but Zak just made me feel good. Zak made me feel like I was the only woman in the universe. There were always fresh flowers in the vase. There were candles around the bathtub, all of them a different colour with a different scent. I had given him the money to dry clean my wedding dress as he insisted this was the dress I would wear, and we always talked about how special our day would be. He just made me feel like a princess, his princess.

Every day he asked me to marry him and every day I said, "Not yet." I was afraid that he would stop asking but, in a weird way, I wasn't ready to let go of Dexter and the security that came with him. I wasn't ready to hurt Dexter either. If Zak loved me as much as he said, then he would wait. Until then I would selfishly just enjoy them both for their different qualities.

I wondered how Hope would get on with Zak, but he didn't seem in a rush to meet her. He said there would be plenty of time for that when he became an uncle. I struggled to think of him as an uncle, or picture him bonding with her the way Dexter had.

If I was careful and didn't say anything daft or make any stupid mistakes, then I could get away with this little secret for a while longer. Who was I kidding? This wasn't a little secret; this secret was elephant-sized.

Unfortunately, even as I was having these thoughts, fate was preparing to drop me right in it. Both men had keys to the bungalow. Zak to let himself in on a Friday, and I had got a key cut for Dexter to use when we were getting Hope's new bedroom decorated so he could come in and out as necessary. I had never asked for it back. There never seemed to be the right time to ask for it, and part of me didn't want it back.

Chapter Thirty-four

Roger's leave coincided with me getting Covid.

I knew what it was well before I got myself tested. I had managed to do a bit of volunteering work at a vaccination clinic at the start of January and by doing so had fast-tracked myself a free vaccination. This was a bonus, as my age range hadn't been called forward yet. They were still working on the elderly and people with compromised immunity.

The morning after my vaccination I had felt dreadful and my arm ached so much I could barely lift it, let alone hold a dog's lead. Dog walking was left to Dexter that day. Many people had commented on how much their arms ached after the jab, and they weren't wrong. Every time I moved my arm it hurt, laying on it hurt, reaching up to get the tea bags hurt. Then you got the headache, the temperature, the feeling of absolute confusion. The compulsory paperwork I had been given at the time of the jab suggested that 'yes', these were side effects, but to man up and get on with it, as if you got Covid without having a jab it would feel ten times worse.

I had longed to do my part in the pandemic. Uncle Fred was one of the first to get a vaccination and had pointed out that the clinic he attended was desperate for volunteers to help get the queues moving quicker, clean the chairs, hand out coffees, that kind of thing. Dexter had said I should do it.

He said there was no feeling in the world like the feeling of helping, of doing your part. He also said that I should just be honest and say I could only do it for a few hours while Hope was at school as I had a dog and needed to be at the school for 3 pm. If they said they didn't need my help, then nothing would be lost. It turned out they did need my help, and I loved giving it.

All the volunteers took turns with the different tasks to make it fair and to give everyone a bit of a change during the day. I would have an hour standing at the door ticking people off the list, then I would spend an hour cleaning chairs when people stood up and went for their vaccination. Everyone had to wait 15 minutes after the jab to make sure there were no side effects, and then I would give out refreshments served in paper cups which then had to be thrown away. It was a waste, but it was a hygienic waste. Everything had to be safe, especially as the first people to be called up for the injection were the most vulnerable.

Dexter was right. It was wonderful to be needed, to take part in this hopefully once in a lifetime disaster. He loved hearing my stories about the old people that came in. How they would be nervous to start with and how I was able to put them at ease. He seemed to both listen and take pride in what I was doing. It was weird, almost like Aunt Lucy had come back in the form of a young ginger and it felt good.

The side effects after the Covid jab hadn't felt good and having what I presumed was proper Covid didn't feel good either. As I didn't actually do much these days, I presumed I had picked up the virus from Hope or one of her classmates or parents at the school, I didn't know where it had come from, but had no doubt what it was.

It had started as a restless night of weird dreams; I was dreaming of a threesome with Zak and Dexter one minute and the next it was a fivesome, with Hugh Grant and Boris Johnson adding to the dynamics. It must have been a huge bed, but like all my fever dreams of the past, I could see my Aunt Lucy and my dad at the bottom of my bed, clear as day, and I wanted to get to them, but every time I tried one of these darned men got in the way.

When I woke up my sheets were wet through, my head ached, and I just knew that I wouldn't be doing the school run for a long time. I eventually took a lateral flow test, which told me what I already guessed. I had Covid.

Lateral flow tests were not readily available for everyone to take yet, but as I had worked in a clinic, they had insisted that all their volunteers took one before each shift. This was expected for all front-line workers like nurses, care assistants, teachers and bus drivers. Once you had produced a positive lateral flow test you then had to take yourself off to a testing centre to have your result confirmed, usually by a polymerase chain reaction test, or PCR, for short. I couldn't bring myself to do that even though I knew it was wrong. I felt so ill. I knew I couldn't look after Hope either. She should, by all accounts, stay with me as she would have to 'isolate', but I decided to try my luck and phoned Belinda. Maybe she could come and get Hope when she woke up.

I phoned Belinda's mobile, but no response so I phoned the landline, resigned to the fact I would have to fight my corner and prepare my already sore throat for a shouting match. Aunt Lucy was looking down on me that morning and Roger picked up the phone. I had no idea he had actually arrived back, and the relief came out in a giant sob. Eventually I managed to tell him my sorry tale.

Apparently, nobody knew Roger had arrived back. He was a day early and arrived just after midnight.

"Belinda isn't going to be pleased that I didn't tell her I was arriving early, and I know Mark is in there with her as they have both been coughing for hours. Let me come and get Hope now. I will get her up and dressed and then bring her back here for pancakes before school."

"I am isolating. Shouldn't you stand outside my front door in a space suit and let me throw her and her bits at you?"

"Sally, I am going to get it one day. May as well get it when I am on leave. It would save an awful lot of hassle. Stay where you are, I'm on my way."

Roger phoned later to find out how I was and to tell me that as predicted Belinda had thrown her toys out of the pram when she and Mark got up and found Hope in the house. He couldn't understand the woman, but Hope sent her love and Belinda sent a growl. He was pretty sure Belinda had the virus as well, but Mark had run out the house like a frightened ferret when he saw Hope and Belinda had refused to get tested, so we would never know.

So that was that then, I had Covid. I also had a dog whom Roger had chosen not to take with him, a secret boyfriend and a soulmate to text. I texted them both, "I am contagious, stay away," and then let Prince out in the back garden. Fortunately, he was satisfied with doing his business in the garden, unlike some of his Romanian dog friends whom Facebook suggested would only do their business on a walk. The garden would have to work. I knew he wouldn't mind.

With all my jobs now done Prince and I jumped into bed. His dog breath was on my face again, but I couldn't be bothered to move him and figured that with my unbrushed teeth and fever, his breath was probably far better than mine anyway, so it would be rude to complain. There was water and paracetamol on the bedside cabinet, along with an emergency packet of salt and vinegar crisps. I knew I was ready to doze, and we both drifted off to sleep quickly.

The Covid virus came in many forms and not everyone experienced the same symptoms. Some had a hacking cough, others a high temperature, others suffered cold-like symptoms or a sore throat, others a headache and some people lost their sense of smell and taste. I had a very sore throat with no cough, but the worse part was the fever. I don't know how Prince stayed on the bed so long, I seemed to go from one weird dream to the next and was drenched with sweat. At one point I sat up and tried to shake my head, hoping to shake away the dream I had just had, but it hurt too much. I noticed that Prince was on the dog bed beside me. It must have been really hot in the bed for him to do that. I wished he knew how to fill a glass with water.

Just as I was thinking that I heard the front door close quietly and the bedroom door opened.

"Zak?"

"I hope that was just because you are delirious, Sal."

Silently, Dexter put the lead on Prince and took him out. I must have fallen asleep because when I woke up Prince was back on my bed and there was a plate of sandwiches on the cabinet with some paracetamol and a glass of fruit juice.

For the next five days that lovely man walked the dog and made sure I had food and fresh fruit to eat. It was all done silently. No words were spoken, but I knew we were both thinking the same thing, and I felt miserable.

I knew I could have opted out of the truth. I could have said that I was delirious, that I had been dreaming about Zak, and I could have just laughed the whole thing off. That would be a lie though. I knew that this had all happened for a reason. This was yet another sign. I needed to talk to

Dexter. I needed to tell him the truth and I needed to say how sorry I was for not being honest with him sooner.

Chapter Thirty-five

It wasn't until day six of Covid that I started feeling well enough to actually get out of bed. I made sure I was sitting in the lounge when Dexter arrived, and I told him the truth. I told him about the emails, about how Zak was a different person now, how he had become 'born again,' how there was something still very physical between us and even how he had been proposing to me constantly, but that something was holding me back.

Part of me hoped this would give Dexter an opportunity to talk me out of it and beg me to marry him instead. But he didn't. He said he wasn't angry with me for not telling him, but he certainly wasn't happy about it either.

"I smell a rat, Sal. How do you know he isn't just saying he is born again because he knows you have a faith?"

"Well, I really don't have a faith, do I? I haven't stepped inside a church since Aunt Lucy died, apart from attending two funerals."

"Yes, but surely you mentioned your trips to church with Aunt Lucy the last time you dated. A leopard can't change it spots, Sal."

What was it with people and those darned leopards?

"What you feel for Zak is lust, not love. He is the live version of your cartoon Prince, possibly even a reminder of your dad. He spoils you like your dad. But do you feel safe with him, Sal? Deep down, do you trust him?"

He didn't push me for an answer, and I didn't give him one.

Once my ten-day isolation was over, I was able to start my routine again. I was able to collect Hope from school and have her during the week. I did still take Prince out with Dexter and Tigger from time to time, but things weren't the same now. It was as if we went through the motions just to make Hope and Uncle Fred happy.

Roger had gone back to his ship now but had insisted that he would continue to put money into my account, as he still wasn't sure when Belinda's next mood swing would come and wanted me to be ready. I didn't mind. I may have had reservations at the start but being lazy suited me. Since getting Prince I was far too busy to work anyway. We had some fantastic adventures together and couldn't imagine him settling into a doggy day care like a regular pooch. He still had anxiety issues and still panicked if I went to the loo without him.

I started to see Zak again at the weekends and he continued to propose to me. He said he didn't come near me when I had Covid as I had asked him not to and, being the law-abiding citizen that he now was, knew that he wasn't allowed because of the regulations. I respected that. He was grateful that Dexter had been looking out for me though, as was Mum who seemed to have developed a soft spot for Dexter and mentioned his name during conversations far more often than she mentioned Zak's.

The latest wave of Covid infections had finally slowed down and Mum and Phil's plans to come over finally seemed to be coming together. The American business was now sold, and they planned to move back once the money had come through and international travel had been opened up again. They were looking forward to being proper grandparents and were keeping themselves busy looking at various UK rental agencies online, with the view to renting for a year before finding their own property.

I was enjoying this season of everything feeling 'right.' I had a boyfriend who was crazy about me, and I still saw Dexter. I had a darling niece and a faithful dog. I was being paid to stay at home and now my Mum was making plans to come home. It was all falling into place very well indeed.

I thought of Aunt Lucy and how much she would have loved this. Her much-loved nephew and nieces all getting on well together. I regretted not making more of an effort to really 'get to know' Roger when she was still alive, and I acknowledged that Hope was the common link. Without Hope nobody would have made the effort.

Even in the outside world things seemed to be falling more into place as we prepared to come out of this latest lockdown. Most of us had received a double vaccination and there was now far more medication available if you did get the virus, which meant less people were ending up in intensive care or dying. Things were much less scary, though clearly, we were not out of the woods yet and the virus was still very much at large.

More and more restrictions were being lifted. There were now no longer restrictions on how many people could attend weddings and funerals, or on how many people you could meet up with outside or even the number you could have inside your house.

I felt excited at the prospect of being able to hug people again, shake hands again and sit on a bus without jumping clean out of my skin if someone tried to sit next to me. What an unsociable nation we had become.

There was talk about nightclubs opening again which would please Belinda, and I wondered how long it would be before she asked me to have Hope back at the weekend.

I hoped that this would be the beginning of a period of stability, not just for me, but in the lives of other people as well.

Chapter Thirty-six

When we did eventually come fully out of lockdown, it was strangely disappointing. There were no street parties, no people randomly hugging each other, no firework displays. The newsreader started the day by reminding people this was the day the government had said we could get back to our new normal lives and that we could now hug if we felt we should hug. In other words, it all now landed on our shoulders. If we visited someone and infected them, if we didn't wear a mask and passed on the virus, if someone we hugged died, it was all our fault.

So that was that, then. We were now living with the virus. Masks could come off if you felt it was the right thing to do. You did not now need to work at home, unless you felt it was the right thing to do. And yes, hug if you felt it was the right thing to do. It was all about whether or not you felt it was right.

It seemed to me that the government was shifting all responsibility onto us in a kind of, "Well, we've done our bit… if you get the virus now it's probably your fault" kind of manner.

Coming out of lockdown and starting the 'living with the virus' period was cleverly planned for the week the kids were due to break up for their summer holidays. People recognised that the timing was so that, in six weeks' time, the Government could declare that they were right and that opening up when they did had made no difference to new virus infection rates. Well of course the numbers would go down when all the little germ-bags were out of school, not mixing with their friends and picking up germs to lovingly spread within their family units.

Coming out of lockdown wasn't the only thing that was disappointing. So were my weekends with Zak. The magic of not having to lift a finger was still there, he did the cleaning and the cooking, and I let him. We snuggled up and watched movies, we had siestas and life in the bungalow was great, but he would never leave the bungalow. I wanted to show him off; the fact I was with someone as handsome and loving as this was something I wanted the world to see, but he would never walk the dog with me or go shopping with me and I was beginning to think I was an embarrassment to him. When I suggested we go to church, he would smile or kiss the end of my nose or do anything but acknowledge what I had said.

I tried not to overthink the church thing as I was aware that, since Covid, everyone overthought everything. I had been to church with Aunt Lucy and the people were normal, they didn't all have halos balanced on their head or walk around the supermarket with a Bible in their handbags praying over their trolleys, so there was no reason Zak should change dramatically when he became a Christian. Zak just didn't seem to have the warmth that came from having the title 'Christian'. Every true Christian I had ever met had been loving, they cared a lot. Yes, Zak cared about me, but he made lots of unnecessary comments about people on the TV or in the papers and was definitely not into 'climate change and all that bollocks'.

I remembered singing 'All things bright and beautiful, all creatures create and small' at Aunt Lucy's church. Yet Zak wasn't always gentle with Prince, and he was a creature. He was definitely neither bright nor beautiful but a creature none the less, and Christians were meant to be kind to animals. I was sure it was decreed somewhere in the Bible that we were put on earth to look after the creatures, I remembered asking Aunt Lucy if spiders counted. Prince had finally started to come out from under the bed when Zak appeared after some coaxing with cheese, but Zak often shoved him off the bed or pushed him out of the way with his foot and that bothered me.

In the same way he didn't appear the slightest bit interested in Hope. All he wanted to talk about was me and the wedding. Then there was the photo thing. When we were almost married last time, we had a lot of fun taking selfies. He was all over my Facebook page and he was the first thing I saw when I got my mobile out, his face smiling at me before every text. But now if I attempted to take his photo, things got quite ugly. I was dating the best-looking man in the whole of Sussex and yet I couldn't show him off. It was painful.

After every doubt I had, I would then make excuses for him. He wasn't a pope; he was just a normal man. Maybe he kicked Prince off the bed because he was uncomfortable. Not everyone liked dogs on the bed and wasn't this what I'd always wanted anyway? To be someone's princess, to be with a man who was focused on me and me alone, so why would I be worried that he didn't rate Hope higher than me. Maybe he just didn't want me to show him off. He just wanted us to be an inclusive couple.

Finally, with my emotions so constantly up and down that I was beginning to feel seasick, I got up one Saturday morning while Zak was still asleep and stomped over to

Belinda's house. She had locked the door from the inside, which didn't help my mood at all. I just kept my finger on the doorbell until she finally opened the door. She and Hope both came to the door. Hope was far more excited to see me than Belinda was, but they listened as I rambled on listing all my Zak concerns one by one.

While Belinda was upstairs taking a shower, I took the opportunity to ask Hope about Mark.

"What does he look like then, this Mark? Uncle Roger says he is very handsome."

"I only saw him once Aunt Sally when you were sick, but he kind of looks like a real-life Prince Eric from The Little Mermaid."

Suddenly there was another voice and Belinda was standing behind her, smiling.

"What if Prince Eric proposes to me then Sally? Have you thought about that with all your moaning about Zak? What if Mark proposes to me and I'm the one who has the dream wedding, because Zak has given up waiting for you?

"You've just given me a list of things that you perceive to be wrong in the guy, but they are all crap. Say 'yes' before he changes his mind and finds someone that appreciates him. I would love someone that doted on me hand and foot."

I decided after leaving Belinda that she wasn't wrong and that I needed to put up with the things I didn't like. They weren't crap, they were valid irritations, but maybe I was running out of time. What if she wore my fantasy wedding dress out of spite? She had looked at – and mocked – my wedding portfolio so many times that she could easily make something similar, just because she could.

We had neither talked about, nor mentioned the main thing that was stopping me – Dexter. But on the way home I prayed that I would be able to put my insecurities to one side about Zak. I hoped that would make me less confused.

Chapter Thirty-seven

Not long after that encounter my insecurities about Zak started to ease, as I started to notice changes in him. I felt quietly confident that my prayers were getting through, and that God and Aunt Lucy had put things in place to make me less anxious.

One Saturday Zak insisted I go and have a pamper day, get my nails and hair done, make myself feel nice. He didn't offer to pay, he never did, but it was a lovely gesture, and I did like a good pampering. I appreciated the fact my appearance mattered to him. It felt nice.

He asked if I could leave my bankcard and when I hesitated, he looked hurt. He explained that he wanted to do something nice for Hope, so I gave it to him and gave him a quick snog as well. He was right to be hurt. He was a different Zak now.

When I got back, I found he had spent the whole time I was away putting together a Wendy House for Hope in the back garden. He had painted it lilac and hung some sparkly purple curtains in the window. I was thrilled. Only last week Hope had said her favourite colour was now purple. I hadn't mentioned it, so it must have been a lucky guess on his part, but I knew she would be thrilled.

Zak was low-key about the whole thing.

"Never met the kid, Sally, but she clearly means a lot to you. Hopefully, this will make her happy."

It did make her happy and Hope wanted to say 'thank you', so I asked Belinda if she would like to pop over one weekend with Hope so that she could thank him. Belinda just laughed and said she wasn't into this love and slush stuff, and they would both get to meet him one day. There was no rush. She also said she was hoping that Hope would be my flower girl, before she got 'too old'.

I had been thinking a lot about Hope being my flower girl. Because I had been thinking about finally saying 'yes' to marrying Zak a lot as well. He was obviously a different guy. He was talking a lot more about his faith, explaining that he knew we shouldn't be sleeping together, that we should be getting married in church under the eyes of God, but he just couldn't wait and that made him feel too guilty to go to church. His head was messed up and he needed to rethink his commitment to God. I got that; I really did. My own head was so often messed up.

He also explained about the photo thing. He had done wrong to a lot of people and his photo had been all over the papers. He didn't want to be recognised. It might affect me and Hope if people realised he was back in the area. I promised that I wouldn't use Facebook and that I just wanted a photo of him in my purse and in the bungalow, but he said 'no' and I could tell he meant it, so decided not to approach the subject again. After all, as Zak had said, there would be plenty of wedding photos.

My relationship with Dexter was also beginning to change for the better. Some of the tension had gone and we were more comfortable with each other now and, although he still wasn't thrilled about the Zak situation, he was more accepting of it. Prince and I enjoyed our walks together, but I knew that he preferred to have Tigger with us, and it was wonderful to watch them both play together. Dexter still picked Hope up with me after school when he could, as having Hope along as well as the two dogs added to the chaos and was even more fun to watch.

Dexter often ended up at the school gates before me and it made him a bit cross that I was being paid to pick up Hope from school and couldn't even get there on time. We both knew why. It was because I was trying to look and act like the kind of girl that should be dating someone like Zak. I was always putting products on my hair to make it shinier, putting it in plaits to make it bouncier or having my nails painted a different colour. He had a right to be cross and I knew that I was just terribly distracted these days.

I decided that Dexter was just being a bit bad-tempered because he couldn't go back to Romania, which he desperately wanted to do but, apparently, it was Uncle Fred that was keeping him in England. The old man was getting frailer.

"Funny Sal, he isn't even my biological family, but I feel he looks at me like a son and he did help me out so much with Mum. I owe it to him."

What a beautiful soul he was.

He sometimes tried to persuade me to go to Romania, saying that it would do me good to be part of a team and that I would enjoy it. In his mind, being the apple of my father's eye, my aunt's eye and now allegedly Zak's eye had prevented me looking outside my own little world. He wanted me to get a taste of what it was like out there as part of a dedicated group with a common purpose. Making a difference as one person was one thing, but when you were part of a team, you were able to cheer each other on, support each other and share successes and failures together.

When one day I asked what his perfect wife and wedding day would be, he smiled.

"I want someone who is a little bit quirky and willing to step out of their comfort zone to make a difference to someone's life. Absolutely not anyone who would turn up with a portfolio of their perfect wedding. When I meet my future wife, we will plan our perfect day together. It will be about us both. Sex would also be about us both, everything we did would be about us both. One team. Soulmates for life."

One evening when I was getting Hope ready for bed, I thought I would find out what Belinda had been saying about me and Zak behind my back, and if she was as up for us getting together as she made out.

"What does your mummy think about me and Zak, Hope?"

"Oh, Aunt Sally it is so exciting, Mummy says your prince has come back and she can't understand why you just can't marry him."

"Well, it's complicated."

"Can I see a photo of Zak, Aunt Sally?"

"That's complicated as well."

I knew I should have kept the old photos I had of Zak but had used them to make a bonfire on returning from the court case, after deleting the whole of his face from my mobile phone's sim card.

"When things are not so complicated can we choose my bridesmaid dress? Let me show you the one I want."

I waited patiently for her to load photos of bridesmaid dresses onto my laptop. I wasn't convinced I wanted to wear my original dress anymore and was getting far more laidback about the whole wedding portfolio idea, so I wouldn't stop the kid choosing her own dress.

Quietly hoping and suspecting she would go for her new favourite colour of purple; I was a bit taken aback when she pointed to a white dress. Did she think she was getting married? It was very sweet, white netting that came to the knees, almost the style of a ballerina dress.

"Please Aunt Sally, I really want this dress. If it is too expensive, why don't you let Dexter pay half and then I can wear it again when he gets married."

I laughed.

"Dexter isn't getting married. He hasn't even got a girlfriend."

"Yes, he has. Her name is India."

"No honey, India is just a lady he talks to when he picks you up from school. She is one of the other mummies. She isn't his girlfriend."

"Well, I think she is. Twice last week when you were late again, he kissed her. He kissed her once on Tuesday and once on Wednesday, just before you arrived. He is spending the night at her house next Friday night. I heard him say it. Why are you looking so angry, Aunt Sally? I am telling you the truth. I'm not lying."

I knew she wasn't lying. I also knew it wasn't her I was angry at.

Chapter Thirty-eight

So that was that then. Dexter was seeing India. He had kissed her twice and he was spending the night with her next week.

Pure fury kept me awake that night; he didn't think to mention this the other day when we were talking about his perfect girlfriend? So much for having a best friend that I could share everything with. OK, maybe I wasn't totally honest or up front about Zak, but he was Dexter for goodness' sake. I didn't think Dexter did secrets.

Also, his description of his perfect wife could not have been more inaccurate if he tried. There was nothing quirky about India. She was immaculate with her straight shoulder length hair which always seemed to hold the perfect number of highlights. I was pretty sure that under her perfectly applied lipstick, her lips had been pumped up to make them look fuller. There was no way she would get her perfect hair dirty in Romania or kiss a stray dog with those lips.

The thing that made me most angry was... why was I this angry? Nothing made sense. I was acting like a jealous lover. He had lied to me, that had to be it. Knowing how much I hated lies, he had told me that it was Uncle Fred keeping him in this country, not pouty-lips India. Turns out it had nothing to do with Uncle Fred.

Would she be like Zak and allow me to be friends with Dexter? Would she be generous with him?

Sleep finally came two hours before the alarm clock went off, so I wasn't in the best mood as we arrived at the school gates and even less so when India waved at me. Cheeky cow. I would need to be professional when it was school pick-up time. I would need to act normal. No hints. I wanted to know how long Dexter could keep this secret without spilling the beans. I also wanted to make sure I was there on time for every school pick up to make things as hard as possible for them.

When school ended, I was there before any of the parents. I was there before the gates opened. It was a bit embarrassing really, and Dexter's first reaction was one of shock.

"Bloody hell Sal, is that really you? Did you really get here before me?"

I just smiled. I needed to play it cool whilst making an inner pact to never be late again. If I was in a wedding race, then leaving him and India alone was giving them a head start. What if Mark did propose to Belinda and she said, "yes." What if Dexter proposed to India and she said, "yes." I didn't want to be the only person who wasn't getting married this year. There was little I could do about Belinda and Mark but if I could get in the way of Dexter and India then at least I was doing something. That had to be better than doing nothing. I also needed to say, 'yes' to Zak soon. If there was going to be a wedding this year, then it was going to be mine.

Dexter and I walked in silence for a while with the dogs and Hope playing happily ahead of us. It was me who finally broke the silence in a less than tactful way.

"So, how's your day been? Doing anything nice Friday night?"

"I am getting more and more worried about Uncle Fred, Sal. This morning, I went around there, and he was having breakfast. Nothing wrong with that apart from the fact there were already two breakfast bowls in the sink. Plus, he has run out of medication again, which means he has been doubling up."

"Oh no, you better not leave Tigger with him anymore when you go to back to Romania then. Who knows what size he will be when you got back. Is there anyone else you can leave Tigger with? Anyone special to you."

He laughed. "Well, you could look after him?"

Typical. Saving his fun times for her whilst I got the dog and the dog poop that went with it.

He continued, "Anyway, I have already told you Romania is off the agenda for now."

"I bet it is."

"I have involved social services to have a care package put in place for Uncle Fred. I don't mind keeping an eye on him, but I think it would be good for him to have other visitors. He does get bored. Sal, stop making polite conversation. What are you dying to tell me."

Eerily accurate as ever.

"I am ready to say, 'yes' to Zak, ready to put the past behind me and finally become his wife."

"You have to do what you have to do Sal, as long as you love him as a person, not just his looks. As long as it is love and not lust, and as long as you are not doing it just to get a wedding."

Ouch.

He linked arms with me as we walked and then continued with the conversation.

"Want to know a secret."

"I probably already do but go on then."

"It's not just Uncle Fred I am staying here for. It's you, Hope and Prince as well. If you are going to marry that con artist then I want to make sure I am around, just in case."

"Thanks for the encouragement."

That night after much prosecco I had a conversation with Prince.

"Dexter is a toad as well. He lies to me, so I am going to do this marriage thing with Zak. You are going to have a new Daddy, mate and you are just going to have to get used to the fact your days of sleeping on the bed are coming to an end."

Did Prince growl, or was I just being paranoid?

Chapter Thirty-nine

With another Christmas fast approaching, my wedding plans were already well under way. This time, coincidentally, it would be a Christmas wedding. Another sign that it was meant to be.

Our engagement celebrations were behind us now. We hadn't really celebrated with anyone but ourselves as nobody really supported our decision, so we took ourselves to a nice hotel in London and lived like royalty for the weekend. We started at one of the theatres, watching a show and celebrating with champagne in the interval, then had more champagne with a meal, followed by even more champagne back at the hotel. It was an expensive weekend for sure, but it was a double celebration. I was getting married plus I was now convinced that this was the right decision.

My final fitting meant my original dress needed to be taken in slightly, but it was now returned, cleaned, protected in a transparent wedding dress dust cover and locked away out of both Belinda and Hope's reach. Belinda and Hope remained the only people who were genuinely happy about my decision to marry Zak, and that made Belinda the person I confided in most. I had told her my wish was that Zak would be more involved in this wedding, to stop me being so nervous about history repeating itself, and he really was.

Together Zak and I chose the cake, the wedding venue, even the Christmas tree and lights which were to be the star attraction at the venue. Every evening, we would look at my portfolio and as things were booked and paid for, we would tick them off.

The wedding was going to be on Christmas Eve and the invitations were out. Mum and Phil were coming over to spend Christmas and New Year with us. It was like a fairytale. Me getting married Christmas Eve to someone as gorgeous as Zak. Zak seemed even more excited than me. One day he went out to a local garden centre and brought some Father Christmas centre pieces for the tables, and on another occasion, he brought home some tiny chocolate Christmas puddings as wedding favours for the guests. Something I had not even thought about.

We were both spending far too much money, I knew that, but I was as bad as he was and neither of us could stop. Zak had his own debit card for my account now which was fine because he planned to get a job after we were married, and it would then become a joint account for us to both put money into and take money out of. Everything we did would be joint. We two would become one and I couldn't wait.

I was excited, Zak was excited, and I had never seen Belinda as excited as she currently was. It wasn't a smile from the heart, it never was with her, and in some ways I thought she looked smug, but at least she was smiling, so three cheers for that. She came with me to buy Hope's white bridesmaid dress, and it was her idea that we got some crystal beads added so that it would sparkle like my dress. When we went for Hope's final fitting, I took my dress as well and we both looked like princesses. Hope insisted that Belinda take a photo of us together so that she could show Dexter.

Belinda was clearly shocked that we were both still seeing that 'Muppet' and I just smiled. The fact Hope even suggested such a thing meant that she and I both assumed that yes, we would still be seeing the Muppet after I was married. He was our friend, and there was always room for friends in a marriage.

Both Princes were going to be page dogs and, once the photos were taken outside of the registry office, Mum and Phil would take the real Prince back to Roger's house where they were all staying, and where he would patiently wait for them to get back from the reception. It wasn't going to be a late night so I was sure it would be fine. I could hardly ask Dexter to look after the dog while I got married. Even I had more tact than that. Prince would have to manage for that short time.

Although Dexter was accepting of the wedding, he kept casting a shadow on it by asking some really direct questions that made my toes curl.

"So, he has a bankcard for your account which he doesn't put any money into right?"

"It will soon be our account, not my account, and he is struggling to get work because of his criminal record. It's not his fault."

"Then whose fault is it?"

Another time he asked why I thought Zak wasn't inviting anyone to the wedding. All the guests were people I knew.

"So, he has no parents, no grandparents, no brothers, or sisters? A spaceship landed one day and just dropped him off, did it. Why don't you look on the internet, find out exactly why he doesn't want his family to come to the wedding?"

OK, he had a point. But Zak didn't invite anyone to the first wedding either and I honestly didn't think about it then or care now. It was my wedding and if Zak wanted to spend the day with my family and friends then, in my mind, it was a selfless and lovely thing to do. I was pretty confident that there would be no dirt about Zak's family on the internet, and even if there was, it was better that I didn't find out at this stage. Besides he was a new person now, all that was in the past.

The only thing I was worried about was the photo thing. Surely, he would allow people to take wedding photos. What else could he do, hide behind the wedding cake? It was probably big enough to hide behind, another thing we didn't need to waste money on, but did. He would have to have his photo taken with me, there would be no choice.

With the wedding only two weeks away and Mum and Dad about to land, Dexter and I took the dogs out for the last time. Well, the last time while I was going to be single anyway. We decided this last dog walk for a while should be with Hope. As the three of them ran ahead, Dexter slipped his arm around my shoulders.

"Be happy, Sal."

Before I could respond Hope came running over.

"Aunt Sally, show Uncle Dexter that photo mummy took of us. Show him how beautiful we both look in our dresses."

We sat down and I showed him the photo that Belinda had forwarded to me. I smiled as I looked at it and passed the phone to Dexter. He looked sad. Hope picked up on his expression as well.

"Why are you looking sad Uncle Dexter? I am going to wear it to your wedding as well when you marry India."

Dexter laughed "Marry India? You don't want to be telling her husband that."

"I saw you kissing her Uncle Dexter, twice. You kissed her and hugged her and then you said you were going to her house on Friday night."

"India had to have a big operation, honey and was very scared. Her husband needed someone to sit in with the kids while he picked her up from hospital. I gave her a couple of reassuring kisses. Oh, for goodness' sake Hope, they were both such small kisses. It wasn't like I was snogging her."

He smiled and ruffled her hair, and she giggled. The way he said it was so sweet, but I couldn't focus on that, all I could focus on was the knot in my stomach. This was a different feeling to guilt; it was something much worse which I didn't understand but it needed to go away as it was making me feel nauseous. Was it regret. I hoped not. It was too late for regret.

Hope didn't try and cover up her mistake. She was too young to appreciate the damage that might have been caused by her jumping to the wrong conclusion and the subject quickly changed.

"Uncle Dexter, when I move away will you bring Aunt Sally and Prince to come and visit me?"

That snapped me out of any downward spiral which may have been imminent, and I interrupted their two-way conversation.

"Why do you think you are moving Hope? Is there a For Sale sign on the door?"

I couldn't believe even Belinda would stoop as low as to sell the house from under Roger's feet.

"No, but mummy has packed two suitcases. I asked her why I didn't have a suitcase, but she said that my clothes were in with hers and then hid both the cases in the wardrobe."

Dexter looked at me and I shrugged. I had no idea what she was talking about but would make it my business to find out.

Chapter Forty

Iarranged to see Belinda the following day, which was the last Friday of school before Christmas. This was partly because I knew how much Christmas clutter Hope would have and Belinda's house was closer, and partly to ask Belinda about the suitcases. I was also going to offer to help with the housework. It was a big ask, her having Mum and Phil. There would be a lot of work involved. I knew housework wasn't her thing and was not sure if Mark was a help or a hinderance. Not everyone was lucky enough to have a Zak.

I had told Zak I would be back late and smiled as I visualised him rushing around the kitchen conjuring up something special for dinner.

There were many reasons to smile and as I got closer to the house I felt my smile broadening. Mum and Phil were about to arrive from America for my wedding, a wedding that was going to happen. I was also excited about finally meeting Mark, just in case I didn't get a chance to talk to him properly at the wedding. And I was intrigued to see what Belinda was going to wear to the wedding. She had not sent me an RSVP for either her or Mark and according to Hope her mummy wasn't even planning on buying a new dress. I dreaded to think what she would turn up in and hoped it wasn't her silver 'rah-rah' skirt or green neon crop-top.

Belinda was already waiting for us in the driveway. Taking all Hope's Christmas bits and pieces she put them in the hall promising her little girl that they could go through them all later and that she was going to treat us both to McDonald's. Belinda didn't treat anyone to anything ever, so I resisted the temptation to insist on coming in and carrying out a house search for the suitcases and, instead, obediently agreed to a trip to McDonald's. Hope walked between us, making sure I had one hand and Belinda had the other, chatting all the way.

It wasn't until I had finished eating the biggest burger on the menu, just in case this was the last meal she ever brought me, that I remembered I was meant to be eating dinner with Zak. That prompted me to ask about Mark and if we could swing into the house on the way back so I could perhaps meet him. My request was met with rolling eyes.

"You have your own boyfriend why do you want to meet mine? He isn't in, anyway. Don't worry, you'll get to know all about him soon enough."

What did that mean? I didn't want to know all about him. I wasn't after an interview, just a viewing, I wanted to see what all the fuss was about and why everyone thought he was so good for her.

When I approached the subject of her moving away, she laughed and told Hope that the suitcases were full of stuff for the charity shop because she was getting rid of Aunt Charlotte's things, and that Hope should chill.

"But Mummy, you said my stuff was in there."

"Yes, stuff that you have grown out of, stuff for selling. Just loosen up, kid."

I was not sure if Hope believed her or not, but she didn't mention it again and neither did I.

I texted Zak to tell him I was on my way home but took the long route back trying to digest my burger and I was a bit concerned that when I opened the door that I might smell burnt food instead of bubble bath. Instead, I smelt nothing. Zak was asleep on the sofa with Prince curled up on the floor beside him. Prince gave me a look as if to say, "What time do you call this then?" before going straight back to sleep. I was pleased that they seemed to be bonding.

Zak was the most handsome man I had ever met, but when he was asleep, he was beyond gorgeous. On this occasion he was out cold, his eyelids were smoothly closed, and his lovely long eyelashes looked like they had been painted on. I wondered how this vision of gorgeousness could be mine? I was the luckiest woman in the universe.

I remembered once reading about an exhibit of David Beckham in the National Portrait Gallery in London.

It was simply called 'David' and was a 107-minute film of Beckham just sleeping. I think he might have momentarily moved once or twice during this time, but essentially, he just slept. People paid good money to watch him because he looked so lovely asleep. They thought it was a good investment of their time and money.

Seeing Zak sleeping right now I completely got that. I wasn't sure how long I should watch him. Part of me wanted to kiss him, part of me wanted to stroke his hair, part of me wanted to lay down next to him and part of me wanted to coax him into the bedroom.

This was the perfect time to take his photo. He wouldn't mind. He wouldn't even know. I would take the photo whilst he slept and carry it around in my purse. I wasn't Victoria Beckham; I wasn't going to allow his photo to be placed in the National Gallery. I wasn't even going to put it onto

Facebook, so what harm could it do? None. I didn't take a photo – in the end, I took six. Then I walked back to the front door, slammed it, and yelled "Honey, I'm home."

Zak's name was now on the house deeds. All the paperwork had been done and the new deeds had been registered with the Land Registry. Zak had been far more relaxed since then. He had insisted that this be done before the wedding as he desperately wanted it to be "our home" when he carried me over the threshold. Wasn't that something he had said before the first almost-wedding? It was a constant battle trying to ignore these dark thoughts, but a battle that was getting easier each day.

He was so relaxed that we spent less time organising the special day and more time doing fun things. One Saturday we took ourselves out for a nice champagne brunch to celebrate our soon to be special day, followed by cocktails. By the time we got back the only thing we could manage was to stagger into the bedroom and go to sleep. When I woke up Zak was no longer beside me. I could hear him banging around in the kitchen while I was left to reflect on my feelings.

I suddenly felt scared. I felt sure Zak had changed, but what if he hadn't? What if he left me at the altar? What if this didn't work out and I lost this beautiful bungalow? I missed Aunt Lucy, the one person who could be happy for me wasn't going to be at the wedding. I felt cross that there was nobody coming to the wedding who felt happy for me, apart from Belinda and Hope. I felt the loss of Hope as much as I felt the loss of Aunt Lucy. Hope wasn't dead, but things weren't going to be the same when she didn't live with me, and I knew I would miss the sparkle and joy she brought to my world. That was the same emotion I felt about Dexter. I already missed him. Was I going to enjoy this new world of just me, Zak, and Prince?

I told myself I was being ridiculous because I was, and put it down to a combination of exhaustion, alcohol and a touch of insanity. I was fast approaching the day I had been planning my whole life and here I was spiralling into depression, which I needed to knock on the head. I listened as Zak continued to clatter about in the kitchen, serving me as always, letting me sleep whilst he conjured up something wonderful for us to eat. I leant over and took his photo out of my bedside cabinet. I had probably gone a step too far having the photo printed and framed, but he wouldn't find it. Not hidden in this cabinet on my side of the bed and under Aunt Lucy's Bible.

Zak had recently promised me that yes, of course, he was going to be in the wedding photos. It was his wedding. The wedding photos would be perfect of course, but this one of him sleeping would always have pride of place. It was going to go in the front room on top of the TV. But for now, it would have to go back in the cabinet.

I threw it back in the cabinet quickly when the door opened thinking I had been caught red-handed, but it was just Prince. He jumped on the bed and started licking my face and breathing his dog breath all over me thinking he was giving me a treat. This clown of a dog would keep me going when Hope left. I wouldn't be sad for long. Prince was clearly adjusting and so would I.

Chapter Forty-one

On the lead up to Christmas there was a lot of talk about a new variant of Covid, and there were whispers that this Christmas was going to be like the one before – cancelled. The variant, discovered in South Africa, was called Omicron and the usual pattern was emerging of us being told not to worry, whilst behind the scenes you could see things unfolding.

People were banned from travelling to South Africa and anyone returning from there got shoved into an overpriced hotel upon their return which, of course, they hadn't budgeted for. From all accounts, these hotels were nasty.

This was not the countdown to Christmas anyone was looking for, and certainly not the countdown to the wedding I wanted. My anxiety levels began to rise accordingly. Fortunately, the closer we got to Christmas the less likely it seemed that another lockdown was going to happen and, despite my worst fears, Mum and Phil's plane landed and they were allowed off the aeroplane. Ironically, nobody even took their temperature or asked for any evidence that they had received their Covid jabs.

Roger also managed to wangle some more leave for the wedding and Christmas. It was a busy time and with less than a week to go I knew I was getting overly tired and emotional. Belinda suggested that she have Hope for the week. She said

Hope could share her bed, there would be room, but I was reluctant to let go. I loved Christmas, I loved the buzz that Christmas week brought, and I didn't know how Christmas would change for either Hope or me when I was married. Nobody pushed me. Mum noticed how quick I was to burst into tears at the drop of a hat. She said that I should focus on the wedding and that they would wait until afterwards to spend time with Hope, as they weren't rushing back.

In many ways, keeping Hope for the lead-up to the wedding proved to be a godsend. It kept me grounded. She made me smile, and her excitement at being a flower girl reignited my enthusiasm. She kept drawing sketches of how the wedding day would be, always matchstick men, women and dogs, all with big smiles on their faces. We decided not to pin these pictures on the wall as we planned to overdo the Christmas decorations again, so we just made a 'happy wedding faces' pile of pictures on the kitchen table.

Like me, she had been worried that Christmas would be cancelled, but now her main concern was whether I would have time to get her a Christmas present. It didn't matter how many times I tried to reassure her, she genuinely thought I would forget.

Like her Aunt Sally and her great Aunt Lucy before that, Christmas was a big thing to Hope, even with so much going on. So, we decorated the bungalow as if it was just another 'normal' Christmas.

A normal Christmas meant putting up countless Christmas decorations and many, many fairy lights. These went on the tree, around the tree, around the windows and, at one point, around Prince. It was all good fun, and he didn't mind one bit. He liked the attention and loved being part of a family. We were his pack, and he loved us.

Somehow, we managed to get the star on the top of the tree, which involved me standing on a chair and Hope kneeling on my shoulders. I knew both Dexter and Zak would freak out if they saw me, as would any Health and Safety officer that happened to walk past at that moment, but we did it and we were happy. We both felt a certain pride in this year's Christmas tree. It was flawless.

With Christmas clearly on her mind Hope couldn't help asking me again.

"Are you sure you have brought me something for Christmas, Aunt Sally? And what about Uncle Dexter? Will he see me at Christmas? I know you and Zak will be all married and busy but what about Uncle Dexter?"

"Uncle Dexter is spending Christmas with Uncle Fred, honey, but he gave me some money which I have added to my money, and we have brought you something super special."

We had brought her a purple jewellery box with a spinning ballerina and inside the box was a silver necklace – a locket with a dog's paw engraved on the front and photos of Prince and Tigger inside.

Dexter had chosen it in case Zak didn't want us to continue to take the dogs and Hope on walks. She could remember Tigger and the happiness he brought her. I knew that neither Hope or I would forget those walks, but it was important to him, and I knew she would love it.

The jewellery box and locket were already safely at Roger's house wrapped up and under the Christmas tree and I was sure by now there would be a mountain of other presents under there for her as well.

Seemingly reassured, Hope skipped off declaring she was going to decorate the rest of the house with the leftover tinsel, which I didn't doubt for one minute and I set to work making a pancake lunch as a special treat.

She was strangely quiet when we ate, and I wondered what had happened in between our excitement about the tree and me making pancakes. Had she broken something? Was she still worried about Christmas day? Just as I was going to reassure her again that I honestly hadn't forgotten to get her a Christmas present, she looked at me seriously and frowned as she said what was on her mind.

"Aunt Sally, I didn't believe you when you said you had brought me a Christmas present, so I looked under the bed, in your drawers and in your wardrobe."

Oh God, not the wedding dress. She hadn't coloured in the wedding dress, had she? Had she been gone long enough to do that? I could feel the colour draining from my face.

"Hope, what have you done? Just tell me."

"It is what you have done, not what I have done. Why have you got a photo of Mark in your bedside cabinet? That is very naughty. He is Mummy's boyfriend, not yours."

"That is Zak, honey. He is my boyfriend. Maybe he looks like Mummy's boyfriend when he is asleep? He does look a bit like Prince Eric as well sometimes." I hadn't thought about that before, but he really did.

But Hope had made her mind up that what she had seen was a photo of Mark. And her mind would not be changed.

Could they really both look so much alike? I hoped so. But I started to get a strange sinking feeling in my stomach.

I texted Belinda and asked her to send me a photo of Mark. When she asked me what I was banging on about, I told her what Hope had found and what she had said. I got no picture, just a message saying, "Don't be so bloody stupid."

I responded, "Ask him if he has a twin," before texting Zak and asking the same question.

"Zak, I need to know if you have a twin, or a cousin that looks like you. Do you?"

He didn't respond. Hope, meanwhile, remained adamant that I was some kind of monster who had stolen her mother's boyfriend.

Before putting Hope to bed we watched Santa Claus: The Movie and drank hot chocolate with marshmallows. That cheered her up at least. I laughed along automatically and pretended to smile as I tucked her into bed, but that knot in my stomach was getting bigger by the moment. I felt sick and as I bent down to kiss her goodnight everything was spinning. I felt confident that my blood pressure was at boiling point.

With Hope in bed, I took a bottle of prosecco out of the fridge and replaced it with another as a precaution. I promised myself that if my worst fears were true, I would become a lesbian, only allow dogs over my threshold and write a book called 'Really, Sally? Again?'.

By the fourth glass I worked up enough courage to send a shot of Zak's photo to Roger, with a smiley face and the breezy question, "Who is this, Roger?"

He instantly pinged back a single word.

"Mark."

Followed a minute later by another text.

"Why have you got it?"

Chapter Forty-two

I honestly don't remember how I felt at that moment. I was too shocked to have feelings and just sat there, unable to move, barely breathing. I looked at my filled glass of prosecco but momentarily couldn't lean forward to pick it up let alone drink from it. My daze was only broken when the mobile pinged again. Another message from Roger.

"Sally, something is wrong. I am on my way over."

Roger was true to his word. He arrived soon after, bringing Mum and Phil with him. Mum walked up to me and just held me tight whilst gesturing to Phil to pour the rest of my almost finished bottle of prosecco down the sink. Dear mother, I was in shock, I wasn't blind.

Belinda had gone. Mark, or whoever he was, had picked her up just after Roger had received my text. She had handed Mum a letter with my name on it, walked towards the car with the suitcases and driven off. I guessed that they weren't on the way to a charity shop with Aunt Charlotte's old clothes and, whatever she had said before to Hope, her little girl's clothes hadn't been in those cases either.

Phil had apparently tried to pull her out of the passenger seat, which was both very brave of him and totally out of character. Poor man hadn't stood a chance. He just got a mouthful about how Hope would be OK because she always was. He had chased the car down the road shouting, "What about Sally?" which was also out of character. At that point a hand had appeared out of the window with the middle finger raised.

Mum was pale, she looked dreadful as if she was bearing the weight of my heartbreak on her shoulders, the tears fell freely when she spoke.

"It's almost Christmas. Why would a mother leave a child at Christmas? Could our daughter really stoop this low."

Phil put his arms around us both and held us close.

"We only have one daughter now, Grace. I have washed my hands of Belinda."

By now everyone had seen the photo of sleeping Zak, and there was no doubt that he and Mark were the same person. Roger did some digging on the internet to find out more about the kind of person he was. There were no surprises. After he had been sentenced, his parents had talked to a local newspaper about how they had to be rehomed after he embezzled their savings and how they had disowned him. A son who could steal from his own parents was well matched with a sister who could abandon her own child at Christmas. Seemed like the perfect couple. No wonder he didn't want to invite anyone to the wedding. He didn't have anyone to invite. Dexter tried to warn me and that just made me feel worse.

I knew I was close to breaking down completely, but I also knew that I had to be strong. I couldn't let everyone down like Belinda had. I would never stoop so low. I had to get through Christmas and give that little girl the Christmas she wanted. The Christmas that she deserved.

While Hope slept, we decided, as a family, we would tell her the truth in the morning. She wasn't stupid and there was no point giving her some made up story.

We all knew how much she loved her mother, so the story line would be that Hope was right, Zak had tricked her mummy and me and was seeing us both. Belinda was cross with him but still loved him so they had gone away together so that people could enjoy Christmas and then everyone would have a grownup conversation after Christmas. We hoped Christmas would distract her from asking too many questions.

I vowed to keep it together until after the New Year, and assured everyone that I would be OK.

I accepted that I would have to move into Roger's house for a while as nobody would relax if I was at home alone. But now was not the time, and nobody thought waking Hope would be the right thing to do.

That night Phil stayed over, spending the whole night sleeping on the settee. I knew he wasn't getting much sleep because every time I left the bedroom he would sit bolt upright and look at me. I was touched, but honestly had no intention of running away. I didn't have the energy for one thing, and I was determined that nobody was going to take either my or Hope's Christmas day away.

The following morning when Mum and Roger returned, we grownups all put on an act, one worthy of a BAFTA award. It transpired that Mum, Phil and Roger also had more of an active imagination than they had ever let on, making things up as they went. We all over played how much we were looking forward to Christmas and how Aunt Sally didn't have a broken heart; she was just happy that Belinda was happy. Yeah right.

Whether Hope believed us or not was unclear, but at the end of the day she was a kid and, as long as Santa knew which house she would be in and she put her stocking at the end of the right bed, she seemed to accept anything that we said. We all stopped off for a McDonald's breakfast and then made our way back the house, Roger's house, the house we would all be celebrating Christmas. It would be crowded but we would manage.

Once settled Hope made a gingerbread house with Phil and Mum, while Roger and I went back to the bungalow to start the process of cancelling the wedding. I should be getting good at this by now – cancelling the happiest day of my life. But my head was all over the place and I couldn't focus. All I could do was hand Roger names and phone numbers: of the registry office, of the reception, the florist and the handful of guests. As it turned out I hadn't invited many people, as nobody was happy for me, so it didn't take long. Once again, it was too late to cancel the wedding cake but there would be enough of us in the house to make sure it didn't go to waste.

I fought the temptation of ringing Dexter. He wouldn't judge me. He would rush over. He would let me sob on his shoulder and tell me it would be OK, but that wasn't fair was it. Dexter had enough on his plate preparing Christmas for Uncle Fred. No let them be. The kindest thing I could do for Dexter was to vanish out of his life and let him be his lovely self with lovely people who deserved his kindness. I wasn't a child. What was that expression? You made your bed, now lie in it. I decided to take my own advice and left Roger to it.

Hope had a lovely Christmas day, she adored her jewellery box and pendant from Dexter and I and she loved all the gifts that Roger, Mum and Phil had brought her. Incredibly, we even managed to find a gift from Belinda in the wardrobe. The gift tag said, "Sorry I couldn't be here but have a blast. I love you. Mummy."

That was a clear indication that she never intended to be here for Christmas. That she and Zak would be gone by then. This meant I would have been officially jilted at the altar. This hurt. How could anyone recover from actually being jilted at the altar? I felt a tear roll down my face as I thought of the impact that would have had on Hope but quickly wiped it away before it started a tear tsunami.

I was terrified there might be a gift for me in that wardrobe with a less festive Christmas tag, but there wasn't. Possibly we would learn more when I opened the letter, but I wasn't ready to do that right now. Especially at Christmas.

Hope's gift from Belinda was a dog from the Teddy Bear Workshop along with some vouchers so she could buy it some clothes. She was thrilled and wanted to go shopping there and then. She kept asking if we could ring Dexter. She couldn't understand why I didn't want to speak to him, why I didn't want to wish him and Uncle Fred a 'Merry Christmas', why I didn't want him to know about the 'change' in my wedding plans and why she couldn't thank him for her present.

Her whining was getting to me, and reality was beginning to set in. I knew I would struggle to keep my promise of 'staying normal' through to the New Year. How could I act normal when I didn't feel anywhere close to that? I needed headspace to think about what had just happened, and with so much going on around me this was not the place I would get it. I could feel myself breaking into a thousand pieces and I knew I was going to lose the plot big time… and very soon.

That is why, on Boxing Day, in spite of vowing never to do so, I stooped as low as Belinda.

I lied to my family knowing that my actions would ruin the rest of Christmas for everyone, but hoping and trusting that they would keep up their act for Hope. I knew this was the biggest lie that I had ever told and that they would never trust me again, but at that moment, the lie seemed necessary.

To stop me snapping at everyone, to stop the continuous tears, to allow me to think, to keep me sane, it was a lie I needed to tell.

Over breakfast on Boxing Day, I told Roger that we had better let Hope video call Dexter to wish him and thank him for the gift before she drove us crazy. I asked if he would mind doing the call with Hope and gave him the number. I wasn't in the mood for Dexters' sympathy and Roger understood that. He took the details without challenging me. In the meantime, I would take Prince for a walk and join them later.

I had already fully charged my mobile, packed the phone charger, put some spare clothes, a toiletry bag and Belinda's letter in my backpack with a few other essentials. I had a couple of tins of dog food in there as well so hoped I didn't collapse under the weight of the bag and give the game away. Nobody would suspect anything was wrong as I always took this backpack with me when I walked the dog. Nobody did. They didn't question me or ask to come with me. They trusted me.

So, on Boxing Day morning, when all arrangements were made, I took Prince for a walk. And I didn't go back.

Chapter Forty-three

It wasn't until a few days before New Year that I finally opened Belinda's letter. I was staying at an undisclosed location in a village in West Sussex and appreciated how lucky I had been to find accommodation at such short notice. Aunt Lucy must have been looking down on me.

Having taken myself to the railway station after leaving the family, only to find there were no trains available on Boxing Day, I had started to panic. Scrolling through the Airbnb app the reality hit me as to how few and far between dog-friendly places were, and when I had phoned a couple, I soon realised that not all dog-friendly places were human-friendly. Especially when being phoned on Boxing Day. Fortunately, one person clearly appreciated money far more than his Bank Holiday peace and actually sounded relieved.

"Yes, come. Someone booked the cottage for two weeks from Christmas Day but has now gone down with Covid. The bed is made up and the cottage has been cleaned. I'll give you the number of the key box."

I transferred some money from my pitiful savings account to his bank account, and then went to find a cashpoint, which then allowed me to make a local taxi company's Christmas dreams come true with the extortionate price they charged to take me.

Prince and I arrived at the cottage just over an hour later to find a complimentary bowl of fruit, tea, coffee, milk and biscuits. Well, that would be my Boxing Day meal. I was pleased I had thought to bring some dog food, though Prince would have happily shared the biscuits. Meals after that were not hard to come by, as we were in a good location with a nice combination of shops and open fields.

The open space gave me lots of time to think, which I desperately needed. And when I wasn't out walking, I chose to watch films rather than the news, which was consistently negative, and not helping my mental health one bit. This week's news topic was 'Covid mistakes and why had the government made so many of them'.

Why did the government take so long to lock us down? Why did they insist on so-called 'herding' before turning to the inevitable lockdown? Why were there not enough oxygen cylinders? Why were the borders not closed sooner to stop the spread of infection? Why were asymptomatic cases not recognised sooner? Why were the elderly discharged from hospitals straight into care homes, thus spreading infection?

Did the government have answers to any of these questions? Did anyone?

I didn't feel I was in any position to either listen to meaningful conversations about mistakes or give an opinion. But many people did.

I felt sorry for the scientists, and I even felt sorry for the government, particularly the prime minister, Boris Johnson. They didn't see this virus coming. Nobody saw this virus coming. Nobody, anywhere in the world, was ready. Just by being in the wrong job at the wrong time, Boris ended up being the person people were pointing fingers at. He certainly was no longer flavour of the month, or flavour of the year, and wouldn't be anytime soon.

Sitting in my Airbnb accommodation with Prince, I had my own list of questions. But, in this case, Boris wasn't the subject of the finger pointing. It was me. No one could argue that my situation was the fault of the scientists', the government or even Boris. There was only one person to blame for the mess I was in and that was me.

Why didn't I figure out that it was Zak Belinda was travelling to visit? She was always the one travelling to see her 'boyfriend' and he never visited her. Why? Because he was in prison! He couldn't travel anywhere. It was all so obvious now.

Why didn't I work out that it was Belinda who gave him my email address? Why had I dismissed the fact he had 'found' my email address so easily?

Why didn't I notice that every time I complained to Belinda about Zak's behaviour, he suddenly changed? When I queried his Christian beliefs, he had instantly come up with an explanation that did just enough to quell my suspicions.

When I whinged about him not getting involved in planning our future, he suddenly became 'fiancé of the year'.

Why didn't I pick up on how weird it was that Belinda never wanted Mark to meet Hope? Or the remarkable coincidence that Zak didn't want to meet her either? There was nothing wrong with Hope, she was lovely. Why didn't I insist Zak meet her?

Looking back, I realised that, of course, Mark was angry about Hope being in the house when I had Covid, as he didn't want Hope to see him. What were the chances it was he that gave the darned virus to me anyway – neither of them took a test and Belinda was very poorly according to Roger?

I needed to stop thinking about 'Mark', a person who simply didn't exist. The same man who had been part of my life had also been part of Belinda's life. And that man was Zak. In my mind, still a toad of the vilest variety.

Why didn't I work out why toad knew that Hope's new favourite colour was purple. Of course, he bloody knew! He knew everything. Belinda told him.

How could I have brushed off Hope telling me about the suitcases, and why would I have believed Belinda's lame charity shop story?

Why didn't I work out sooner that he only wanted his name on the bungalow to get half of its value, which would happen now? He was a convicted con artist, and I had stupidly handed over half my cherished Aunt's beloved bungalow to a conniving toad, and that was something I would have to live with for the rest of my life. Even after that, I imagined, as Aunt Lucy would be waiting, ready to air her disappointment once I winged my way through those pearly gates.

Why didn't I notice that my savings account was getting lower and lower?

These questions kept going around and around in my head. I was lucky that our temporary residence was a cottage in the countryside with a huge back garden and a gate that led into the fields. Some of the fields had angry looking cows in them, but just sharing their field broke the endless cycle of these questions and made me think of something else. Other times I chose some of the fields without the cows so that Prince could have a run. It was refreshing watching him having such a wonderful and carefree time. Ah, to be a dog.

I was running out of money and would need to go home eventually, but I was still overwhelmed with embarrassment. Embarrassment over Zak. Embarrassment over lying and running away, but the biggest embarrassment was over being so stupid. That was the worst bit. When things go wrong, it's always good to have someone to blame. But there was nobody else to blame for my stupid mistakes. Belinda? She wouldn't have been able to do what she did if I wasn't so unbelievably stupid. No, this was all down to me!

Unlike Belinda, I had contacted home regularly, if briefly, which was something that she hadn't bothered doing. Amazingly, nobody was cross with me. Worried yes, but not cross. Phil had even offered to transfer some money into my account in case I wanted to stay longer, but I knew I had to face my demons. I knew I couldn't run away forever. Plus, the cottage was prebooked and would no longer be available. I only had a few more days to get my head together.

Mum and Phil loved being hands on grandparents and said that Hope was filling their hearts with happiness. Her current project was planning my next wedding to a 'real prince', which was keeping her very busy.

Most of the time I felt I would be OK, but sometimes I felt so low I didn't think I could go on. When I felt like that Hope would ring, Prince would give me a slobbery kiss or Dexter would send me a text. It was as if someone was making me see that it wasn't all about Sally. I had to go on and somehow that was enough to keep me going.

Despite all my negative feelings, texting and speaking to Dexter still gave me a buzz. I tried hard not to smile when his name flashed up on my mobile, but it was impossible.

Hope had been quick to fill him in on Boxing Day, describing Zak as being "evil and no prince at all". Then Roger had phoned him when Hope was in bed, just to confirm what he had already worked out, and to tell him that I had done a runner.

It didn't take Dexter long to ring me and I hadn't picked up his calls straight away due to my feelings of humiliation and embarrassment, but eventually I thought I owed it to him to let him know I was safe, so he wouldn't worry. He never said, "I told you so" and never made me feel bad about myself. I wished he would as it would somehow clear the air, but he just listened. For hours he would listen and at the end of the call he would say something like, "It will be all right" or "I am here for you" or "This is just one season, there is a brighter season ahead."

The only time he voiced an opinion was when I told him I was almost ready to come home but needed to read Belinda's letter first. People would want to know what was in the letter and they deserved to know. I was in a bad place and thought he was telling me off.

"Sal, you can't do that. You can't read the letter on your own."

I had been crying all day thinking about that darned letter and when Dexter sounded cross it just made me cry more. It was my letter not his and I could open it when I sodding well felt like it. The combination of tiredness, confusion and, yes, anger that Dexter was cross made me start sobbing and I couldn't stop.

Although Dexter was begging me to tell him where I was, I just kept crying hysterically. I was so wound up that I was finding it hard to speak. In the end he had to raise his voice more just to make himself heard.

"Sal, if you want to have a hissy fit, it's your choice, but for God's sake, I need to come and rescue that poor dog. Where are you?"

Hissy fit! Is that what he thought? I was having a hissy fit?!?

On the verge of hysteria now but not wanting to hang up, so he could hear what he had triggered with his insensitivity, I waved the phone around madly to make a point.

"Look, a field! I am in a field with lots of cows in it! Cows are my new best friends! Cows don't cast judgement and accuse me of having a hissy fit."

Then I hung up.

Did Dexter really think I was selfish enough to have a hissy fit in front of Prince? Prince was safely back at the cottage, probably standing on the back of the sofa looking out of the window and wondering where I was.

Should I ring him back and tell him that I was just distraught, not stupid?

I thought better of it. Now was not the right time to tell someone I wasn't stupid. Especially when I had just announced that my new best friends were cows.

Chapter Forty-four

Trying to push the cows and Dexter to the back of my mind, I took Prince for the last walk of the day before leaving him home alone again so I could wander off and spend money at the nearby off-licence. I wondered if the day for cutting back on wine would ever happen. This was going to be another evening where the bottle was my best friend, my only friend, not including the four-legged variety, of course. I needed courage if I was going to open that letter, which I was. Aunt Lucy used to call it, 'Dutch Courage'. Then she would add, "But as you aren't Dutch you won't need it."

Sitting beside Prince on the sofa I switched on the TV and wondered if I was the only daft dog owner to put so much effort into making things seem 'normal' for the sake of the dog. I wasn't actually watching the TV; I was focused on the letter, but needed to make sure that my beloved doggo didn't suspect anything was wrong and that this was just a normal evening in front of the TV.

Feeling quietly confident that he didn't suspect a thing and was enjoying the quiz show, I felt it was safe to open the letter. A quick swig of wine... three, two, one... I took a deep breath and opened the envelope.

Sally

Take care of my kid. None of this is her fault. It's your fault.

The thing with you is that you are such a spoilt bitch you don't see the damage you cause.

Mum and Dad moved away from you because they thought you were deranged and wanted to protect me. That turned my life upside down, making me move away from everything I knew, from my Aunt Lucy, my friends and the only life I had ever known.

Then you did the 'poor me' act in front of Aunt Lucy and it worked. It really made Roger angry when she left you the bungalow. She was our aunt as well, and that money should have been split three ways.

Nobody ever wants to rock your boat though, precious Sally. But I am rocking it. You are a greedy cow.

I went to the prison and spoke to Zak, and he was pissed off with you as well. He agreed it was payback time. He was happy to go along with my plan.

All his life he put himself at risk, taking from rich people to make it fair. They had far more money than they needed. Zak was doing well, taking from the rich and giving himself a chance in life until you and that ginger loser messed things up for him.

Neither of us dreamed just how easy you were going to make it for us to get our own back. Two more days and we would have wiped your account clean; three more days and we would have left you jilted at the altar. But you had to take that photo, didn't you? Even though the man you supposedly loved told you not to. Selfish till the end.

I expect Mum, Dad and Roger will give me the silent treatment for a while, but they will get over it. At the end of the day, I am their daughter, Phil's only real daughter.

I have never just left Hope. I always make sure there is someone to look after her and there are plenty of people around. They will all calm down eventually.

We are going to spend some time living the life we deserve. We have enough money, and more will come in when you sell the bungalow. Yours and Zak's bungalow! We have other money-making ideas too, but don't take too long selling it, half of that belongs to Zak and to me.

Don't let Hope forget me. She is mine, not yours and one day I will come back for her.

Princes and dream weddings? How old are you? Grow up.

Belinda

I wasn't sure she needed to sign it; it was too unfeeling to be from anyone else? I also wondered what emotions she thought this letter would trigger in me. She wanted to break me, for sure. At first, I resisted the temptation to give in and let her win, but things in the letter soon started playing on my mind. I knew they were just words, made up words, lies. But then I found myself questioning my conviction.

Not wanting to ruin Prince's evening chill time I put my shoes on, hoping he wouldn't notice the tears streaming down my face, and went into the back garden, closing the door behind me so that he didn't follow. It was colder than I expected but going back for a coat would have him presume this was an outing he was invited to, and that absolutely wasn't the case.

The words of the letter cut deeply. Had Mum really agreed to move to America with Phil, away from what she loved, because it was the only way of getting away from me? I didn't think I was that difficult. I was self-obsessed with the wedding thing, but was it really affecting everyone else? Had they tried talking to me about my obsession? I couldn't remember.

Had Aunt Lucy really felt trapped by me? Did she really give me the bungalow out of pity? That couldn't be true, could it? I cared for her. We looked after each other.

Maybe Belinda was right, and Roger secretly hated me. Appearing normal in front of Hope this Christmas, pretending everything was OK had come naturally to him, maybe he had been acting for years pretending that he understood me and was on my side?

And now Belinda had gone, Phil had lost his only daughter. Sure, he had recently washed his hands of her. But that wasn't fair, she was his flesh and blood. I was his stepdaughter; it wasn't the same thing.

It was so confusing. I was becoming convinced that I was a monster. I needed to stay away from people, live on my own so they could rebuild their lives without me. I needed to rehome Prince before I destroyed him as well.

By now I was sobbing uncontrollably. Was I having a breakdown? Would anyone notice if I lost the plot somewhere in the cow-filled countryside? Would they come looking for me? I was confused, I was lonely, I was cold, and, I realised with a start, I wasn't alone.

There was a shadowy figure in the garden, walking towards me through the dark.

Dexter.

At first, I was so happy to see him. I just ran up to him and let him hold me.

"Sal, you are freezing."

"I am getting snot on your coat."

"I don't care, just let me hold you."

"How did you find me?"

"When you were madly waving your phone around and proclaiming that cows were your best friends, the camera picked up the name of the cottage. I didn't need to be Sherlock Holmes to find out which Airbnb had that name, and where it was."

"Oh."

"I'm taking you inside."

Then something snapped inside me. Dexter couldn't stay with me. I was a monster, my parents moved away to get away from me, I broke hearts, I ruined lives, I conned people. Before I knew it, I was screaming at him, begging him to leave and begging him to take Prince with him.

Dexter didn't say a word. He just scooped me up and physically carried me into the house. He sat on the settee and held me close until I had calmed down. I thought Prince would freak out because of the noise I was making but he knew he was safe. He even looked relieved that Dexter was there.

Once I had calmed down, Dexter persuaded me to let him make a hot chocolate for me, which I agreed to, but before he could bring it back, I was asleep. I woke up a few hours later in bed with Dexter beside me. He must have carried me there. I didn't object, I didn't feel threatened. This was Dexter. I was safe.

Chapter Forty-five

For the rest of my time at the cottage Dexter stayed with me, sleeping on the sofa. It was brave of him, as my mood swings were constant. One minute I was sobbing uncontrollably and the next I was smiling and enjoying the fresh air. We both loved the countryside. All three of us spent as much time as we could exploring and taking in the quietness of our surroundings.

Dexter contacted Uncle Fred every day for a Tigger update. Tigger seemed content with just being let out in the garden rather than taken for his walk. Fred's care package didn't really cover doggy care, but the ladies who visited seemed to enjoy the distraction and Dexter had asked Mum and Phil if they could pop in occasionally as well, which they did with Hope in tow. Hope missed having Prince around, so that provided happiness all around.

During one of my crazy moments, I cut my hair short with a blunt pair of kitchen scissors. It was my way of saying that I did not intend to think of myself as a princess ever again. The result was a trip to the local village hairdresser, who managed to salvage something from the mess I had made. Dexter thought the new version of my short hair looked great, but it felt weird. It was curly now not straight, and I knew it would take me a lot of time to get used to it.

In another crazy moment I insisted that Dexter arrange online interviews with every member of my family so I could ask them directly if Belinda's statements were true. Dexter took a photo of the letter and sent a copy to everyone via his mobile so they could all see it before we talked. They were all suitably appalled and did what they could to reassure me.

Phil and Mum really did prefer America and told me that Belinda did as well most of the time. And even though they didn't always understand my active imagination, they were broken-hearted when I decided to stay in England with Aunt Lucy. Mum seemed genuinely upset when reliving the moment that they left the country without me.

Roger had told me that it was his idea for Aunt Lucy to give me the bungalow. He honestly didn't need it and would probably have given his share to charity if she had refused to listen. At that time, Aunt Charlotte was happy with Belinda and Hope living at their place and worried that Belinda might one day move away, and who would look out for Hope. He knew Belinda would be sorted in the short term and he shared Aunt Lucy's concern about me being homeless.

Everyone was very patient with me and my questions, always answering them with what seemed to me to be genuine honesty. The trouble was that in the headspace where I was now, I was paranoid and not always convinced everyone wasn't just telling me what I wanted to hear. My interrogations seemed to be exhausting everyone apart from Dexter, who seemed to take everything in his stride.

Dexter later revealed that he had gone through this with his mum a long time ago when she suffered a meltdown after his stepdad left. He had seen her turn the corner and knew that I would as well. He was confident that this low stage I was in wouldn't last forever.

The good days we had during our short stay at the cottage outshone the bad days.

One night I lay on the grass looking up at the stars; only I wasn't looking up at the stars, I was having a private chat with Aunt Lucy. I wanted to say, 'Sorry'... Sorry if she thought I had only been caring for her because I wanted the bungalow, and sorry that I had then given the bungalow away.

Before long Prince was panting in my face and Dexter was lying next to me. So much for a private chat, but it was nice. I enjoyed them being part of my life and after trying to remember the names of some of the planets, we just lay there and enjoyed the silence. We would all miss being in the country.

I had never really been out of the city before and loved the country air. It was different somehow. The cottage we were staying in was for sale, and I was beginning to fantasise about buying it and living here with Prince and Hope. I could take her out of school and Dexter could teach her online, she and Prince would love to live here.

The fresh air, space and exercise helped me to clear my head. Maybe it was possible to go through life without being married, and I could live with that. I couldn't live without the special people in my life or my friends or my dog, but did I need a husband or a wedding?

Dexter was also fantasising about buying the cottage, which was a fantasy far more realistic than mine, as he hadn't signed half his money away to a conniving sister and a con artist. He dreamt of making it into a dogs' home – a home to foster dogs, so that Ruff 'n' Rescued could at least get them out of Romania and the shelters they were in. So that the dogs could feel what it was like to sleep in a bed or on a chair, what it was like to feel warm, to feel safe and to feel loved until their forever home became available. Only someone very special and unselfish could think like that. How could you foster a dog, love it, and then give it away? Dexter could.

We also talked about us. Dexter told me that he loved me, but I wasn't ready to listen. It was the worse news that anyone could have given me at that time. My best friend wanted to be my lover and then what? I would just lose him as well.

I wasn't sure if he understood my rejection or not, but it was not discussed again at the cottage, or for a long time after that.

Chapter Forty-six

When my time at the cottage was over, I moved straight back into Roger's house. It was a squeeze, but we managed. I never slept in the bungalow again.

It was the first day of spring term when Hope stood in front of the class during 'news' time – when each child got to talk about highlights of their holiday – and announced, "My mummy has run away with my Aunty's prince."

That day, Mum and I were both outside the school gates at home time waiting for Hope to appear and the school headmaster came out and asked if he could have, 'a word'. He had left Hope in with the After-school Club children, and she was having fun making things at the craft table.

He said that Hope's announcement had been as entertaining as all the stories she told. However, if it was repeated by another child at home then that parent or carer could well raise the situation, possibly with himself, or may even contact social services. It could be perceived as a 'safeguarding' issue. We both took turns trying to convince him that this was not a safeguarding concern. In fact, Hope's wellbeing was our major focus. We told him we had nothing to hide and would be willing to go along with anything social services suggested. Mum phoned them the next day.

Neither of us were particularly bothered about what either the school or social services thought about Belinda's parenting skills, but this pushed us into doing something 'official' about the situation we were in.

Having someone from social services come to the house was terrifying. We had deep cleaned the entire house from top to bottom, and we were both shaking in our boots as we waited for Sharon, our allocated social services lady to arrive. Fortunately, Sharon was lovely and not as shocked to hear our story as we thought she would be. Belinda clearly wasn't the first mummy to temporarily put her parenting duties to one side, or worse.

After talking to us, to Hope and to the school, Sharon said she would need to speak to Belinda and confirm she agreed to have a private family arrangement put into place. I couldn't believe what she was saying. Could this little girl's future really lie in the hands of my sister? How could we expect her to be helpful, or even reasonable? I gave up right there and then, I had no fight left and knew it would end badly. Mum felt differently to me.

"Belinda has said more than once that she would never 'just leave' Hope. I think just me texting the words 'social services' will get a reaction, and we know that she is glued to her phone right now in case there is any news on the bungalow being sold."

She sent Belinda a text:

Social services are here to discuss Hope.

The phone rang instantly.

Belinda knew better than to be rude in front of social services, but her responses weren't particularly warm or friendly either.

No, of course they didn't need Jez's permission. He wasn't even named on the birth certificate. He didn't want to be.

Yes, of course she gave her permission. Why would she want her kid anywhere but with her family and yes, of course, she gave consent for us to be able to make decisions and access information about Hope. What kind of Muppet did they think she was?

Yes, she would send confirmation by email. Just get someone to text her the email address.

Then she hung up. I presumed Mum would get an earful later.

Sharon took Belinda's attitude in her stride and basically seemed pleased with what she heard. She said maybe in the future a formal child arrangement order could be discussed, but this was all she needed for now and she would keep in contact. We were touched at how unjudgmental and warm she was, and, in many ways, it was a relief that we now had an official person with a name to go to. I also felt relieved that Mum and Phil were still here. They would have to go back to the States eventually, even if just to finalise things, but for now we were a team. Team Hope.

Mum and Phil were paying Roger rent for the house, which seemed fair as there was no room for the poor chap to sleep now, and he would need to book into bed and breakfast on his next leave. Although he looked in good shape, Roger felt he was getting a bit tired of navy life and would leave once his four-year contract expired. He talked about opening his own bed and breakfast somewhere in the country, another of his dreams he hadn't fulfilled yet.

Roger, Phil and Dexter had all offered to help me keep the bungalow. They even offered to put their names on the mortgage with me if I remortgaged it. We could pay off Zak and still pay the mortgage. But it wasn't for me anymore. I could never live in that bungalow now. It felt contaminated. Zak and Belinda had ruined it. They had taken away the innocence of my childhood and made it dark. But neither of them could take away my memories. My memories were in my heart and that was all I really needed to remember my Aunt Lucy.

Having Hope around helped me a lot. She made me smile and kept me grounded in the same way she did at the start of the pandemic. There were some terrifying moments in 2020, but you couldn't sit glued to the television, watching the daily briefings and counting the deaths when you had a child. You had to play it down, dress up, watch uplifting films and save news bulletins for the nighttime when she was asleep. You were forced to make the whole thing sound like nothing more than a huge inconvenience. "Oh dear, the virus hasn't gone away yet. Guess we will have to stay at home a little longer."

The bungalow needed emptying, but I never went alone. I always had Dexter and Hope with me. You couldn't scream, shout and kick innocent items of furniture in front of a confused child. I was growing up. It wasn't all about me and my feelings anymore. It was about her.

We three went to the bungalow every weekend to sort things and get it ready for when it was finally sold. It had been up for sale for a while now. Belinda had been in regular touch with Mum, convinced we were lying about it not being sold and Mum had sent her a photo of the For Sale sign and a link to the estate agents we were using. She sent no message of reassurance, just the sign and the link. Neither she nor Phil felt ready to engage in any conversation with her yet.

We tried to make the weekend trips fun for Hope by getting her involved. One idea we came up with was to put everything into a pile in the middle of the front room and she had to decide which charity shop should get which item. This project lasted a while as every charity shop had its own box with a relevant hand drawn picture on it. Her old clothes went into a Save the Children box marked by a drawing of a baby with a dummy in its mouth. We also had some unwanted dog bits as Prince had forgotten he was a street dog and was ultra-fussy about his toys – if they were not rubber, he wasn't interested. Dog teddies and rope toys needed to go and were put into an RSPCA box with a drawing of a dog on the front.

Every time we emptied a wardrobe or set of drawers, we would all wash the items down, give it a lick of paint and try and sell it if we could or, if not, put it on the 'Free to Collector' page of our local community website. One day when I was clearing a drawer I found my first engagement ring from Zak, wedged right at the back. I must have thrown it there during my first meltdown and forgot all about it. Jokingly, I tossed it into the middle of the room.

"There you go Hope, what charity will we give this hideous ring to?"

Suddenly, Dexter seemed to materialise from nowhere and picked up the ring. There were tears in his eyes as he whispered, "It's Mum's." Then, ruffling my hair in his usual 'no hard feelings' manner, he put the leads on Prince and Tigger and disappeared leaving Hope to continue packing boxes, and me to wonder how many more times I would hurt this poor man.

Another thing Hope liked to do at the bungalow was to colour. The highlight of 2020 for her had been the rainbows in the windows. She had enjoyed seeing them and she had enjoyed painting rainbows on pebbles. Rainbows were a sign of better days ahead during those trying times. Nothing seemed to be purple anymore. She had moved on. Now everything was rainbow-coloured.

We had decided very early on that the dining table would be the last thing to leave the bungalow. It was too useful to get rid of too soon. It was that table that we sat around drinking hot chocolate, that we ate our various takeaways on, and which Hope coloured unlimited rainbows on.

One weekend after getting back from yet another charity shop run, we all sat around the table colouring rainbows. We were shattered and waiting for our pizza to arrive. Dexter and I coloured silently barely able to move our felt tip pens yet alone our mouths, but Hope wanted to chat.

"I have a good feeling about this year, Aunt Sally."

"That's good to know."

"Do you remember when we were all locked in what I said to you?"

"Honey, we did a lot of talking."

"Do you remember me saying that when the rainbows come down, I would help you find a prince so that you could be a princess, just like Princess Meghan."

I smiled.

"It didn't quite go to plan did it."

"But he wasn't a real prince. He was a baddie pretending to be a prince, I think that this year you will find an actual real live prince."

I momentarily found myself wondering if there were any real live princes that were still single until I remembered that I was going to become a lesbian.

"You are very kind, but I think I am going to stick to the two I have for now, one real dog and one pretend dog. Two princes are enough for one Sally."

"You have been at the wrong end of the rainbow for too long. But now you are going to climb over."

"Am I? Is it a long way to climb?"

"Yes. Sometimes you get to the middle, and you slide back to the wrong end again. If you are strong and keep going you will make it to the right end of the rainbow, the happy end."

I loved that, and smiled as I visualised Boris Johnson on his podium back in the spring of 2020. Would the news have been received differently if instead of saying, "I must level with you, I must level with the British public. Many more families are going to lose loved ones before their time."

What if he had said, "We are currently at the wrong end of the rainbow. But if we are strong and keep going, we will make it to the right end, the happy end"?

Would that have made it easier on our ears and our brains somehow?

Maybe I should drop him a line so that he could add that to his long list of things he could have done differently.

Chapter Forty-seven

By the end of the summer, I was beginning to think that Hope's prediction had been correct. This year was going incredibly well.

The bungalow had finally been sold. Zak's solicitor had confirmed that half the money had been transferred to Zak's account and my solicitor assured me that the other half went into my account, which it had. I could get on trying to plan the next chapter of my life.

Belinda had phoned Mum to confirm that the money had gone through and had asked to speak to Hope. She had also phoned Hope on her birthday and sent her a gift. That seemed enough for Hope. She was pleased her mummy was still out there and had enjoyed talking to her, but also seemed pleased that she wouldn't be bringing the 'baddie' back any time soon.

I was feeling well enough to start job hunting again. Everyone thought I shouldn't rush myself; that I was still too fragile. But I didn't feel fragile, I felt strangely liberated. I had got rid of Zak, I had got rid of the bungalow, I had got rid of the stupid idea of a dream wedding to a non-existent prince, and I was quite excited about the prospect of spending my life single and doing my own thing. As Sally the person, not Sally the dreamer.

The house was quite crowded with everyone living together and I was hoping the money from the bungalow would cover a deposit for my own place. There were only a limited number of flats that took pets, but at least there were a few. Some were not too bad, with access to a downstairs garden. I just needed to look in the right place. What choice did I have? I had to work. Reality had now hit home. I was no princess, and I needed to work to live. There was nothing special about me, everyone did it.

The only time I felt fragile was when Dexter started talking about 'us'. I now believed that he really had loved me since we first met. Deep down, I'd probably known that for a while. He had indeed got his teeth straightened and grown his hair because of me, in the hope that I might be distracted from the exhausting idea of finding a prince or, at least, accepting that Zak wasn't one. I loved him as well, I knew that now, but I didn't want to rock the boat. If I got too happy, then things would go tits-up – they always did. If the boat rocked even a little bit, I was the one who would get tipped overboard. That was the way it worked. It was much easier keeping my head in the sand, making myself believe that Dexter was still just a friend.

One evening, things came to a head. We had been talking about the misunderstanding about India and how I had been outraged that he had suggested his perfect wife would need to be quirky and then opted for someone who couldn't be less quirky if she tried. Then I had asked him for an example of someone 'quirky' who put themselves out for others.

"You, Sal. You are the quirkiest person I know. What grown woman dresses up as a bride and a Disney character? You, are not exactly a run-of-the-mill, normal kind of female, are you? And I love that."

Rude, but accurate.

He pointed out that me giving up my job, compromising the sanctity of the bungalow, and all the things that I did to make Hope feel secure and comfortable were the most selfless acts he had ever seen. He added that he loved the fact I could tell a story about anything at all just like that, and my sense of humour – I always made him laugh. Apparently, I was a ray of sunshine who had the ability to light up dark places just by being me. That was a strange thing to hear, as that was how I often felt about Hope.

He wanted to know if I loved him as much as he loved me. I knew I loved him, he was my safe place, my strength, my support. Of course, I loved him, but couldn't he see I was only just beginning to dry out from my last rocky boat ride? I knew that my continuously changing the subject and deflecting his approaches were beginning to wear thin.

Finally, he sighed deeply and told me that if I didn't love him then he needed to move on. He would return to Romania, but this time to live. Just like the strays who meant so much to him, he needed a forever home. He needed to belong, to have a purpose and I was the only thing keeping him in this country now.

Uncle Fred had passed away at the end of spring and he had nothing to hang around for, apart from me. He couldn't wait forever. Ruff 'n' Rescued needed him, and he needed to be needed. He could take Tigger with him, and he could buy a place somewhere near the shelter.

"Unless you tell me to stay Sal. If you tell me to stay, I will."

With that, he changed the subject.

Nothing more was said. Days turned into weeks. My thoughts were all over the place, but I still couldn't bring myself to face up to what he had said and the choices he had laid out for me.

Finally, after weeks of waiting for me to answer, Dexter dropped his bombshell.

"Sal, I will make it easier for you. I am going back to Romania, for good. I hoped that my love for you would be enough to overcome your fears, but you are not ready, and I can't wait forever. Tigger and I leave tomorrow night. Let's pick Hope up from school and I'll tell her."

So that was the decision made. The horse was bolting and the barn door closing rapidly behind it. As usual, it was nobody's fault but mine. Dexter had been honest; he had told me that he loved me, but I didn't trust him not to hurt me. As usual, it was all about me.

I was hoping that Hope would kick off, have one of her hissy fits and tell him not to go. Strange thing about kids, when you want them to throw a wobbly, they don't, and when that's the last thing you want, they go for it big time and won't stop.

Hope had such a long list of people she had once loved and lost that emotionally she didn't flinch. Through the eyes of a child, Aunt Charlotte and Aunt Lucy were in heaven together, knitting apparently and watching daytime television. Roger was in the navy and doing a good job, "keeping sailors fed on chocolate brownies" and Belinda would be back, hopefully after dumping Zak and not bringing him with her.

As far as she was concerned this news that Dexter broke to her was exciting.

"No way, Uncle Dexter! You are going to make new kennels; you are going to rescue more dogs like Prince and find them a forever homes. That is fantastic." She asked him to put lots of photos onto the website and asked if we could visit him next summer and that was that.

Somehow, I managed to keep it together, hug him goodbye and even smile as I waved him off. Then I took to my bedroom and cried for a week. It wasn't as easy consuming vast amounts of alcohol living with Mum and Phil – another reason I needed my own place. Somehow the thought of having my own place that had once filled me with hope and excitement seemed hollow now.

That Sunday I decided to go to church. I wasn't sure which church I wanted to go to as the only one I knew was the one Aunt Lucy and I used to attend, and I hadn't been there since Aunt Charlotte's funeral service. It was a nice enough church, but my whole focus was on moving forward, not looking backwards and definitely not remembering funerals.

Hope was still Hope, but she didn't need me now as Mum and Phil were the perfect grandparents and I felt like a loose end. I felt like I was heading for another downward spiral and that scared me as Dexter wasn't around to rescue me. The one thing I had learnt about going to church with Aunt Lucy was that it was a happy place. There were songs, happy people and a happy feeling when you left. Right now, I desperately needed happy.

It took three Sundays to find a church that suited me. The first one had a congregation of elderly people. I was clearly the youngest person who had entered that building for a while. The average age seemed to be the wrong side of 70 and the vicar was so old he didn't look like he was going to make it through the sermon. At one point when we were meditating on God's word his head lopped to one side and I thought he was finished.

The second church I tried was the opposite, and I felt like the oldest person who had ever walked through the door. The worship went on and on and the youngsters were bouncing around, dancing, waving their arms and some of them were even waving flags. It was very happy, which is what I wanted, but exhaustingly happy. After the service people would 'go down in the spirit', whatever that meant. All I knew was that you had to climb over bodies to get a cuppa after the service. It all seemed a bit weird.

Just like Goldilocks with her third bowl of porridge, the third church seemed just right. This church had people of all different ages, including families with young children, and I felt this could be somewhere to bring Hope if she ever showed an interest. The church service started with some easy-to-learn songs and had some easy-to-understand children's talks which suited me, as grownup sermons usually hurt my brain. When the children went out halfway through the service there were prayers, some testimonies and a very short sermon which wasn't too painful, and then the children came back in for the last worship song. It was perfect.

Meanwhile, Dexter didn't seem to be missing me at all. Not that I asked him to. Hope was forever shoving the laptop under my nose to show me what he was up to. He was working hard, I would give him that, and I wondered if he even had time to miss me. Did he miss me when he did have time? Did he even think about me?

From time to time, I thought of Zak, but I didn't miss him a smidgen. It was more a case of 'I wonder if you have spent all that money yet, you toad'. I tried hard not to think of Belinda as, even though I still couldn't get my head around how hateful she had been to me, I felt bad having negative feelings about Hope's mum.

It was weird the way we all handled this. We regularly bad-mouthed Zak, but Belinda was just never spoken about. Phil had said he had replaced her name with Hope's name in his Will and that any money would be put into a trust until

Hope was 18. It didn't make any difference to me what he did with his money. I had learnt over time that money was overrated. It was just a shame you needed it to live. But it was comforting to know Hope would be taken care of. Mum had a photo of Belinda and me on the television in a double frame, so she still viewed Belinda as her daughter, which she was, so that was fine with me. Only she didn't talk about her or appear to make any effort to contact her. When Belinda called to speak to Hope, any conversation she had with Mum seemed very short.

I tried to keep my feelings of heartbreak about Dexter to myself and put on a jolly act. My face was aching with fake smiles and pretend laughter. Dexter was my soulmate, he was part of me, the better part of me and I missed him. Mum wasn't fooled by my fixed smile; she could see right through it. It was she who suggested I go out to Romania and find him. That produced a real laugh, a laugh from the belly. Who went to Romania? The insane and hardy might. Maybe I had a touch of insanity, but I was meant to be fragile. I wish Mum would make her mind up. Was I fragile or not?

"If I am meant to go to Romania, mother, then Aunt Lucy will send me a sign." It was weird the way I had somehow replaced God with Aunt Lucy. It was never God himself that would give me a sign; it was Aunt Lucy. I wondered if God minded the fact Aunt Lucy had taken over his position since entering through those pearly gates.

Hope had come up with an equally crazy idea. They were approaching the autumn half-term holiday at school and on the first week back they were going to be participating in something called the 'Romanian Shoebox Appeal'. Children were being encouraged to bring in things like sweets, yo-yos, playing cards and teddies to be put into an empty shoe box along with gloves, hats and winter gear. The box would then be wrapped up in Christmas paper, so that an underprivileged Romanian family would have something to open at Christmas.

Apparently, Hope had put her hand up and said that she and I would take the shoeboxes out to Romania to save on the postage.

"Can we, Aunt Sally? Then we can visit Uncle Dexter afterwards."

Ironically, my new church was also going to be doing the Romanian shoebox appeal and on the Sunday after my declining Hope's kind offer of hand delivering the school's shoeboxes, the church played a video which showed the genuine happiness these humble shoeboxes brought to the children and elderly who received them. So, it wasn't just dogs that struggled in Romania then, there was some real poverty going on out there.

The video was followed by a talk about the appeal, which concluded with the vicar announcing, "In a fortnight, we will be driving over to Romania with these shoeboxes, and we are in desperate need of volunteers. I believe someone here was being encouraged to go to Romania. They have been looking for a sign. Well, here it is."

I presumed he was talking about a sign from God not Aunt Lucy, but he was clearly talking to me. This was it then. I was going to Romania.

Mum had jumped at the chance of a trip to London with me to pick up an emergency passport, especially when she found out why. After securing the guarantor signature from an ex-nursing colleague from the hospice confirming I was who the paperwork said I was, I applied for Fast Track. I got my appointment for two days later and we booked our train tickets.

It was a lovely day. Mum had insisted on paying for the Fast Track service and she took me shopping in Oxford Street to kill time as we waited for a text to say the passport was ready. She pointed out I was going to Romania, not the Bahamas, and I would be needing some thermals. I was struck with how excited she was about me going. She clearly had a soft spot for Dexter.

It was nice being able to really shop again. Going through the various lockdowns we had missed this normality. Even when the shops had eventually opened it had taken courage to walk into one. The virus had certainly shaken us up, we had been facing something we had never faced before or knew anything about which had made us all feel a bit insecure and vulnerable. Now was the time to put those insecurities behind us.

Chapter Forty-eight

Just a few weeks after the trip to London I found myself on a minibus heading for Romania, and all the feelings of the lockdowns had come flooding back. I was scared, I was insecure, I felt vulnerable.

Was this another episode of insanity? What was I doing, for goodness' sake? I barely knew the girls I was travelling with, even though we were all from the same church. They were much younger than me, and the girl driving the bus was the youngest of all. It was so dark she couldn't possibly see where we were going. I started going down the road of an overactive imagination; ending with me upside down in a freezing cold ditch in the minibus, while everyone at home carried on, thinking I was on an exciting adventure having a good time.

I seemed to be the only one feeling vulnerable and my five female comrades were upbeat and happy. Annie, Maddie, Kerry, Julie and Esther were all as lovely as you would expect church volunteers to be. They wanted to be doing this, they wanted to be bringing happiness to a handful of folks in Romania and, unlike me, they didn't have a hidden motive. They couldn't help singing countless songs of worship to display their love and faith as we travelled along the dark roads. 'Sing Hosanna' was definitely one of their favourites. "Give me oil in my lamp, keep it burning…" Only so many times one could stomach the same lines over and over again and, as nice as they were, I wished they would shut up.

In my fairy-tale-like imagination I had visualised myself boarding a gleaming white ship. It would be like taking a trip from Portsmouth to the Isle of Wight – possibly 45 minutes, one hour at the most, across smooth water. The people from Romania would be waiting for us on the other side, standing there smiling and waving Union Jacks at us in the sunshine. Once off the boat we would book into a five-star hotel then, after a hot shower and cooked breakfast, just knock on a few doors with our shoe boxes.

This was not a 45-minute journey. We had been travelling for hours, starting with the minibus, then the boat, then back in the minibus again. In fact, it seemed like we had been on the move for days. And when we finally entered the small village where we were staying, there was not one Union Jack, let alone any Romanians, or anyone else, to wave it. It was freezing cold, and I could already see the poverty surrounding me, a stark contrast to the comforts of my hometown. This was totally unfamiliar to me, and I felt like a scared five-year-old again. I didn't want to leave the minibus and step out into the unknown. The van was cold, but it was safe.

Why was Mother so excited about me doing this? Had she no concerns about me wandering around a strange foreign village without a bodyguard? From the time I told her, to watching me pack my case, she hadn't been able to control her excitement. Phil had to physically remove her from my bedroom eventually, just so I could get on.

Hope, however, was not excited for me at all and had screamed and sobbed demanding to come with me. Looking around me now. I was relieved I hadn't caved in and taken her. It was hard enough keeping my own fear, and the emotions that went with them, at bay without having to worry about anyone else. She would have been sick on the boat, sick in the minibus and now looking at the accommodation I felt quietly confident she wouldn't have approved of that either.

This definitely wasn't a five-star hotel, in fact it was barely a hotel at all. The bedroom was minimal; a single bed with a heavy duvet, which was lovely once inside, and one rock-hard pillow. There were minimal shower facilities down a cold corridor and the 'ensuite toilet' was a loo and a sink, both of which had definitely seen better days, though they seemed clean enough.

Delivering shoeboxes was not as easy as I had imagined and nothing like I expected. As usual, what I had expected had been right off the scales in terms of reality. I had imagined being a Father Christmas-like figure, knocking on doors, bringing joy to everyone I met and leaving with a smile on my face and a happy heart. I did bring joy to people, but I had no idea of the scale of poverty I was about to see, and the job was both physically and emotionally draining.

At first, I was useless. Each time I entered a home with obvious signs of poverty I burst into tears. The girls were kind and patiently taught me that these people had been looking forward to this event all year. They wanted to see us smile, open the boxes with them and share their joy over the content. Eventually, I did manage to pull that off, keeping the tears in check – at least until I got back to our accommodation.

After a few days the whole project got easier, this absolutely was the highlight of their year and when they welcomed us into their homes, which they graciously did, they wanted us to be positive, happy and bring warmth into their homes along with the gift. This was what teamwork was about. This was what selflessness was about. This is what Dexter had been doing for most of his life.

With the trip nearing an end and a genuine fear that I might actually just get onto the minibus and go home without even having tried to find Dexter, I realised that the only way forward was to come clean with my travelling companions. That evening before dinner I talked to Aunt Lucy and, including her friend God this time, asked that they would help me find the perfect person to tell and the courage to remember that honesty really was the best policy.

I could never work out the difference between an answer to prayer and a coincidence. This always baffled me. Whichever one it was, when I went to the dining area there was only one place left, at a table with three other girls. These were three of the girls I had initially travelled to Romania with: Annie, Maddie and Esther. I knew they were lovely and that they always insisted on saying grace before they ate. But that was all I knew about them.

What I didn't know was how they would feel about what I was about to say. Would they think that I had bloody cheek volunteering to do this trip for my own benefit? Would they insist I pay back the cost of the trip? Would they throw me into a nearby lake and see if I would drown – like Christians did back in the day to see if people were witches or not? Was that even real or did I just make it up?

I was rapidly changing my mind. Forget the courage bit, honesty couldn't possibly be the best policy. I was almost ready to run away, when Annie spoke up.

"So, Sally, what made you decide to volunteer for this trip?"

Half an hour later, they knew everything. It just came out. It was only the bullet points of my life, and I hoped that I hadn't been talking so fast they couldn't keep up. I told them how Dexter had always been there when I needed him, how he was so good with Hope, how much love he had in his heart and what he did as a job. I told them that the shoebox distribution volunteer work and finding Dexter was well out of my comfort zone, but I felt I had to step outside that zone and do this. I opened my heart to them, and they let me.

Saying it out loud like that just intensified my need to see him and I found myself sobbing, while the girls looked on with tears falling down their cheeks as well. I appreciated this sounded more like a good story or TV drama. But it wasn't a story. It was my life. I was the leading lady, and I didn't want to mess up the last chapter or episode.

Then I told them that I was sorry that I might have come on this trip with my own agenda, but I had honestly enjoyed the experience far more than I expected, and whatever happened or didn't happen with Dexter I would sign up and do it again next year. Only this time it would be for all the right reasons.

The four of us stayed up very late that night and together we worked out how far away Timis was from where we currently were staying. It was Hope that told me Dexter was in Timis. Unlike me, she listened to what people said. She said, or at least I thought she said, the town was called, "Teemee sore arse," but Timis for short. That was enough to be going with. It transpired the county was called Timis and the actual city was Timisoara. Ironically, we would actually pass Timisoara on the way out of Romania back to the UK.

Not knowing the outcome of my visit, we all agreed that it felt safer not to leave it until the last minute. If we were going to do it, we had to do it sooner rather than later. It was a four-hour drive away, which the girls felt was doable. Google had confirmed that there was a project going on there to build a 'sanctuary' for dogs who were unable to be rehomed due to behavioural issues caused by trauma. The shelter would be called the Ruff 'n' Rescued Sanctuary of Hope. The stars were lining up.

My concern was that if my 'happily ever after' went to plan, then I would be OK, but the girls would have to then drive all the way back to the youth hostel. It seemed like a big ask, mainly because it was a big ask. But they all were insistent that they wanted to be involved.

The only feasible plan was to do the journey after dropping off shoeboxes the following day. This was usually done by 3 pm, so we could be there by 8 pm. Esther and Maddie both drove, and Esther was willing to drive there, and Maddie equally willing to drive back. Annie would just come for the ride so she could sing or tell bad jokes and make sure everyone stayed awake for the journey back. As a bonus, she had visited Romania on previous charity trips and knew a few key words in Romanian. I was humbled. They barely knew me, but they were willing to help me in this way.

Knowing that this was very much a Christian organisation I was volunteering with, I was a bit worried that there might be some kind of cleansing ceremony that would have to take place upon their return. If they got caught, then would they have to confess their sins and be cleansed. Perhaps even thrown out of the church. They could get into all sorts of trouble because of me.

They all three laughed when I told them my fears. Maddie giggled as she said.

"What do you think they will do girls, make us walk on shards of glass, or will it be the hot coals this time?"

They explained that everybody was allowed free time, and they had done well over and above the call of duty, so had a legitimate claim to this free time. The subject of whether or not they had a claim to 'borrow' the minibus never came up.

Nobody would say anything and when they got back, they would tell the truth; that I had a friend I hoped to visit and would make my own way back to England. That was easy for them to say. What if my friend had already found someone else and I had to walk back to England? I would cross that bridge, and channel, when I came to it.

Annie said it was probably the most exciting thing she had done in her entire adult life. I liked Annie. I couldn't decide if she was an older version of Hope or a younger version of me, but she had already come up with the happy ending to this whole scenario. Dexter would accept me back with open arms, he would propose to me in the morning, and we would be married by Monday. Failing which, I had my passport so could ring my parents and arrange for them to book me a flight back. Good point, I had parents, I wouldn't need to walk back. It was fun being part of a team and I could see why Dexter enjoyed it so much.

It was good sharing this adventure with Mum over the phone. She couldn't be more excited, but neither of us mentioned the Dexter part to Hope. As far as Hope was concerned, I was still on a mercy mission with the shoeboxes and wouldn't be back for a while. Apparently, she had already stood in the front of the class and told everyone, "Aunt Sally is turning into a nun. She goes to church. She prays and now she is giving gifts to people in Romania even though she doesn't even like the cold, and she can't buy prosecco out there." I wished they would stop choosing Hope to stand in the front of the class. They needed to give another child a turn.

She wasn't wrong about the cold though; I didn't like it one bit and had never experienced a chill like this before. I was also uncomfortable with the number of dogs that were wandering around whilst seemingly nobody cared. I knew that Dexter's charity had run a neuter campaign earlier in the year, and I could see why.

Mum said Hope hadn't contacted Dexter for a while. She was too focused on her courageous nun of an Auntie's trip to Romania, and she was proactively colouring in posters for next Christmas's shoebox appeal. Mum thought me turning up would be a bolt out of the blue and a complete shock for him. I had been sending him the odd text, but no hints of what was going on, so she was right. The shock would kill or cure him for sure.

I hoped Dexter knew me enough to know that I was well out of my comfort zone, and it was because of him that this latest spell of insanity was happening. I was hoping this, the biggest, most out of character, challenge of my life, would be enough to demonstrate to him just how much I loved him.

We were about to find out.

Chapter Forty-nine

That trip across Romania to Timisoara was an eye opener for me. I felt very humbled that these girls were willing to put themselves out like that. They knew nothing about me, and they hadn't judged me. On top of that, now that we felt free to discuss our lives, we all got on so well. I felt like I had known them for far longer than I had, and we talked for the whole journey. Having gone through the last few years presuming I was the unluckiest woman alive; it was now apparent that I wasn't. Life was just complicated. It sucked for so many of us, and you just had to make the most of every day.

Esther's parents had separated when she was young and her mum was now living abroad with her brother, leaving her as sole carer to her father, who had Parkinson's disease. He was having respite care whilst she was away, and I was amazed that being given the opportunity for a much-needed break she had chosen to use it to serve others. She had decided that when she got back, she would put him in a care home full time for both their sakes. She didn't feel able to look after him anymore and felt she would like to spend time being his daughter, not his nurse. She knew this would upset him and was dreading it.

Maddie had Crohn's disease and was under the care of a specialist team at her local hospital. She hadn't been sure that she would be able to make the trip, but her new medication seemed to be working. This was her last chance with medications, and if it failed, she would need to have a life-changing operation after Christmas, which could result in a stoma bag. She didn't seem to dwell on this, she just focused on helping others while she could.

And dear Annie had also made mistakes in love, far bigger and more dangerous than mine. She had found herself in a coercive relationship and, since leaving her partner, had moved twice fearing he would find her. She now realised that he had probably moved on physically or romantically years ago, but it had left her scarred and still scared. She only really relaxed when out of the country, so spent a lot of time travelling.

I had learnt a lot this trip and even if Dexter had moved on, even if I went home tomorrow in the same minibus I came in without his love, my parents were in good health, I was in good health and while I may have lost some money and a bit of pride along the way, I wasn't living in fear. I vowed there and then not to make up my own ending to this story, but to just embrace however the story ended. Things could be so much worse.

We had packed some sandwiches and snacks so had a munch break and a few stops for stretching and comfort breaks along the way, so it was almost 9 pm when we arrived. Esther asked what my plan was, now we had got there. Then they laughed at my stunned expression. I had a plan?

Maddie had a pretty good map on her phone which showed where we were and where we suspected Dexter was. We didn't actually know where he was, but it showed clearly the Ruff 'n' Rescued base, and we already knew the new sanctuary was being built very close to that. The base was about three minutes' walk away, so unless Dexter, in some ironic and mean twist of fate, had moved onto another dog rescue centre somewhere, he shouldn't be far.

I felt Annie touch my shoulder as she encouraged me.

"Just ring him, Sally. We haven't come all this way to watch you get cold feet."

My feet were indeed very cold, in every interpretation of the phrase.

I rang his number and after what seemed an eternity, Dexter picked up the phone. I put him on speaker and Maddie put her hand over Annie's mouth as a precaution. Annie had a habit of giggling, and from what I had seen, her gasping out loud wasn't an impossibility either.

"Sal, what's happened? Is Hope, OK?"

"Hope is fine. Just thought you would like to chat. How's it going?"

"I am exhausted. I am in bed already. What's the time?"

Eeek… He wasn't meant to be in bed. Who was he in bed with?

"Dexter it's only 9 pm. Shouldn't you be watching TV, or out clubbing maybe?"

"Clubbing? After all the heavy maintenance work I have done today? I just need my mattress and a soft pillow."

I let myself drift off as I visualised him in bed on his soft pillow, until Esther prodded me back into the real world. She was pointing frantically to a shopping mall with a big A on the front.

"I looked up where you are working on my Google map Dexter. I was interested. There is a big shopping mall near the new sanctuary isn't there? It has a large red A on the front with a couple of palm trees in the car park. Can you see it from where you are?"

"Sal, can we talk about this tomorrow?"

"Trust me, tomorrow will be too late."

"No, I can't see it, but it isn't far away, Sal, have you been drinking?"

"So how long would it take you get there if, say, you fancied hanging out with me under one of the palm trees?"

"OK, now I am hanging up. You are drunk."

Suddenly the girls couldn't contain themselves anymore and all three of them shouted "No!" at the top of their voices.

"Dexter, I am here. I have come to Romania to find you. Please don't leave me in the car park all night. Dexter?"

Silence.

What had happened? Had he hung up? Fainted? Had the shock really killed him? I hoped that wasn't the case. I hoped that he was on his way.

The girls decided me meeting him under the palm tree was probably the best idea I had managed to come up with since arriving, as it was well lit. We would see him approach, if indeed he hadn't died, and I wouldn't end up getting out of the van and throwing myself at some innocent Romanian who just happened to be walking by.

We sat in silence waiting, though none of them knew who they were waiting for. Finally, Annie pointed at an approaching figure, "Does Dexter look like Ed Sheeran?"

And there he was, my own Ed Sheeran, looking slightly confused but walking at speed towards the palm trees in the car park. "Go get him, Sally," said Annie, pushing me out the door and before I knew it, I was walking towards him.

We sat on a wooden bench under the palm trees and, without making eye contact with him so as not to forget my prepared speech, I told him how much I loved him, how much I needed him, how I had travelled to Romania to deliver shoeboxes just to be close to him, but how I knew close wasn't enough. Then I told him I wanted to be with him forever. I loved him in a way I had never loved anyone before. I now knew the difference between love and lust and… blah blah blah and blah blah blah blah blah.

Finally, Dexter couldn't take any more and gently turned my face towards him.

"Sal, shut up and kiss me."

So, I did as I was told, and it was lovely. I had often heard the expression, 'did the earth move for you?'. The earth didn't move, but I was pretty sure the bench did. Our first real kiss was long and wonderful and in the background was the sound of excited women cheering accompanied by a minibus horn. Then, hand-in-hand, we walked over to meet my new friends. On this visit Dexter had opted to stay at a hostel. He knew the owner well and was sure there would be some spare bedrooms available. He insisted that the girls spend the night in the hostel and insisted on paying for them.

Yes, it was disappointing not having him to myself, but this was Dexter. Of course, he wasn't going to let them travel back through a strange country in the dark.

Maddie phoned the shoebox appeal coordinator, a sensible middle-aged man named Bill, who, after gasping, "You have done what?!?," followed by, "Are you even insured to drive that minibus?" concluded that, yes, they had better stay the night. The rest of the team would have a slow morning while they waited for them to return before delivering the few remaining boxes and then planning their homeward journey, presumably with an empty seat.

With the girls safely tucked up in bed I joined Dexter in his room. I knew there were rules in the Bible about sex before marriage but was pretty sure that the girls would be disappointed if they found me stepping out of a different room in the morning. I was in Dexter's bed. There was nowhere else in the world I would rather be. I was safe, and this was a far better ending than anything I could ever have come up with. That night the earth did move for me, and I didn't want it to ever be still again.

The next morning all three of the girls were smiling at me and giving me a thumbs-up, which I ignored, but was pretty sure with my wonderful new shade of pillar-box red they would have worked out I hadn't slept in my own room. We all talked and laughed over breakfast and then Dexter gave us a quick tour of the dog sanctuary they were building. It still looked very cold and unhomely to me, but he assured me it was much better than the dog pounds they were currently in, and this would be like stepping into paradise for them.

Everyone at the sanctuary seemed to know who I was and seemed pleased for Dexter. So pleased that they actually gave him the day off. So, after exchanging mobile numbers and hugs we waved goodbye to my new friends. I hoped that Bill would be understanding, and that they really had been joking about the hot coals.

NOTES FROM A PANDEMIC

2020 was a big deal, and yet we learned to carry on as if the lockdowns never happened. But they did happen, and it taught me some valuable lessons, perhaps most importantly, not to take anything for granted.

When we were in lockdown, our freedom was taken away, airports were closed, Christmas was cancelled, and we weren't even allowed to hug another person. It caught us all by surprise and mistakes happened. People died because of those mistakes and, in memory of them all, we should not forget.

Good things happened as well, though. The feelings of solidarity, of love, rainbows of hope in the window, the feeling of triumph when the vaccination was announced... All these things were uplifting, small victories that provided light in dark times.

Without the pandemic would we have even noticed that what we had before was so good?

Chapter Fifty

It was all a bit like my life, really. There are parts of my life which I wish had never happened. I know that I made mistakes, but even during those times when I felt so alone and stupid, I was never short of love, I was just looking for it in the wrong places.

Lots of very special things happened when Belinda and Zak tried to destroy me. To begin with, my relationship with Mum and Phil became very special. Phil is Dad now; he has been with me most of my life and cared about me far more than I initially realised. Without Zak I would not have known these things. I would not have sat down and talked with Phil. I did not realise how much he did for me and for Mum before Belinda was born. He was always in the background supporting us.

I know Mum and Phil are furious with Belinda. They have cut her out of their Will. But something else I have learnt is that money isn't that important. I am touched by their love, and I am grateful that they want to leave me money, but I don't need it.

Without realising it, the bungalow became a shrine to Aunt Lucy, but it wasn't the bungalow that made Aunt Lucy special, it was her love. The special bond we had was something neither Belinda nor Zak can take away from me. People's businesses went under during Covid. Many lost their homes, but the virus couldn't take their spirit and determination; it couldn't stop them starting again.

Hope helped me survive the storms. Seeing everything through her eyes, witnessing her 'just get on with it' attitude in dealing with whatever came her way, seeing her ability to enjoy life... She means everything to me. According to the dictionary, 'hope' means: "A feeling of expectation and desire for a particular thing to happen." With Hope, the expectation is that only good things happen. She fills my heart with joy and light. People say that I was there for Hope through gloomy times. I say this is rubbish; it is Hope that got me through the dark times.

Zak and Belinda, as far as we know, are still together, but would Belinda ever tell us if they weren't? As far as we can work out, Belinda enjoys travel and, with or without Zak, that's apparently what she is doing. Does it make her any happier not having a base? Probably not. There is no security in that and the money from the bungalow won't last forever. Who knows how they will get their cash or what victims they might use to get it, but you can't make decisions for other people. People have to make their own decisions, and if they choose to continue down that path, it is their responsibility.

Zak is just a name. My life with Zak is in the past and I have no feelings towards him, good or bad. He is just nothing, a negative being that passed through my life and has now gone.

Belinda, for all the terrible things she did, is still my half-sister. More importantly, she is and will always be Hope's mother. When the time comes, if she does come home, I will have to face her. How will I react? I don't know, but I know I am not capable of carrying her type of hate and evil in my heart.

While I don't understand or have any real sympathy for Belinda and the path she has chosen, I do, in a way, pity her. I know that she is the loser in all this. The longer she is away and the more of Hope's life she misses the more she is depriving herself; these are times she will never get back.

Nobody speaks badly about Belinda in front of Hope, but Hope is growing up. She is working it out and there will be a time when she will start to ask questions. I think she will be told the full story. Nobody is willing to lie for Belinda. How she reacts will be up to her.

And as for Dexter, now officially 'my' Dexter, we couldn't be happier.

I went through another minor bonkers stage where I didn't want anything from my past and insisted that we got rid of everything, as I just wanted to start life with a clean sheet.

Dexter's response was, "Fine, let's light a bonfire and start with Hope, Prince and Tigger."

We didn't do that, but we did buy our own place. With my half of the money from the bungalow, and Dexter's combined inheritances, from his mother and a small sum from Uncle Fred, we had quite a decent amount to put down on a deposit.

That was one of our first 'couple compromises'. I was drawn to new flats, ones that were painted floor to ceiling in bright magnolia paint, which had white shiny floors and windows that sparkled. Dexter was drawn to falling down places on the outskirts of the town which would be 'fun' for us to fix up. Seemingly his fun and my fun were two totally different funs.

The compromise was a large, older, detached house that backed onto a park. It was close enough to Hope's school, but far enough from town for us to think we were living in the countryside. The house is not falling down by any means. But it was lived in by a frail elderly couple who have now moved to sheltered accommodation. That means a lot of work is needed, but we three are doing it together. Dexter and I do the work with Hope telling us how it should be done.

The best thing about the house is that it has a large lounge and pride of place on the largest wall is given to Aunt Lucy's picture of heaven. It is special for many reasons, but mainly because it makes me feel I have brought a piece of her with me.

Dexter still teaches English to students abroad from home because he enjoys it. I like to watch him work. He is fantastic with children, and I do sometimes feel guilty that I am probably too old now to give him any of his own. On the occasions, I have mentioned it, he just looks at me with a twinkle in his eye and says, "We will see, lots of kids out there that need adopting, Sal." Hmm… Could this be another 'couple compromise' ahead?

For now, we have a different pitter-patter of tiny feet in the house. I found a job where I could make a difference. It's certainly not the type of work I was expecting and isn't in the care industry – at least not the people kind. I've opened a business where I look after other people's dogs, something which both Dexter and Hope are happy to be involved in when their work and school allows.

It was meant to be a maximum of four small dogs at a time. Four small dogs that belonged to people who needed to go into hospital for treatment or go on holiday, etc. A temporary arrangement, for which I would charge a reasonable fee.

Dexter, however, has a habit of volunteering us to be a 'foster home' for all kinds of dogs from Ruff 'n' Rescued.

He says it makes him feel better about not being out there helping with the shelters though, I dare say, one day he will go back. Maybe we both will.

We both attend the church, not regularly but sometimes when I feel I want to be close to Aunt Lucy. And, as promised, I did help with the shoebox appeal this year, stupidly taking Dexter with me, where I was persuaded to temporarily house a Romanian Mioritic Shepherd dog named Albert. He arrived a few weeks later on the happy van.

We were told that Albert would be rehomed quickly. People have come and looked at him with the potential of adopting him. But he is such a big, clumsy clown of a dog that by the time he has bowled them over in the doorway with his enthusiastic greeting, knocked their cups off the table whilst passing or crushed them by throwing himself on their laps as if to say, "See, I'm not too big," nobody ever felt brave enough to say 'yes'.

Prince and Tigger seem to thrive on seeing new dogs and I swear they show them around the place and settle them in.

So, this is my new world. No princess-like lifestyle, just grubby hands and matted hair. No chance of my man waiting on me hand and foot either, or me not having to lift a finger. My man is content watching me pick up dog poop and struggle to get Albert off the couch. Our home is no palace and there are no shiny floors, no nice settees, just a lot of dirt, a lot of happiness and a lot of laughter.

Dexter proposed to me last week, which was totally unexpected. I no longer wanted to be married and told him that often. I don't need to be married. As long as I have Dexter, I have everything. Apparently, he and Hope had other ideas and they came up with the perfect proposal together.

Hope came steaming into the kitchen shouting, "Aunt Sally come quickly one of the dogs has got out of the gate and Uncle Dexter is looking for it in the park."

Panic set in, I was convinced it was Ruby, a cockapoo that was the well-loved only 'child' of a gay dentist who left her a pile of special food and a list of instructions on a weekly basis. This was the only client I had that paid a proper fee as he trusted me. I knew he would throttle me if anything happened to his fur baby.

I was jogging after Hope through the back gate and into the park when she suddenly stopped, let me catch up and held my hand.

"Uncle Dexter has something he wants to say to you, Aunt Sally."

I looked at Dexter and counted the leads in his hand. Nobody was missing, he certainly had the required six dogs with him, and Ruby was definitely one of them.

As I looked at Dexter my heart did that funny thing it did at times, and before I knew it, he was kneeling in the mud and looking up at me with a ring box in his hand.

"Sal, you are the quirkiest person I have ever met. I fell in love with you from the moment I saw you. I wanted to propose to you in front of all these witnesses, so you felt obliged to say yes."

I glanced around at the witnesses, six dogs and a little girl. If I changed my mind none of them would be any good on the witness stand and the case would be thrown out of court. I wasn't going to say 'no' though and I wasn't going to change my mind, not ever.

The man that kept me safe, the man that had always looked out for me, always supported me, always had my back; of course I wanted to marry him.

First, I said 'yes', then I burst into tears. When he opened the box, the ring was breathtaking. Apparently, it was Hope's design, and he had arranged for it to be made to order, which must have cost a small fortune. It was a simple design of a gold wedding band with six small, but beautiful stones embedded in the band. Two small red rubies in the middle with two small diamonds to the left and two small diamonds to the right of the rubies.

Before Dexter had the chance Hope whipped the ring out and placed it on my finger.

"That represents our family Aunt Sally, you, me, Dexter, Prince, Tigger and Albert. You and Dexter are the two red rubies, and you are surrounded by your family."

First, I hugged Hope, then I kissed all six dogs, ensuring that I officially welcomed Albert to the family before kissing Dexter. It was suitably disgusting, but that was just how it went. All of us rolling around the wet grass, kissing, crying, slobbering, barking and covered in mud attracted a lot of onlookers who took photos and videos before congratulating us.

So, Sally is finally getting married. No date is set yet, and Hope is arranging everything. Her new favourite colour is red and so that's what the wedding theme will be. The engagement ring was a dead giveaway really. I still get to wear white, as does Dexter, but my flowers will be red roses to match his red shirt. Hope, my only bridesmaid, will be in a red silk dress carrying white roses.

She doesn't care what Mum, Phil or Roger wear as long as the men have red ties and Mum has a red handbag. Hope is also planning to invite Belinda, who will also have to carry a red handbag. It's unlikely Belinda will even reply – and the rest of us would prefer she didn't – but to see her carrying any handbag at all would be something. No mention of Zak. Oh, and the original Prince, the toy dog who is still around, and all three real dogs will wear red tartan bow ties for this dog-friendly event.

As a young child I dreamt of a fairytale wedding. I wanted to marry a prince, and that part of the fairytale has come true. I now get to marry a genuine Prince – and actually get to live with three princes. Transpires that Dexter's surname is Prince. I had only recently found that out when I came across his passport. Being the self-absorbed Sally of old, it had never occurred to me to ask him what his actual surname was once I found out it wasn't Greene. He was always just Dexter.

Oh well, I guess you have to kiss a lot of toads before you find your handsome prince.

As Hope would say, I am no longer at the wrong end of the rainbow.

Acknowledgements

I would like to acknowledge my editor, Ian Corks, for the hours he has put into helping me make my dream happen. You have been both supportive and awesome, doing over and above what an editor should do. For most of my life I have been grateful for your support... and I am grateful again.

Also, my husband Brian, for coping with the many times I have just sat at my keyboard typing and completely ignored him. Thank you for your patience and for agreeing to support me in following this dream, come what may. I love you.

I would also like to recognise the work done by the many charities dedicated to rescuing dogs. I am eternally grateful to Paws2Rescue for giving me my own rescue dog, Princy. No longer with us but always in my heart. My storyline doesn't do them justice. They do all that is in this book and so much more.

Adopt. Don't shop.

And, finally, I would like to remember two dear friends: Chris, who inspired me to 'just do it' and Gerry, who was so excited I was writing a book but couldn't work out why. Your belief in me helped push me over the finish line. So sorry that you are both no longer here to see it in print.

About the Author

Sandra Salter is the wrong side of 50 and has lived in Hove, East Sussex UK all her life. She is married to Brian and has two children, two stepchildren and three grandchildren, all adored. Sandra has always had an active imagination and longed to write a book. Still working, she thought the sensible thing would be to wait until she retired and had the time. Then came Covid, and she felt the time was now. This is Sandra's first book.